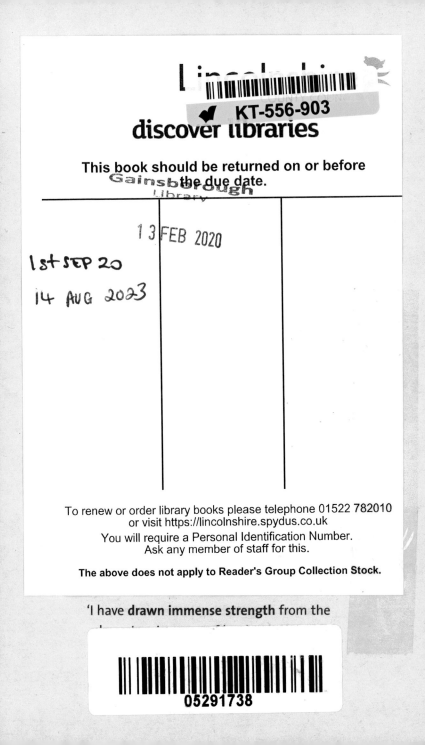

'I have **drawn immense strength** from the

Blessing in Disguise

Danielle Steel has been hailed as one of the world's most popular authors, with nearly a billion copies of her novels sold. Her recent international bestsellers include *Child's Play*, *Spy* and *Moral Compass*. She is also the author of *His Bright Light*, the story of her son Nick Traina's life and death; *A Gift of Hope*, a memoir of her work with the homeless; and the children's books *Pretty Minnie in Paris* and *Pretty Minnie in Hollywood*. Danielle divides her time between Paris and her home in northern California.

By Danielle Steel

Moral Compass • Spy • Child's Play • The Dark Side • Lost and Found
Blessing in Disguise • Silent Night • Turning Point • Beauchamp Hall
In His Father's Footsteps • The Good Fight • The Cast • Accidental Heroes
Fall From Grace • Past Perfect • Fairytale • The Right Time • The Duchess
Against All Odds • Dangerous Games • The Mistress • The Award
Rushing Waters • Magic • The Apartment • Property Of A Noblewoman
Blue • Precious Gifts • Undercover • Country • Prodigal Son • Pegasus
A Perfect Life • Power Play • Winners • First Sight • Until The End Of Time
The Sins Of The Mother • Friends Forever • Betrayal • Hotel Vendôme
Happy Birthday • 44 Charles Street • Legacy • Family Ties • Big Girl
Southern Lights • Matters Of The Heart • One Day At A Time
A Good Woman • Rogue • Honor Thyself • Amazing Grace • Bungalow 2
Sisters • H.R.H. • Coming Out • The House • Toxic Bachelors • Miracle
Impossible • Echoes • Second Chance • Ransom • Safe Harbour
Johnny Angel • Dating Game • Answered Prayers • Sunset In St. Tropez
The Cottage • The Kiss • Leap Of Faith • Lone Eagle • Journey
The House On Hope Street • The Wedding • Irresistible Forces • Granny Dan
Bittersweet • Mirror Image • The Klone And I • The Long Road Home
The Ghost • Special Delivery • The Ranch • Silent Honor • Malice
Five Days In Paris • Lightning • Wings • The Gift • Accident • Vanished
Mixed Blessings • Jewels • No Greater Love • Heartbeat
Message From Nam • Daddy • Star • Zoya • Kaleidoscope • Fine Things
Wanderlust • Secrets • Family Album • Full Circle • Changes
Thurston House • Crossings • Once In A Lifetime • A Perfect Stranger
Remembrance • Palomino • Love: *Poems* • The Ring • Loving
To Love Again • Summer's End • Season Of Passion • The Promise
Now And Forever • Passion's Promise • Going Home

Nonfiction

Pure Joy: *The Dogs We Love*
A Gift of Hope: *Helping the Homeless*
His Bright Light: *The Story of Nick Traina*

For Children

Pretty Minnie In Hollywood
Pretty Minnie In Paris

Danielle Steel

BLESSING IN DISGUISE

PAN BOOKS

First published 2019 by Delacorte Press
an imprint of Random House
a division of Penguin Random House LLC, New York

First published in the UK 2019 by Macmillan

This paperback edition published 2020 by Pan Books
an imprint of Pan Macmillan
The Smithson, 6 Briset Street, London EC1M 5NR
Associated companies throughout the world
www.panmacmillan.com

ISBN 978-1-5098-7779-9

1 3 5 7 9 8 6 4 2

A CIP catalogue record for this book is available from the British Library.

Typeset in Charter ITC Std by Palimpsest Book Production Limited, Falkirk, Stirlingshire
Printed and bound by CPI Group (UK) Ltd, Croydon, CR0 4YY

Visit **www.panmacmillan.com** to read more about all our books
and to buy them. You will also find features, author interviews and
news of any author events, and you can sign up for e-newsletters
so that you're always first to hear about our new releases.

To my beloved, wonderful children,
Beatie, Trevor, Todd, Nick, Sam,
Victoria, Vanessa, Maxx, and Zara,

May the blessings in your lives
be abundant, and not disguised,
and may bad things always lead
to good ones!

I love you so much,
Mom/ds

BLESSING IN DISGUISE

Chapter One

Isabelle McAvoy sat at her well-organized desk with photographs of the important people in her life in silver frames around her. Her oldest daughter, Theo, in Putnam's arms when she was three months old, a photo of Xela at two, hands on hips, looking outraged. That photo made Isabelle smile every time she saw it. It was so Xela, the drill sergeant among them. Theo was the dreamer, as quiet and shy as she had been since she was born, and so like Putnam, her father. It was as though they both had landed from another world and weren't quite equipped for this one. There was a photo of Declan, next to one of Oona as a baby, where she was smiling broadly. She was the happiest person Isabelle had ever known. From the very beginning she had radiated joy and good humor. There was also a photograph of Isabelle with all three of her daughters, taken during a trip to Italy a few years before, with Theo looking wistful, Xela annoyed, Oona laughing, and Isabelle the bridge between the three. Their personalities hadn't changed, and at thirty-seven, thirty-two, and twenty-six now, they had grown into the women they had promised to be as children.

It was hard for Isabelle to believe how the years had flown. Theo had been pursuing a life of self-sacrifice and caring for the poor in India for sixteen years, Xela was consumed by her passion for business and entrepreneurial talent, and Oona had been nurturing her children, her husband, and his family in Tuscany, and loving it. Only Xela remained in New York where they'd grown up. Isabelle had her own career as a private art consultant, after years as a curator in a highly respected downtown gallery. Now she had her own clients. They ranged from famous art collectors to the newly rich, hungry to buy important paintings to show off their wealth and impress their friends. Some of them genuinely wanted to learn what Isabelle could teach them. Others just wanted to spend money, and a few had a deep appreciation for art. She enjoyed working with all of them and ran her business from her home, a small, elegant town house on East Seventy-Fourth Street she'd owned for twenty-seven years. She also used it to showcase the art she sold. The house was impeccable, it suited her, and the girls had grown up there as well. It was thanks to Putnam that she had been able to buy the house and start her business, which had flourished ever since. She hadn't amassed a huge fortune, but had enough to live well, help her children when they needed it, and enjoy a pleasant life herself. Her innate sense of style showed in the simple, chic, understated way she dressed. She was still beautiful at fifty-eight.

On her desk was a photograph of Isabelle with her father, Jeremy, as well. They were in front of the remarkable "cottage" in Newport, Rhode Island, where she'd grown up. Her mother had been a schoolteacher and died when Isabelle was three. Her father had been a curator at the Boston Museum of Fine Arts, with a specialty in Impressionist art and a subspecialty in Renaissance art and history. Her earliest memories were of trips to the museum with him. Two years after his wife's death, he had made a dramatic career change and accepted the job of property manager for one of the Vanderbilt estates in Newport, which included the mansion euphemistically referred to as the Vanderbilt "cottage." It was a spectacular home more like a small château, filled with priceless antiques and art. With the job came a modest house on the grounds where Jeremy and his daughter could live. Jeremy had been looking for an opportunity like it for a while. He thought it would be better for Isabelle to grow up in the country rather than the city of Boston in a small apartment with him. He also wanted a job where he could spend more time with his daughter than his curating at the museum would allow. When the right position turned up, he jumped at it. They moved to the Vanderbilt estate in Newport. He was responsible for the art, antiques, the grounds, the staff, and keeping everything in perfect order and ready at the drop of a hat for his employers, who only used the house once a year for a few weeks in August. The rest of the time, the Vanderbilts lived in their other homes in New York, London, and the South of France, where they spent June and July.

For eleven months of the year, Isabelle had free run of the grounds and was in and out of the main house frequently with her father. She would study the paintings for hours while he was busy. She'd sit quietly on a chair, examining the paintings minutely, and her father would tell her about them, and something about the artists. She learned a great deal from him, and her early favorites were Degas and Renoir. It never struck her as odd that she lived amidst such opulence, although none of it was theirs. She had no pride of ownership, and nor did her father, only a deep appreciation for the beauty of their surroundings. In some ways, it was like living in a museum. As she grew up, her friends were the house-keeper, the butler, the cook, and maids and housemen, though she and her father ate dinner alone in their own house every night. She went to the local school but made few friends. It was complicated explaining to them where she lived, and why.

It came as no surprise to her father when she decided to major in art history at New York University, and volunteered on weekends at the Metropolitan Museum of Art.

She took her junior year abroad at the Sorbonne, where she spent every moment possible at the Louvre, the Jeu de Paume, and the Impressionist exhibits that her father had given her a profound love for ever since she was old enough to talk. She described every exhibit and museum she went to in detail in her letters to him, and he was proud of her. He had saved up for her education for years, and he approved of her plan to work at the Met or an important gallery in New York after she graduated. She landed an internship at a greatly respected gallery in Paris for June and July after she'd finished her year at the Sorbonne. It was there that her life's journey began. And now, so many years later, she was still influenced by the choices she had made at twenty, and by the people who had crossed her path so long ago.

*

Isabelle had begun her internship at the Verbier Gallery in Paris that June feeling breathless to be in its hallowed halls. The most important collectors in the world entered their portals regularly to view the remarkable paintings being presented to them, at prices beyond anything she could imagine. Her duties were menial. She had to clean the coffee machine, order lunch for the sales representatives from the bistro nearby, and set it up in the gallery's dining room. She was taught how to wrap a painting for delivery, or for crating to be shipped, using all the packing materials they showed her, and under the careful super-vision of one of the regular employees. They all wore the same white cotton gloves she had been given to handle the art. The truly important paintings weren't left in her care, but she saw them after they were removed from a viewing room. She'd been told that if she encountered a client, which would be rare, she was to say only good morning or good afternoon. She was fluent in French by then, having learned it during her year at the Sorbonne. She looked like a child with her long blond hair in a braid, and the short navy skirt and white blouse she wore to work every day. She looked younger than her twenty years.

She'd been at the gallery for a week when there was a considerable stir one afternoon, before a client came in. She didn't hear his name, and wouldn't have recog-nized it anyway. All she could glean was that he almost never came in, as it was rare for him to leave his château in Normandy. Although he was an important collector, and a frequent client of theirs, he hadn't been to the gallery in two years.

The gallery's director, Robert Pontvert, and two assist-ants were on hand when he arrived. They showed him discreetly to a viewing room, and shortly after, Isabelle was asked to bring cold mineral water for the client to drink. She noticed the four beautiful Monets on display, and a slim, quiet man, concentrating on the paintings without saying a word. She set the water down on a table, as the man turned toward her and smiled. She then disappeared without a sound, as she'd been told to do. He emerged an hour later, with the gallery director looking pleased. The client stopped briefly to study a small painting of a nude on the way out. It was part of their current exhibition, and after he left, Isabelle heard his name for the first time. Putnam Armstrong was American, from a wealthy Boston family, and had lived in France for twenty years. He had just bought two of the Monets, and there was a celebratory atmosphere in the gallery after he left. Armstrong had slipped out as quietly as he'd arrived. He drove away in a beautiful old silver Rolls he had left with the doorman outside.

Isabelle had forgotten about him by the next day. She tended to her duties, watched other clients come and go, and two days later, the director of the gallery summoned her to his office. She was sure she had done something wrong, although she had no idea what it might have been. She had followed all the directions she'd been given impeccably. She wondered if someone had seen her looking at the paintings they kept in a locked room. She'd been careful not to touch them, and only studied those that were set up on viewing stands, but she was suddenly terrified she might be dismissed.

"Did you see Mr. Armstrong, the client who was here two days ago to see the Monets?" Robert Pontvert asked. She nodded, too frightened to speak at first.

"Oui, monsieur," she said in a whisper, waiting for what would come next.

"He looked at a small nude on the way out, and wishes to see it again. He wants us to send it to his château. It's a two-hour drive from here, in Normandy. Can you drive?" he asked her sternly. She had gotten her international license before she'd left, in case she wanted to go on driving trips, but had only used it a few times. It was easier to take the train.

"Yes, sir, I can." He didn't tell her Putnam Armstrong had requested that she deliver it. He had identified her as the girl who brought him water in the viewing room. It was a demand he'd never made before. He normally didn't care who delivered the paintings to him. But whatever he wanted, the gallery would supply. They had delivered the two Monets to him the day after he bought them. They knew that payment by wire would be made within days by his bank. He was one of their most reliable clients. He could never pass up a truly spectacular work of art.

"Good. You can take the painting to him tomorrow, with the gallery car. Leave it with his butler, Marcel Armand. He'll be expecting you."

"Should I wait to bring it back if he doesn't keep it?" she asked cautiously, not wanting to make a mistake. It seemed like a daunting task to be entrusted with a painting to take to a château, and she wondered why they had chosen her.

"Just give the painting to the butler, and come straight back. You won't see Mr. Armstrong. He'll look at it whenever he wants and let us know," Pontvert said precisely, and she felt like she was being entrusted with the holy grail.

She barely slept that night, worrying about it. What if she got lost and couldn't find the château? Or if she had an accident and it was destroyed? Or what if she was robbed at gunpoint on the way? The worst scenarios possible rushed through her mind, and she was at the gallery the next morning in her navy skirt and a freshly washed and starched blouse, looking anxious and pale. The painting had already been wrapped and was carefully put on the floor of the backseat of the Citroën so it wouldn't fall on the way, which had been another of her fears. She was given a map and told that the château would be easy to find, half an hour outside Trouville. A few minutes later, she left the gallery and was on her way.

She didn't start to relax until she'd left Paris and found herself in the countryside. It looked a little like New England. As she approached Deauville, she glanced at the quaint Norman houses. She followed the directions she'd been given, and two hours after she'd left Paris, she found herself at the imposing gates of the château. It was a beautiful June day, and she had caught glimpses of the sea along the way. She pressed the button on the intercom at the gate, and was instructed to proceed to the end of the drive, which was a surprisingly long way after the gates swung open for her and she drove through. There were enormous old trees on either side of the drive along the way, and she saw a park and manicured gardens at the château come into sight. All she had to do now was find the butler, hand him her precious cargo, and go back to Paris.

As she got out of the car, she saw an older man with gray hair appear on the top step and guessed he was the butler. He was frowning at her, as though she were an intruder. She hurried up the steps to explain her mission to him, and he nodded. She went back to the car to get the painting, and as she did Putnam Armstrong appeared and came down the steps to greet her with a quiet smile.

"Did you have trouble finding us?" he asked pleasantly, as though she were a welcome guest. Putnam had spoken to her in French, and she responded in English, knowing that he was American.

"They gave me very good directions." She smiled at him, and he looked surprised.

"You're American? I thought you were French." He didn't tell her that she looked like a young French girl in a school uniform, with her flat navy shoes the French called "ballerines." "Thank you for bringing me the painting. It's been haunting me ever since I saw it in the gallery. I wanted another look. It's a bit of a trek here."

"It was a beautiful drive," she reassured him. "I enjoyed it." She opened the back door of the car and carefully handed him the painting, as the butler continued to observe them as though she might attack his employer. He appeared to be fiercely protective of him.

Putnam stood holding the painting for a minute and looked into her blue eyes, the color of the summer sky, almost as though he had seen her before in a different context and was remembering someone else. Then he spoke to her in a soft voice. He seemed like a gentle person, and she had the feeling he was shy.

"Would you like to come inside for something to drink? Juice, water, something cold?" he offered. The day was warm and she'd had a long drive. Isabelle wasn't sure how to respond, if she were meant to decline or if it would be more polite to accept. They had given her no instructions to cover the possibility of his inviting her into the château. It hadn't occurred to the gallery owner, or to her, that he might. She looked hesitant, but his smile was warm, and the invitation seemed kind and sincere.

"Just for a minute, if you don't mind." She followed him up the steps as the butler glared at her, as though she were a thief or a gold digger. He would have stopped her from entering if he could, but it wasn't an option as Putnam Armstrong led the way into the château. She found herself in the long entrance hall, filled with impressive paintings that covered the walls, and she stared at them in awe. The hall was somewhat dark, and he flipped a switch to fill it with light so she could see the paintings better, then led the way into an enormous living room, with even more paintings on the walls, beautiful antiques, and two huge fireplaces. Beyond it, she could see a terrace overlooking the sea. The château sat on a cliff above a beach, and she could see sailboats and other boats, as she smiled back at him.

"It's so beautiful." She admired the château and the scene beyond, and he was pleased by her reaction.

"That's why I never leave. I hardly ever go into Paris, only once or twice a year. It's so peaceful here."

And lonely, she thought, although she wouldn't have dared to say it. She wondered if he had a wife or children. But there was something very solitary about him, and a sad look in his eyes when he gazed at her. The butler reappeared then and asked her with a pinched expression what she'd like to drink. She asked for water as Putnam walked her out to the terrace and invited her to sit down. He had put the wrapped painting on a desk in the living room and seemed in no hurry to open the package, nor to have Isabelle leave, now that her mission was accomplished. And he made her feel it would be rude if she left immediately. The view was spectacular, and he watched Isabelle with pleasure as she looked out to sea.

"What brought you to Paris?" he asked, curious about her. She wasn't at all what he'd expected. He had thought she was someone's niece helping at the gallery for the summer. Instead she turned out to be a surprisingly poised, very pretty young American, whom he had begun to suspect was older than she looked. Initially, he had liked the idea of a young summer intern delivering the painting so he wouldn't be obliged to get trapped in conversation with one of the regular gallery employees, which was why he had asked for her. But this enchanting young woman had appeared, and he was enjoying talking to her instead of fleeing, as he normally did.

They sat on the terrace in the sun, chatting for an hour and looking peacefully out to sea. When he asked, she told him about her year at the Sorbonne and growing up in Newport, at the Vanderbilt cottage. She explained that as a child she had been surrounded by great luxury, without really being part of it. He said it sounded like the movie *Sabrina,* and she laughed at the idea, and said there had been no son to fall in love with, and her father wasn't a chauffeur, he was a museum curator turned property manager. She had always thought he'd go back to working in a museum when she was older and went to college, but he was happy where he was, and grateful to his employers for the life they had provided for him and his daughter for fifteen years. He enjoyed living on the property, and his time outdoors overseeing the groundskeepers, not just the art collection.

"You've had a very interesting life, Miss Isabelle

McAvoy," Putnam said, once he asked her name. He was intrigued by her. She seemed at ease in his environment and undaunted by him, while still respectful, and knowing her place.

He invited her to stay for lunch, much to the butler's amazement. Putnam never invited anyone to lunch and preferred to spend his time alone, reading or walking on the beach. He had a small sailboat he took out by himself, and told her he was an experienced sailor, from his Cape Cod summers as a boy and young man. The butler knew that a boating accident had brought him to France initially, but he knew no more than that. While they shared the simple but delicious meal of cold chicken and a big green salad that the cook had prepared for them, Putnam told Isabelle that he was an only child of older parents and had been left to his own devices and was very solitary in his youth. He mentioned that his parents had been very cold, and it sounded sad to her, unlike her very affectionate father who had lavished time and love on her, and she felt sorry for Putnam and the life he described. After his brief references to his early years, their entire conversation during lunch was about art, which was a safe subject. He showed her some of his favorite paintings after that, and then they looked at the small painting she'd brought.

"I think I'll keep her," he said pensively. "I'll put her in my bedroom." There was nothing suggestive about the way he said it, it was simply the musing of an avid collector. Isabelle was relieved that he didn't offer to show her his bedroom. She had no sense during lunch that he was flirting with her. He just seemed like a lonely man who wanted someone to talk to, and they shared common interests. He had been to the Vanderbilt cottage, before she was even born. During lunch he had told her he was forty-seven years old, but he seemed ageless to Isabelle, as though he was suspended between his old world and his new one, and time had stopped for him. He had come to France at twenty-five and hadn't been back to the States since. He said he had no desire to return to Boston. His parents had died years before, he had no siblings, wasn't close to his other more distant relatives, and his life at the château suited him perfectly. He admitted to being a recluse, and didn't seem to regret it. Once they'd looked at the painting the gallery had sent him, she said she ought to leave. It was four o'clock by then, and she mentioned wanting to get the car back before the gallery closed.

He walked her to the car, and she thought he looked melancholy as he said goodbye to her. Then, in a soft voice, he said, "I really enjoyed your visit. Thank you for coming," as though she'd had a choice in the matter and had accepted an invitation.

"Thank you for lunch, and for letting me stay so long," she said, smiling at him, and meant it. Talking to him had been fascinating, and she was planning to tell her father all about it the next time they spoke. "I'm glad you're keeping the painting. She's so pretty, she belongs here." He smiled in answer and watched her go, waving as she turned into the driveway. Then he walked into the château, thinking about her. Her visit had been like a breath of fresh air. He went down to the beach after that, and took off in his sailboat. She had brought back memories for him, some of which he wanted to forget. Being alone in his boat on the sea always cleared his head.

*

When she got back to the gallery, Isabelle told them that Mr. Armstrong had decided to keep the painting, and they were very pleased.

"We thought you'd run away with the car," Monsieur Pontvert's assistant teased her, but they had in fact been concerned that something might have happened to her, and the painting. It was small but valuable.

"He had me wait while he made up his mind," she said simply, not wanting to explain that they'd spent the afternoon together. She suspected they wouldn't have approved of that.

"I hope the butler gave you something to eat at least." He was never pleasant to the employees they sent to deliver paintings, so she thought it unlikely.

"They gave me lunch." She didn't want to tell them either that she'd had lunch with Putnam on the terrace— they might not have believed her, nor approved.

The gallery closed shortly after that, and she went back to her small student room on the Left Bank, thinking of the day she had spent with Putnam, and how pleasant it had been. His home reminded her a little of the Vanderbilts' cottage. There was something familiar about it. It had been an interesting detour from her usual job, and something to remember and tell her father.

Four days later, Putnam called the gallery to arrange for payment and asked to see another painting that had caught his interest. He requested that Isabelle deliver that one as well.

"You're turning into our best salesperson," Monsieur Pontvert teased her, as he handed her the car keys, and one of the gallery helpers put the painting in the back seat.

She knew the way this time, and the drive went quickly, as she thought about seeing Putnam again. He bounded down the stairs to greet her himself this time, without the butler, who had taken the cook to buy food in the village. Putnam looked happy to see her, and greeted her like an old friend.

He took her for a walk on the beach almost as soon as she arrived, and showed her his sailboat. He was proud of it, an old wood boat that he had restored himself.

"Do you like to sail?" he asked and she nodded. "I'll take you out sometime," he promised, and they walked for a long time before they went back to the house. Marcel, the butler, and the cook were back by then, and Putnam asked for sandwiches to be served on the terrace. They relaxed as they sat in the sunshine, and forgot all about the painting she had brought him. He asked what she'd been doing since he'd last seen her. He sounded as though he was hungry for news of the outside world, but he was only interested in what she did, and was surprised by how menial her job was.

"That doesn't sound very exciting," he said.

"It's not," she laughed, "except for coming to see you. I like being an errand girl, so I can bring you paintings." He smiled at that. She seemed totally at ease in his presence, and Marcel stared at her in amazement when he served them lunch. There hadn't been a woman in the house in years, and never one as young as this. She could easily have been Putnam's daughter, and in twenty-five years, the butler had never known his employer to be a womanizer, even in his youth. There had been one or two female visitors in the early years, but they never lasted long. And none at all in the last decade.

After lunch, they examined the painting she'd brought him. It was by an Italian artist Isabelle didn't know, of a small fishing village with sailboats on the water. They had sent him a photograph of it and he'd said he would like to see it in person. He decided to keep that one as well. She got ready to leave after they'd looked at it, and he asked her to stay for dinner. She didn't know if they'd worry at the gallery, but she decided to stay anyway. She knew how to get into the garage now, with a key they'd given her in case she got delayed.

They had dinner in the dining room at a formally set table, and she looked more than ever like a schoolgirl, at one end of the enormous table, seated next to him. There was an innocence about her, which touched him. They chatted for hours and lingered over dinner, and he seemed regretful again when he said good night to her, and warned her to be careful on the road on the way back to Paris. His attitude toward her was more fatherly and protective than anything else, like a big brother, or an old friend who had known her forever. She felt the same way about him, and she was surprised by how at ease she was.

"Bring clothes and I can take you sailing the next time you come," he said to her as he stood next to the car when she was leaving. "A bathing suit and some shorts. We can go swimming." There was a pleading look in his eyes as he said it, as though he were begging her to return and not sure she would. But as long as he kept buying paintings, they were sure to send her. Whatever was happening at the château, from their perspective, seemed to be working. They asked Isabelle no questions when she returned. Whatever Putnam's reasons for wanting her there, they were his business, not theirs.

For the rest of the month, Putnam asked to see a number of paintings, and for Isabelle to bring them to him. He bought most of them. He took her sailing when she came to see him, they lay on the beach together, and went swimming. He enjoyed her company as much in conversation as in silence.

They'd known each other for a month when she dared to ask him some questions about why he never went back to the States, and why he'd never married.

"I was engaged once," he answered carefully, looking out at the horizon as he said it. "We met in college. She was my closest friend. My only friend, when I was at Harvard and she was at Radcliffe. Consuelo. She was two years older than you are now when we got caught in a storm in my sailboat, and it capsized. I tried to save her but I couldn't. We were in Maine, and I got washed up on an island where they found me the next day. They found her body a week later. I never wanted to be with anyone after that. The responsibility was too enormous. I felt like I'd killed her. Everyone insisted it wasn't my fault, but I didn't feel that way. The responsibility of another human being is too much for me. I feel the same way about children. My parents ruined my childhood with the way they brought me up. They were harsh and never approved of anything I did. I never measured up to what they expected of me. I was always being blamed for something, or ignored. I wouldn't want to do that to someone else. They should never have had children, and neither should I. And then I killed the only person I ever loved." He blamed himself entirely for Consuelo's death, and she could see he had never recovered.

"You're not a cold person," she said gently. "You're a very kind man."

"I have no role models, no idea how to be a good parent. I come from an icy world where form mattered, and never love. Consuelo was different, she was a bright, sunny, happy girl, a free spirit . . . a lot like you," he said, forcing his gaze back to Isabelle with a serious expression. "I don't have that kind of joie de vivre in me. I never did. My parents stamped it out of me. I live in a dark place and rely on other people's light, but I can only tolerate it for so long, and then I need to be alone again. She understood that and she didn't seem to mind. She was a lovely girl. I don't know if the marriage would have worked, but I was happy with her." Isabelle instinctively understood his need for solitude too, and sensed how painful it was for him to be around people. She never intruded on him when he was quiet, and waited peacefully until he wanted to talk again. She wasn't sure how it had happened, but she could tell he had been badly damaged as a child. And instead of letting his wounds heal, he had chosen to isolate himself, so he wouldn't be hurt again. He had built walls around himself a mile high. It was tempting to try and get behind them, but something told her no one could.

"I came to France six months after the accident. I couldn't stand everyone knowing about it and telling me how sorry they were, even though I'm sure most of them blamed me. No one knew about it here. It was easier to leave and start again than to look into their eyes and see my guilt. I bought the château and stayed. It suits me better here. I have nothing to go back to there anymore. My parents had both died before the accident. I was living in their home full of ghosts. I sold it after I bought the château. Sometimes the past is better left behind. I have no bad memories here." But he had no good ones either. All he had now was peace, which seemed a shame to her. He was too young to give up on life. And she wondered when he had. As a boy, or later? "I don't think I'd be good at marriage. I've never missed it. The idea of it terrifies me. I feel safe alone." He smiled at her then, and she thought there was something so achingly poignant about him in his self-imposed solitude, running from the past, and the girl he thought he'd killed, and an unhappy childhood. "What about you," he asked her, "no boyfriend to go home to after your year in Paris? Or a boy here, who'll pine for you after you leave?" She shook her head to both questions. And then he wondered about something else. "Are you a virgin?" She shook her head in answer to that too. He felt comfortable enough to ask her now, and she wanted to be honest with him. He didn't press her about it.

"One mistake, when I was fifteen. I've been good ever since. I learned the price you pay when you do something stupid. A big one. I don't want to make the same mistake again."

"You'll have to one day," he said, "or you'll wind up like me, alone." They were both wounded in a way. He smiled at her as they lay on the beach in their bathing suits after a long swim. They were both strong swimmers.

"It will have to be right next time. Otherwise everyone gets hurt," she said and he nodded agreement.

"You look so young and innocent, I thought you were probably a virgin."

"Not as innocent as I look." She gave him a knowing glance and he laughed at her.

"Not exactly a femme fatale either. The people at the gallery probably think we're having a torrid affair by now. It's funny. Things are never what they appear." He leaned toward her as though he wanted to kiss her, but he didn't, and she wondered if he ever would. He lived behind the walls he'd built around himself, and he had let her inside them more than any other human in twenty years, since Consuelo, but she could tell that he was afraid of letting anyone get too close to him. He was like a wild animal who had been badly injured, by loss and bad circumstances and the cruelty of his parents in his youth. He didn't offer more details about his parents, but the results were plainly evident, from the seclusion in which he lived, and had chosen instead of marriage and children of his own.

June fed into July with more visits and more paintings, more lunches on the terrace and quiet dinners. The butler was used to her visits now, and was stone-faced at her arrival, which was an improvement. He wasn't sure why she was there and didn't fully trust her, but he saw plainly that his employer enjoyed her company, and he could see why. Isabelle was a sweet girl, or appeared to be, and accepted Putnam with all his scars and limitations. She never asked for more of him than he wanted, or felt able, to give. He felt safe with her.

It was in the last days of July that she reminded him that she was leaving in a week to go back to Newport, to spend August with her father before school started in September. Putnam was silent for a long moment after she said it, as though weighing something difficult in his mind and wrestling with his demons. Then he finally spoke to her.

"What if I asked you to stay? Would you? Not forever," he clarified immediately, not wanting to mislead her. He liked her too much for that. In fact, he was falling in love with her, but didn't want to admit it to her or himself. "I mean for another month, until you have to go back to school in New York. You could stay here with me at the château." It was new territory for him, and for her as well. He had never done anything like this before, and they had never even kissed. She looked confused.

"As friends?" she asked, wanting to know how he viewed it, and what he meant.

"Not exactly," he said, as they sat on the terrace in the moonlight after dinner. Marcel had served their coffee there. And with that, Putnam leaned over and kissed her. It was a searing kiss, filled with all the emotion they had both felt for two months and hadn't expressed, and she responded as the floodgates opened and tossed them toward each other. It was a long time before he pulled away from her with a tender expression. "As lovers, not just friends," he said gently and kissed her again. His gentleness as a person was contradicted by the force of his passion. She hadn't expected him to be so ardent, and she knew her answer by the end of the second kiss.

"If you want me to, I'll stay," she said hoarsely, and he was barely able to keep his hands to himself.

"I've wanted to do that since the first day you came here two months ago, but I didn't want to frighten you or myself."

"I'm not afraid of you, Putnam," she whispered to him in the moonlight. "I love you. I have done almost since the first day."

"I love you too. But I want to be honest with you. We're never going to have a life together. And no matter how much I love you, I'll never marry you and I won't ask you to stay. I can't. I'm too damaged. There's a part of me missing—something in me died, in the accident, and even before that. Or maybe I never had that piece that makes people want to be together. I've always been different, even as a boy. I need to be alone. I don't want to disappoint you. There's no future with me, this is all I've got to give. A month together for now, and then you'll have to go. Can you live with that, Isabelle, without having it break your heart?"

"I can live with it," she said softly, although a part of her didn't believe him and wondered if he'd change his mind one day, after he'd known the warmth of love again. But he was more deeply wounded than she thought.

"Then come and stay. Give up your room in town, and stay with me until you go. Don't say anything at the gallery." They were closing for the month of August anyway, which was why her internship was set to be over at the end of July. "What will you tell your father?"

"I'll think of something, like they asked me to stay on as part of a skeleton crew for August. He'll understand. He never stands in the way of what I want to do, especially if it's to learn something, or gain experience that will look good later on my CV." She had never lied to her father, but she was willing to this time, to be with Putnam. She would have done anything for him. He needed her, and she wanted him.

Three days later, she had arrived on the train with both her bags. She had sent her books home to Newport, with a few mementoes from her year in Paris. Putnam picked her up at the station in his silver Rolls, and Marcel looked stunned when she arrived. Putnam hadn't told him that she was moving in for a month, and he asked Marcel to put her things in one of the guest suites, to give her space to move around. She would be staying in his room with him. She opened the shutters and fluffed things up, arranged some flowers from the garden in vases and put them in the rooms he used, and instantly became a ray of sunlight in the house. Even Marcel smiled from time to time.

Their month together at the château was as perfect as they both had hoped it would be. They swam and walked and dreamed, sailed in his boat. They took long drives in the countryside, and lay on the beach below his house, and made love all night until they fell asleep in each other's arms. She wasn't a virgin, as she had said, but she wasn't experienced either, and he taught her the wonders of lovemaking as though discovering them for the first time himself.

She was totally at ease with him, made him laugh as he hadn't in years, turning his mornings into something glorious, and his nights into passion. Marcel smiled now when he saw her, knowing how happy she made his employer. He was a changed man, or seemed to be. She learned more about Putnam from living with him. He read a great deal and was knowledgeable on a multitude of subjects. And although he couldn't tolerate the company of his fellow man, he was deeply compassionate about those less fortunate than he and contributed large amounts of money, mostly to causes which involved children and young people, and populations living in extreme poverty. He had paid to feed whole villages in third-world countries and improve their living conditions. He explained some of it to Isabelle, and she was vastly impressed. He was a kind man, committed to doing good in the world, and wanted no credit for it. He had never worked, and managed his investments and many philanthropies well.

*

As August drew near to a close, reality hit them both. She had promised her father to be back for the Labor Day weekend and, true to his word in the beginning, Putnam did not ask her to stay. She more than half hoped he would, or that he would be so miserable without her after she left that he would beg her to come back, but he had been honest about himself. He had wanted a month with her, and no more.

On their last night together, he had held her in his arms and cried. "I don't want you to go," he said in a tone of anguish that tore at her heart, "but I can't ask you to stay. I know I can't do it, and I would only disappoint you. At some point, I have to go back into my cave."

"I can wait," she said, crying herself.

"Don't. I don't ever want you to do that. You belong in the world, Isabelle, I don't. I can't. You're young and full of life. You deserve everything life has in store for you, all the good things. But everything you need and should have is what I can't do or be. I will never forget these months with you, and I'll love you forever . . . but you can't stay. You would come to hate me in the end."

"I will never hate you, Put. I love you just as you are." She meant it when she said it.

"Then you have to go tomorrow, without looking back, without asking for more or trying to stay. My heart goes with you. You've already had the best of me, I don't have more in me to give than this."

"It's enough," she said, and meant it for a moment, although in her heart of hearts she wanted more, just as he knew she would. But she loved him enough to respect his wishes and go.

There were tears in her eyes the next day when she said goodbye to Marcel, and he looked gloomy as he carried her bags to the car.

"We will miss you, mademoiselle," he said grimly, and waved as he watched them drive away. Putnam took her to the train and held her so tightly she could hardly breathe, told her he loved her, and helped her board with both her bags. He stood waving for as long as she could see him. When she got to Paris, she took a bus to the airport, and felt lost when she got there, and heartbroken to leave, as he had feared she would. But she was going, just as she had promised him. She called him from the airport, but Marcel said he was out on his boat, and he wished her a safe journey again. She boarded the plane to Boston, feeling dazed by how much she loved Putnam, the three months she had spent with him, and particularly their last month of living together. But just as he had warned her from the beginning, their dream had come to an end. Putnam was a man of his word.

Chapter Two

Isabelle's father was waiting for her at the Boston airport. She hadn't seen him in a year, but he looked no different than he had when she'd left. He said he'd been busy for the whole month of August. His employers had left a few days earlier.

"It's just as well you stayed in France. They had house guests for the entire month, and new projects they wanted to work on with me. They want to change the whole south garden, put in an orchard, and extend the stables. He's getting into racehorses now. She wants the whole ground floor repainted, and they had me moving paintings around. I haven't stopped for a month," he said as he hugged his daughter tight. "So how's my little Parisian? For a minute when you delayed coming home to work at the gallery in August, I thought maybe you'd fallen in love with a French boy," he teased her. She shook her head with tears in her eyes and turned away so he didn't see. Putnam was no "French boy." He was far more than that, but she knew her father would never understand her falling in love with a reclusive man twenty-seven years older than she was, who had sworn to her that there was no future in their relationship. From the moment she'd landed, Putnam had become a cherished secret. She loved him more than ever, even though she knew there was no hope. Perhaps more because of it. He was the impossible dream, the man she loved and knew she could never have. He had just proven it to her when he'd made her leave.

Her father found her unusually quiet once she was home, but he put it down to travel fatigue, how busy she'd been at her job, and culture shock after a year in France. He was sure she'd be fine once she got back to school. Five days after she arrived, she took the train to New York to start her senior year at NYU. She felt more disconnected once she was there. She cried all the time and wrote to Putnam whenever she could, trying not to sound needy and pathetic, which only made her cry more. She was exhausted being back in school, although the Sorbonne had been just as hard. She often fell asleep at night with the lights on and could barely keep up with the work. After a month of tears and exhaustion and missing Put, she started to feel physically sick.

He sounded no better in the letters he wrote her. He was deep in his cave again. He said he missed her terribly and the house was a tomb without her. But she knew that however miserable he was, his solitude was familiar and comfortable, like a shroud he had wrapped himself in and refused to shed. It was frustrating knowing that all she had to do was go back, and they'd both be happy again, but he wouldn't let that happen. He had had more than his quota of happiness and couldn't bear any more. He had to retreat into the darkness again, for reasons of his own.

The first month of school was agony, and the second month was worse, although she didn't tell her father. On the first of November, she realized what had happened. She had denied it to herself since she'd left France. She was two months pregnant, and it must have happened in their final days together. With trembling knees she went to the infirmary and had a blood test, praying she wasn't pregnant, and hoping she was at the same time. If she was, what would she do then? He had already told her she had no future with him—but what if there was a child? Would he let her come back then?

She called for the results of the test the next day, and after they told her it was positive she went to her dorm room to lie down. She was in shock. She had some serious thinking to do. This explained everything she'd been feeling for the past two months, the crying, the fatigue, and the nausea she'd been experiencing for the past few weeks. But at least Putnam wasn't a child, he was a man. Sooner or later she knew she'd have to tell him and see how he felt about it, and if the news would change his mind about them. She didn't want to make any decisions without him. She had nowhere to turn. She didn't want to tell her father until she had spoken to Put. He had a right to know first.

She spent two weeks of sleepless nights and then called him in France. She hadn't been to a doctor yet, but had calculated that the baby was due in May, with luck right after graduation, so she could finish her senior year and get her diploma. That is, unless he wanted her back in France immediately, which was what she really hoped. She hadn't gotten pregnant on purpose and they'd been relatively careful, but relatively wasn't good enough.

She called him late at night his time, and she knew he'd be up. The sound of his voice rippled through her like gentle waves. He was surprised to hear her. He had told her he preferred writing letters to talking on the phone, and she had respected that since she'd left.

"Is something wrong?" he asked her. Tears sprang to her eyes.

"Yes . . . no . . . I don't know. There's something I have to tell you," she said, detesting the sound of her own voice. There was silence at his end. "I'm sorry to tell you this over the phone, but I just found out I'm pregnant."

"Oh my God." She could hear the panic in his voice. He sounded like a horse about to bolt. "How did that happen? . . . Never mind, stupid question, I know how it happened." She smiled at that. "What are you going to do now? Is it too late for an abortion?" He had counted

34

backward too. She was almost three months pregnant, and it wouldn't be possible after that.

"I was in denial for a couple of months. I thought I just missed you. Turns out it's more serious than that. Do you want me to come back?" There was no point beating around the bush. She needed to know, and his answer was instantaneous.

"No, I don't. I love you as much as ever, but I told you, I can't do that. I can't handle marriage or full-time anything, let alone the responsibility of a child. I'm not going to force you to have an abortion. I can't do that. You have a right to do what you think best, but your coming back to me now, pregnant, or with a baby six months from now would drive me right over the edge. I know what I can't handle, and that's it. If you decide to have it, I'll help you of course, and provide for the baby, but I'm not able to be part of your life, or a child's. Please don't base your decision on me." He was as honest as he had been since the beginning, and as she listened to him, she cried. She had hoped for more than that from him. But he had always been honest with her about how impaired he was. "We should have been more careful— it's my fault that we weren't." He took full responsibility for that, but not for what would come next. He had made it clear. She had to face this on her own. She wanted to be honest with him too.

"I went through something like this five years ago,

when I lost my virginity. I made some terrible mistakes then, and I don't want to make the same ones again. I was a kid and I had no choice. My father decided what he thought was best, and he was wrong. I can't do that again. I love you. I'm going to have the baby, Put. I just can't see doing anything else." She was sobbing as she said it, and he felt terrible for her, but it didn't change his mind.

"I'll do whatever I can to help you, Isabelle. I'm not going to leave you stranded, or deny our child. But I can't take it on either. Marriage or our living together with a baby is not in the cards."

"I understand." She said it, but didn't really.

"Are you truly going to have it?" He sounded devastated, for her as well as himself.

"I have to, Put. I can't do anything else."

"What happened before?" He was worried about her, and she had never told him about it except to say she had made a mistake in the past.

"It doesn't matter. It was a long time ago. I was fifteen. I'm grown up now. The baby is due in May. I can finish senior year and graduate, stay with my dad and take the summer to get organized, and then get a job in the fall."

"I'll give you whatever you need," he said without hesitating.

"I don't want anything for myself, just for the baby. I'm not going to be a burden to you, and I don't want you to think I did this to get something from you."

"Well, you certainly did that," he said, teasing her for a minute, and she smiled through her tears. "No one's ever been pregnant by me before." He sounded shocked. "I never thought I'd have a child. You should think about this for the next few weeks, and make sure it's what you want to do. And even if you had a difficult abortion before, it could be fine this time." She didn't answer for a minute, and there was iron in her voice when she did.

"I'm not getting rid of our baby, Put. I love you. I can handle this." She sounded sure and he was stunned by her strength.

"Have you told your father?"

"Not yet. I wanted to talk to you first."

"Well, keep in touch and let me know what you decide."

"I already did," she said quietly, angry at him for a minute. She had been hoping to hear "Come home," not "Keep in touch." But his message was clear and always had been. If she had this baby, she would be doing it alone. He would provide financial help, which she was grateful for, but he would not be around or part of their child's life, or hers. She wasn't even sure if he would ever want to see it, and suspected now that he might not. She was on her own.

"Do you want me to send you something now?"

"No, I don't. I don't need anything until the baby is born, and I'm going to work, Put. I'm not expecting you to support me now. That isn't part of the deal."

"We'll talk about that in a few months. And for God's sake, take care of yourself. Should you drop out of school?"

"Of course not. I need a degree to get a decent job."

"I'm so sorry, Isabelle. This is rough. I didn't want this to happen to you. I loved our time together, but it comes at too high a price for you."

"No, it doesn't. Maybe this was my destiny, to have your child." She was serious when she said it.

"God help the child. I hope it's nothing like me," he said, sounding sad, and hating himself for what he didn't have to give. Isabelle deserved better than that, and he knew it. "Let me know how you are," he said seriously. "And as hard as it may be to believe, I love you, to the best of my abilities."

"I love you too." They hung up a minute later, and she lay on her bed thinking of everything they'd said. In an instant, her path in life had changed. She was no longer a student, hoping to find a job, meet a good man, and get married one day. She was going to be a mother, unmarried, with a child to take care of and think about before all else, and whoever she met and fell in love with in the future would have to accept her with the child she had given birth to out of wedlock. It was what her father had tried to spare her at fifteen, and now here she was again.

She told her father when she went home for Thanksgiving. He was stunned. He wanted to know who the father was, if she had contacted him, and what his reaction had been.

"I assume he's some French kid you met at the Sorbonne," her father said, sounding weary. Isabelle shook her head.

"No, he's American, and very much an adult. He loves me, but he doesn't want to get married or have a baby. He'll help me financially, but he can't have us in his life."

Her father was furious at that. "Is he married?"

"No, he's not. He just can't handle it emotionally. He warned me of that from the beginning. I'm not sure I believed him at first, but I know that he can't do it, Dad. I'm going to have the baby on my own."

"We've been down this road before, Isabelle," he said angrily.

"I'm not going down the same road again, Dad. I'm not fifteen anymore. I have to make my own decisions this time. For everyone's sake. I can do this," she said firmly as her father shook his head.

"You don't know what you're talking about. I couldn't keep my job and take care of you adequately when your mother died. I was never home, that's why I gave up my job at the museum, and we came here. And what are you going to do, take in washing at home?" His words sliced through her like a knife.

"No, Dad, I'm going to work like everyone else. What

do widows do? Or other women who have babies and aren't married? I'm going to get a job in New York, and he's going to help provide what I can't for the child. I don't want to be dependent on him, but I'll need some help. We'll make it work. I'm not getting rid of this baby. Besides, I love him, and he's a good man."

"Not in my book, he's not. If he were, he'd marry you. And too bad if he doesn't want a wife and a child. He sounds like a selfish SOB to me."

"I wouldn't want to be married if that's not what he wants," she said quietly, "and I respect who he is." There was no way to explain to her father how damaged Putnam was. He was a tortured soul.

"You're making a terrible mistake having his baby," Jeremy McAvoy said fervently. She had heard it all five years before. "You're too young to saddle yourself with a baby without a man."

"I'll be twenty-one when the baby is born. That's old enough." He left the house then, and only came back in time to sit down to their Thanksgiving dinner, which Isabelle had prepared, as she always did. He didn't say a word to her during the meal.

She hardly saw him the next day while he worked around the property. He sat stone-faced through the dinner of leftovers from the day before. It was usually a jovial meal. Saturday was no better, worse in fact. He tried to interrogate her about the baby's father, and she refused to answer his questions, knowing he wouldn't understand anything about Putnam. And she felt protective of him. On Sunday, as she was about to catch the bus to Providence and from there the train back to New York, her father turned to her.

"I'm sorry, Isabelle. I need some time to adjust. This wasn't what I hoped for you. I wanted you to have a better life one day, with a man who loves you enough to marry you before you have a baby."

"I didn't want this either, Dad. But it's what happened, and I'm going to make the best of it. He won't abandon us completely."

"He already has," her father said, "whether you see that or not."

"I guess I do. He's different, Dad. He can't handle it." There were tears in her eyes as she said it. "And I'm sorry to disappoint you again." She hugged him then, and he drove her to the bus. It broke her heart to see how crushed he looked as the bus drove away. She thought about him all the way to New York, and about Putnam, and everything that had happened five years before. All she knew was that she couldn't go through that again.

Chapter Three

Isabelle graduated in mid-May, eight and a half months pregnant. She'd had a job at the university bookstore at night for the last six months, and had saved up for things she needed for the baby—a crib, a bassinet, a car seat, and a stroller. Putnam had set up a bank account for her days after she'd told him she was pregnant, but she hadn't touched it. She knew she'd need his help with an apartment in a decent neighborhood, and childcare when she started working. She didn't want to take advantage of his generosity before that, and even then she would only use his money to the degree she had to. He kept encouraging her to buy whatever she needed. But if he didn't want to share a life with her and their child, she was uncomfortable taking money from him. She had sent him pictures from the sonogram, but you couldn't see much except the outline of the baby. They hadn't been able to determine the baby's sex, and they had discussed names for both sexes in their letters. She could tell that he wanted to participate, but always from a distance. He was

Blessing in Disguise

becoming more like a benevolent uncle or friend, watching over her, and less like a lover.

Her father had finally made his peace with it, and he was proud of her at graduation. She stayed in New York for a week afterward to interview for gallery jobs that would start in September. There were two at well-known galleries she liked particularly. All they'd said was that they'd get back to her. She knew she'd have to start as the lowliest assistant. Her only gallery experience was as an intern at the Verbier Gallery in Paris the previous summer. The owner of the Acker Johnson gallery was impressed that she had worked there. He asked if her husband worked in New York, and she said he did, since she had bought a plain gold wedding band and had been wearing it since Christmas. She told people she knew at school that she'd married a French law student during junior year in Paris and claimed to potential employers that her fictional husband worked on Wall Street. No one questioned it, or suspected she was an unwed mother.

She went back to Newport a week before her due date and got things ready for the baby. She had sent everything home that she'd bought so far, and her father smiled when he saw her turning her bedroom into a nursery.

"It looks like we're expecting a little guest here." She had put decals of Winnie the Pooh and Piglet holding red balloons on the wall, and she had squeezed in a chest of drawers filled with tiny little T-shirts and pajamas. It

43

reminded Jeremy of when she was born, and what a happy time it had been for them. He still couldn't understand the man who claimed to love his daughter but wanted no responsibility for her or their baby. Isabelle was far more compassionate and forgiving than he was, and he got angry every time he thought about him.

The day after Isabelle finished setting up the nursery, her water broke while she took a walk in the garden. She didn't understand what it was at first, and she hadn't yet met the doctor who would deliver the baby. She'd been getting all her prenatal care at the university and had an appointment with the obstetrician in Newport the next day. Her father was talking to the architect about the extension to the stables they were building when she went to get him, and informed him that labor had started. He looked panicked when she told him. Her bag was packed, and he drove her to the hospital twenty minutes later, after she called the doctor she was supposed to see the following day.

Nothing much was happening when they got to the hospital and a nurse checked her. Isabelle wanted to go home, but her father insisted that she stay there. If things speeded up, he didn't want her giving birth at home, or for anything to happen to her. He left and said he'd come back in a few hours, and to call him when things got going.

She had a semi-private labor room with no one else in it, and a nurse suggested she walk up and down the halls to get labor going. She thought of calling Putnam, but she knew she'd just make him nervous and there was nothing to tell him. The nurse who checked her predicted that the baby wouldn't come until after midnight, and it was only two in the afternoon by then.

The doctor wasn't planning to come until labor got started in earnest. She'd walked up and down the hall outside her room half a dozen times, stopped to look in the nursery window, and smiled at the sleeping infants. Some looked only hours old, and a few were crying. It was hard to believe that sometime that night, she would have one of her own. She was thinking about it dreamily when the first hard pains hit, and by the time she got back to her room at the other end of the hall, she was doubled over and could hardly walk. A nurse saw her, and came running.

"Did your husband leave?" she asked Isabelle as she helped her onto the bed during another pain.

"He's my father, and he went home to do some things. The baby's . . . my husband is in France," she managed to choke out during a long contraction.

"We have a little Frenchy coming, do we?" She smiled at Isabelle. "Well, it looks like we're going to be saying *bonjour* pretty soon." She encouraged her as Isabelle tried to smile but couldn't. She was suddenly in too much pain to make conversation. Another nurse came in to check her, and said she was making good progress, just as the doctor walked in. She was a young, pleasant-looking woman, and she assured Isabelle that everything was fine. Things were starting to move quickly, and labor was harder and more painful than Isabelle had expected. An hour later, she was in the delivery room, and the doctor and two nurses were telling her to push. It was only four o'clock by then, and she wished that Putnam was there with her.

"It won't be long," the doctor said between contractions, as Isabelle asked for something for the pain, and the doctor said they had missed their window of opportunity. It was too late for a spinal to take effect. "We'll have your baby in your arms very quickly," one of the nurses promised, as another contraction ripped through her, and for the next hour, Isabelle continued to push and had the sensation that she was drowning each time she did. They put an oxygen mask on her, and Isabelle felt like she'd been swallowed by a wave of pain and couldn't even hear their voices anymore. Then she heard a wail from a great distance. She wasn't even sure what the sound was at first, and then someone told her she had a little girl, and they put a different mask on her face to put her to sleep for a few minutes while they sewed her up. When she woke up, a nurse handed Isabelle her daughter, and there was a tiny rosebud face in a pink blanket staring right at her.

"She's so beautiful," Isabelle said in awe of the perfect features in the serious little face. What struck her instantly was how much she looked like Putnam. She had the ethereal appearance of someone freshly arrived from another planet. Her eyes were a deep blue, and she had Isabelle's white blond hair, but everything else about her was pure Putnam. She didn't cry or wail, and her mouth was a tiny perfect circle.

They took the baby to the nursery then, and wheeled Isabelle to her room an hour later. It was six o'clock, which was midnight in France, and she called Putnam from the phone in her room. He answered on the first ring, and had had a sixth sense that it was Isabelle.

"I'm sorry to call you so late," she said in a voice still weak from the exertion of giving birth. She was still shaking, with warm blankets tucked in around her.

"Do I have a son or a daughter?" he asked, sounding hesitant, still not sure which he wanted, and feeling guilty for not being with her for the birth.

"We have a beautiful little girl," she said, exhausted but proud as tears slid down her cheeks when she told him. "And she looks just like you, Put."

"How unfortunate for her," he said politely but sounded pleased.

"She's very little, just under six pounds."

"Did it go all right?" He'd been worried about her for weeks, and how she would get through the delivery.

"It was hard, but she's worth it," Isabelle said, smiling as she held the phone. He surprised her then.

"I want you to bring her here this summer. I want to see her."

"You do?" She hadn't expected that, and he hadn't mentioned it until that moment. He had wanted to see how he felt first, and now all he wanted was to meet his daughter and see Isabelle again. A new bond to them had suddenly formed in him.

"I want to see you both. Why don't you come in August, and stay the month the way you did last year? You'll be recovered by then, and she should be old enough to travel at two months, or is that still too early?" He wasn't sure, and knew nothing about babies or children.

"She'll be fine, and I'd love it." Isabelle was beaming at the thought, and couldn't wait to show her to him. "What'll we call her?" They had decided on Maximilian for a boy, but hadn't settled on a girl's name.

"I've always liked Theodora. I had a great-aunt by that name. It seemed very elegant to me. She was a terrific woman, full of spunk and spirit. How does it sound to you?" he asked her.

"I like the name, and I want to give her my mother's name as a middle name. Theodora Jane," Isabelle said softly.

"Armstrong," he added, sounding very definite about it. She hadn't broached the last name with him, and assumed it would be McAvoy like her, since they weren't married. "Theodora Jane Armstrong."

"Are you sure, Put?" Tears slid out of her eyes and down her cheeks.

"Of course. I may be a recluse, but I'm not a complete son of a bitch. I have every intention of recognizing my daughter. She's the only living relative I care about now, and probably the only child I'll ever have. Thank you, Isabelle," he said softly, "for having the courage to go through with it. I won't let you down, I promise." Although he already had, and they both knew it.

But Theodora was hers now, and made up for everything she had missed. The mother who had died when she was three, the child she could have had at fifteen, and the husband Putnam could have been and chose not to be. Now she had her daughter.

"I think I'll call her Theo. It suits her. She looks like a Theo. Theodora Armstrong. I'll send you pictures," she promised and a few minutes later they hung up. She called her father and told him the good news. He thought it had gone remarkably quickly, four hours from start to finish, but it had seemed interminable to Isabelle.

He came by that night for a few minutes and declared her beautiful, and then left Isabelle to sleep. They brought the baby to nurse and she held her and said her name, and Theo looked at her seriously, and then closed her eyes and drifted off to sleep. A nurse took her back to the nursery as Isabelle fell asleep too. The next day, Isabelle supplied the information for the birth certificate, and gave them the last name of Armstrong, as Putnam had told her to.

Theo was three days old when they took her home to the nursery Isabelle had prepared for her. That night she told her father she was taking the baby to France in August to see her father.

"Putnam wants to see her," she said simply and Jeremy looked relieved. He knew Putnam's name by then, but no details about him.

"I hope he comes to his senses when he does," he said with a determined look, as Isabelle shook her head and picked the baby up to feed her.

"I'm not expecting that, Dad. This is the best he can do." He left the nursery so he didn't say anything he'd regret about his granddaughter's father, but he thought his behavior was deplorable. How could any decent man let a young girl like Isabelle bring up a child on her own? Clearly he had no heart, no matter what Isabelle said about him.

By the following week, Isabelle had heard from Putnam's lawyers in Boston, informing her that Mr. Armstrong was setting up a trust for his daughter, with Isabelle as trustee. He had complete faith in her to make the right decisions, with the assistance of his lawyers and bankers. The attorney who had called her said that Mr. Armstrong would explain it all to her when he saw her, which sounded complicated and mysterious. But all she needed to know was that Theo would be taken care of.

In July, she went to New York and took the baby with her, to interview with the galleries again, and look for an apartment. She found one she liked in a solid-looking pre-war building with a doorman, on a quiet street in the East Seventies near the river. The apartment had two bedrooms. The building wasn't luxurious, but looked safe, and she noticed several children and their mothers coming in and out. Overnight, she had stopped feeling like a young girl. She was suddenly a grown woman. She interviewed three babysitters and hired Maeve, who was leaving her current job in September when the children started school. She was a middle-aged Irishwoman, who looked serious and responsible. And as soon as Isabelle got back to Newport, the gallery she wanted most called to offer her the job as an assistant. The pay was barely enough for her to live on, but with what Putnam was providing monthly for his daughter, Isabelle could pay the rest, and the babysitter. She had everything she needed—a home, a job, and a babysitter to take care of Theo while she was working. Maeve had made a comment that Isabelle was barely more than a child herself. She had inquired about Mr. McAvoy, and wanted to know when she'd meet him. Isabelle said simply that they were no longer together, and he lived in France so he wouldn't be visiting. Maeve looked startled and then sorry for her, to be left by a man with a baby so young.

"Men," she said with a disapproving look, "we can

never count on them, can we? Well, we'll do fine without him, won't we," she said to Theo, who stared at her with interest and then drifted off to sleep. Isabelle liked the fact that she had glowing references, had come through a good agency, and had six children of her own. She was a widow and had brought up her children alone too, in a one-bedroom apartment in the Bronx. Maeve said they were all grown up now: one was a doctor, both her daughters were nurses and had put themselves through nursing school, another son was a cook in a restaurant, and two were priests. Isabelle knew she'd feel safe leaving Theo with her when she went to work. She was going to start at the gallery as soon as they got back from France.

By the time she flew to Paris on the last day of July, her life was organized. Theo was two months old and discovering the world. She was an easy baby, but you had to work hard to get a smile out of her. She appeared to be pondering life and deciding if the person talking to her was worthy of a smile. She reminded Isabelle of Putnam. She was bright and alert, but even at two months, she appeared to be a serious child.

Isabelle saw Marcel waiting for them as soon as she came through customs. He was in awe of the beautiful infant the moment he laid eyes on her, and he gave Isabelle a warm hug.

"She looks just like her father, doesn't she?" He had noticed it too, and Isabelle was impressed when she saw that Putnam had bought an infant car seat, and Marcel had put it in the back seat of the Rolls. It made her smile as she got in next to the baby, and they drove from the airport to Normandy. Putnam hated going to airports, and wanted to meet Theo at home.

He was standing on the front steps when they drove up. Marcel had buzzed the intercom at the gate to let him know they'd arrived, and he ran down the steps, put his arms around Isabelle and kissed her, before poking his head into the car to see his daughter for the first time. She had just woken up and stared at him in amazement but didn't cry. Marcel had actually made her smile when he'd put her in her seat and tickled her face with a fluffy pink toy he had bought for her himself.

Putnam was silent as he gazed at her. He undid the buckles of the car seat and picked her up as Marcel got the stroller out of the trunk and Isabelle set it up. Putnam assured her he had gotten her a magnificent antique crib at an auction in Deauville. He said it was worthy of a princess. Theo regarded him with interest and didn't make a sound as he carried her into the château.

"This is your other home, my darling," he said as he walked her around and took her out on the terrace to observe the view. It was a gorgeous sunny day, and she was wearing a little pink smocked dress with a matching hat that Isabelle had bought for the trip. Theo finally smiled at her father when he kissed her bare feet. It brought tears to Isabelle's eyes to watch them. She had never expected this kind of emotion from him. He was instantly in love with his child. He insisted on taking them upstairs and showing Isabelle the crib, which was a splendid antique, upholstered with billows of pale pink taffeta and lace, and pink satin ribbons everywhere, and a small pink teddy bear, which he had bought for her too. The crib was set up in the dressing room next to his room, so they could hear her easily during the night. It touched Isabelle to see the familiar bedroom where Theo had been conceived.

"Welcome back, my love," he said and kissed her again. He didn't call it home, but neither of them could have imagined this scene a year before. Marcel and the maids fluttered around them like a flock of mother hens, wanting to see the baby, and exclaiming over how perfect she was. And Putnam couldn't deny how much she looked like him, except for Isabelle's pale blond hair. He and Theo looked like twins, and she had the same reserve he did, the same cautious outlook on the world. Theo never seemed entirely convinced that she wanted to communicate with her admirers oohing and aahing over her, just as Putnam always looked as though he was about to run away when people were around him. Theo had many of his facial expressions. It was uncanny how much they looked alike. His genes were very strong.

"I hope she's more gregarious and engaged in life than

I am, or she'll be a very unhappy girl," he said to Isabelle that night over dinner. "But she has adoring parents, which I never did. That should make a difference."

"She has a very definite personality," Isabelle confirmed. "She's very peaceful, and I think the word I'd use to describe her is reserved." It was a funny thing to say about a two-month-old baby, but her grandfather had seen it too, while they stayed with him in Newport. She was nothing like the happy baby squealing with delight that Isabelle had been at the same age.

Isabelle was amazed when he produced a baby carrier the next day and put it on, so he could carry Theo everywhere with him. He even walked her down to the beach, and dangled her feet in the waves, and then put her back in the carrier when they walked along the sand.

He and Isabelle had made love the night before, but she noticed with a little disappointment that the fire had gone out of their lovemaking, and he admitted to being afraid that she'd get pregnant again. He had adjusted to it once, to some degree, but said he knew he couldn't do it twice. He had fallen in love with Theo on sight but insisted that she was unique, and the passion he'd felt for Isabelle the year before seemed to have transferred to their child. He never tired of being with her as the days went by.

He spent a morning explaining Theo's trust to Isabelle and how it would work. Ultimately Theo would be his sole heir, and there would be appropriate amounts of money when she reached certain ages. The investments in her trust would be handled by his bankers, but he wanted Isabelle to teach her to handle it responsibly too.

"I expect her to do some good in the world," he said seriously, "however she wishes to do that, either through philanthropy and gifts to causes she's interested in, or more actively on a personal level. A great deal of responsibility comes with the money I'll be leaving her one day. She has to put it to good use, not just spend it on herself."

It was what he did with the causes he supported. What he said inspired Isabelle to learn more about managing money, and she promised him she would. All she knew about was art. She liked Putnam's view that their daughter should do some good in the world. It made Isabelle realize how fortunate her daughter was. She had always lived side by side with enormously rich people, but had never given it much thought. Now her daughter was going to be one of them. Isabelle didn't want to benefit from it herself, and didn't expect to, but she realized that she owed it to Putnam to teach his values to their child. He intended to as well.

"I want you both to come here every summer," he said to Isabelle one night over dinner. "You can spend the month of August here." It was all the human contact he could tolerate, and it was a strong dose of it for him to have them in the house for a month, but he wanted to see Theo grow up, and spend time with her every year. "And I want you here too," he said generously, although he had barely made love to her since she arrived. It made Isabelle sad at first, but reminded her again of how limited Putnam was, and she was grateful that he loved Theo as much as he did. He treated Isabelle more like a daughter or sister or best friend now. The love of his life had turned out to be his daughter, and Isabelle had turned out to be the unexpected vehicle for the gift. It was an adjustment for her because she was still in love with him. She knew that Putnam loved her and cared about her, but not romantically or sexually anymore. He saw her more as a Madonna now, and he took hundreds of photographs of mother and child that summer. She knew he would pore over them in his loneliness after they left.

"You'll bring her back next August, you promise," he said, almost pleading with her the night before they left.

"I promise," she said solemnly. She knew how badly he needed them and how intensely he loved Theo, even if he was willing to be far from her for a year.

"And you'll let me know if you need anything." They had settled on an amount that he would send her every month, but she wanted to keep it to a bare minimum and support Theo herself to the degree she could. It was important to Isabelle to maintain her own independence and integrity, and he admired her for it, and respected her all the more. Even Marcel had understood that

"Mademoiselle" wanted nothing from his employer. Putnam had given her a pearl necklace that had been his mother's, as a gift for giving him their remarkable child, and she wore it every day, but it was all she would accept from him for herself.

"I don't need anything, Putnam," she insisted. "I'm starting a job as soon as we go back. You're paying for the apartment, and the sitter, that's more than enough."

"You'll need more when she's older," he reminded her.

"I hope I'll be making a decent salary by then." She smiled. She had every intention of working hard and making a good living. She wanted to be one of the curators of the gallery one day, although she would never make a fortune like his or the Vanderbilts', or even what her daughter would have, but she intended to make some money and put it away.

"I want her to go to private school," he said, thinking ahead.

"She's a lucky little girl," Isabelle said, still amazed by her good fortune, and her daughter's, but she knew that he was right too, and one day Theo would have a responsibility to those less fortunate than her. They would both have a lot to learn about what that meant.

On the morning they left, Putnam held them both tightly in his arms for a long time and then carefully put Theo in her car seat and strapped her in. She looked healthy and rounder and gently tanned by the sun, and seemed much bigger than when they had arrived. She was even more alert now and observant of the world around her.

"I'll write to you," he promised Isabelle when he kissed her goodbye. Marcel drove them to the airport, and Isabelle watched Putnam disappear into the house as they drove away. She felt sorry for him as she never had before. She was taking his life's blood with her, and all the joy he'd ever had. He wanted it desperately and it was within easy reach, but he simply didn't have the emotional fortitude to grab it and hold it close. What he wanted most in life had just slipped through his fingers, and he was alone again.

Chapter Four

Their August together in Normandy became an annual tradition. The gallery where Isabelle worked closed in August, so it was easy for her, and she didn't like being in Newport then, when her father was busy with the Vanderbilts in residence.

More and more, Putnam was their benefactor and the safety net under them, even though he was unable to participate in their daily life. He loved hearing about Isabelle's job, and her regular promotions.

Within a few years, she was dealing with some of their more important clients, and her salary was commensurate. She was making a good wage for how young she was. Putnam delighted in watching Theo grow up too, and shared information with her far beyond what most children could absorb at her age. She was bright and seemed to understand everything he told her. He was a doting father when he was with her, and a kindly presence through letters and phone calls when he wasn't. Even as a very young child, Theo had no doubt that her father loved her.

He helped Isabelle in the few ways she would allow him to, and had bought several paintings from her at the gallery. He knew she would appreciate the commissions. She referred to him at work, and among people she knew, as her ex-husband now. She didn't use his last name and no one ever questioned it. In the art world, he was known as an important collector, and her employers loved it when he bought paintings from them.

Away from work, Isabelle focused entirely on her daughter, and even her father had to admit it had worked out well. Isabelle was an exceptionally good mother despite her youth. Maeve had stayed with them, and was someone Isabelle could count on. Theo adored her and loved the stories she told her, and Maeve loved the little girl almost as much as one of her own.

Isabelle had offered to bring Theo to Normandy to spend Christmas with Putnam, but he hated the holidays and was content to see them once a year in August. She continued to spend Thanksgiving and Christmas with her father in Newport. He loved his only grandchild too. He would take her around the gardens and to see the horses, and he told her all about the estate. She was as fascinated by it as Isabelle had been when she was growing up there. It had never dawned on her as a child that she wasn't really part of it. In the same way, it never occurred to Theo either, since her own father's property in France was even larger than the Vanderbilts', the château even more imposing, and the art collection equally impressive. Theo's lineage, thanks to Putnam, was every bit as distinguished as theirs, although she was too young to know that yet. Isabelle's arrangement with Putnam was unusual, but it had worked out well so far.

The only thing that concerned Jeremy was that Isabelle's life was one of duty and responsibility. To the best of his knowledge, there had been no man in her life since Theo was born. She was still in love with Putnam in a remote, surreal way, and her father frequently reminded her that she needed fun in her life too. She always said that Theo and her month with Putnam in Normandy were fun enough for her.

"I love my work," Isabelle countered. She made no effort to meet anyone—she went to no parties in New York, had declined invitations to dinner from co-workers at the gallery, and had unwittingly become as solitary as Putnam, despite her circumstances and her age. Jeremy hoped to see her happily married one day. She had time, but he still thought her lifestyle wasn't healthy for a girl her age. "You did the same thing when we moved to Newport, Dad," she reminded him.

"That was different, I was nearly forty and widowed after a loving marriage. And I went out with women from time to time. I was just discreet about it, so it wasn't obvious to you." She knew he had had a "close friendship" with the main housekeeper, a lovely Englishwoman, when Isabelle was in her teens. But the woman had eventually gone back to England and married someone else. Jeremy had never wanted to remarry, which discouraged most women after a while. Isabelle was far too young to give up on romance in her life, but the passion she had shared with Putnam, and deep affection she still felt for him, were hard to match. Putnam had said the same things to her in the past year or two, and warned her not to become a recluse, like him. But unlike her father, Putnam felt sure she'd meet the right man eventually.

It worried Putnam at times that a new man might not want her spending a month with him at the château every year, so he didn't push her too hard. He hoped that by the time she did meet someone, Theo would be old enough to visit him alone. He was no longer possessive about Isabelle, but he didn't want to lose his daughter to another man who would take his place, and he had expressed that to Isabelle many times. She understood and promised him that he would never lose Theo, no matter what happened.

She did everything to strengthen the bond between father and daughter during the year. Their apartment was full of photographs of him taken during their visits, and Isabelle talked about him constantly to Theo. She read his letters to her, and whenever she said she wanted to hear her papa, they called him, if it was a reasonable hour in France, and now and then when it wasn't. He was always delighted to hear his daughter, no matter how much he disliked taking phone calls from others. They talked to Marcel occasionally too, when Putnam was on his sailboat or walking somewhere on the estate, and Marcel was just as pleased to hear her as her father. He had developed a warm affection for Isabelle too. In Putnam's mind, Isabelle had become his family, and had a role of vast importance in his life. She had lived up to all his expectations and had given him life's greatest gift with Theo. Isabelle had never disappointed or lied to him, and they treated each other with the greatest respect.

In the September after their visit when Theo was four, she started nursery school and called to tell her father all about it. She said she already had two best friends. Isabelle was happy and busy and on the board of a major charity event she had volunteered for, to benefit a new wing at NYU hospital for breast cancer treatment and research. The gala they were organizing was going to be the New York social event of the year, with a major art auction, and an auctioneer from Christie's. Her gallery had donated a small Renoir drawing which was expected to go for a big price. Many galleries from cities all over the United States were involved, and she was on the committee to help set up and organize the booths, and decide who would be placed where. The art to be auctioned was an impressive collection of major and minor works by well-known artists from around the world. Their hope was to make at least five million dollars from the sale, and they had a benefactor who had promised to match what they made. And Putnam had made a large donation in Theo's name to get the event off to a good start, for which Isabelle was very grateful.

The behind-the-scenes politics of the event were complicated, with the more powerful galleries wanting the best spots for their booths, and the lesser ones wanting to show their work advantageously as well. She had just resolved several disputes between rival galleries. Other board members were on the committee for the black-tie dinner before the auction, and a well-known band had been hired to provide dancing afterward. The ticket prices for the evening spanned a broad range, with those in the "platinum" seats paying ten thousand a person and a hundred thousand for a table. They had one table of "diamond" guests for twenty-five thousand each. That table had to be in the front row for the auction, and right next to the dance floor, to satisfy the donors. Isabelle had a million details to attend to.

They had taken over part of Lincoln Center for the evening, and Isabelle had bought a simple black evening gown at Bergdorf that she knew she could wear again at gallery events. But her mind was occupied with far more important things than what she would wear. Each gallery wanted their setup to look impressive, and as soon as the auction was over, the empty booths had to be dismantled rapidly when the dancing began. The evening promised to be magical, but she was one of the magicians who had to make it all happen, which was incredibly stressful, but hopefully rewarding for the hospital in the end. Just as she was hoping to grab a sandwich at three o'clock the day before the event, she was called on the walkie-talkie to come and talk to a dealer who was in a heated debate with another committee member about where his booth had been placed.

"What can I do to help?" she asked pleasantly as she arrived on the scene to find a strikingly handsome man in a blue shirt and jeans arguing with two women from the committee who were at their wit's end, while he flatly refused to accept the booth he'd been assigned.

"I don't give a damn," he was saying to them. "I have the biggest clients in California, and twenty buyers flying in from Las Vegas who took two platinum tables. They don't want to see me shoved in a back row somewhere behind some gallery from Podunk, Iowa. I'm not going to let you make me look bad to my clients." He was almost shouting at them. One of the women was near tears. He was a force to be reckoned with.

"This is about raising money for the hospital for breast cancer," Isabelle reminded him in a pleasant tone, glancing at the name on his badge and looking it up on her list, which described him as a contemporary art dealer in

Newport Beach, California. She'd never heard of him before, but she was unfamiliar with dealers of contemporary art, except for the most elite ones in New York. "Everyone's trying to be good sports about where they're placed, since it's a charity event," she reminded him as he looked her over and assessed whether or not she was important enough to include in the argument. Her looks and calm demeanor told him she was—her beauty alone caught his attention, if nothing else. The two women he'd been arguing with were considerably older. "This really isn't about getting new clients," she said, but they both knew that wasn't entirely true. The booths being set up by a fleet of carpenters and electricians and still being painted would catch the eyes of collectors and potential buyers from around the country. It was part of the draw to encourage galleries to donate work, even if it wasn't fully representative of what they had to sell, since they weren't donating their very best work. It was a major undertaking, and Isabelle had enjoyed working on it for several months. Her employers were delighted she was doing it. She was well respected by her peers and superiors.

"I'm just going to pick a booth I like in the front row and set up in it, if you don't give me a decent one," he said in a bullying tone, and glanced at the name on her badge too. "And what do you do here?" he asked, his eyes blazing, which made him look even more handsome, although he was being particularly unpleasant.

"I'm on the committee that assigned the booths," she said calmly. They had spent weeks on the floor plan, and knew they'd have some problems like this, and were braced for it. She had a sudden idea as she spoke to him. They were trying to keep galleries of the same kind close to each other, so people interested in a particular kind of art, contemporary or modern or eighteenth century, would know where to find it. They had a map of the booths. "We had a cancellation this morning from a gallery in Chicago. The owner had a death in the family, and they're not coming to the event. We have the work they're donating, and we'll incorporate it with another gallery, but they no longer want to set up a booth. Let's see if it suits you, Mr. . . . Stone."

"Collin," he said, sounding slightly more gracious. "Thank you, Miss McAvoy," he said, as the two women looked at her gratefully and she led him away to show him the space.

"Isabelle. It's not ideal," she admitted to him before they got there, "but you may like it better than where you were placed." The event had been set up like an art fair, with less permanence, but with several alleys and long rows of booths. They were auctioning off three hundred pieces of art, like a real auction, with all the handlers that Christie's could supply. "I'm very sorry you're unhappy," she said more sympathetically than she felt. She just wanted the evening to go well, whatever it took. And he wanted to impress his clients who were flying in for the event.

"I have some major high flyers coming in from Vegas, as I said. I don't want to be shoved in a back corner, where you had me."

"I completely understand," she said smoothly as they stopped at the only available booth she had. He frowned as he looked at it, and then back at her.

"This is all you've got?"

"I'm afraid so. It's very centrally located." It was in the middle of the area they were setting up, where two alleys intersected.

"I've got a couple of really big pieces that could work well here," he said, and suddenly smiled at her. "Thank you for not embarrassing me with my clients. I'm opening in LA in a few months, and after that in Vegas, and I want my clients to be excited about us. We're going to two major art fairs this year." She knew that just getting through the red tape of that was a major feat, and this was obviously a major event for him too. It was an opportunity for all the galleries to showcase their work, not just help the hospital. "We're an up-and-coming young gallery, I hope you'll be hearing a lot about us in the future," he said to her enthusiastically.

"I'm sure I will," she said politely.

"Would you like to have a drink later? You just did me a big favor, Isabelle."

"I'm glad I could help. It was just luck that they canceled the booth." If you could consider a death in the family luck, but she didn't point that out to him. "But I'll be here tonight until after midnight, probably two or three A.M. I won't have time for a drink until after this is over." She also had no desire to have one with him. He was stunningly handsome, with movie-star good looks, but he seemed headstrong, arrogant, and difficult.

"Who are you in real life, when you're not working at this event?" he asked, and she smiled at the way he put it.

"I'm an associate at Acker Johnson," she said, knowing full well that the name of the gallery where she worked had enormous prestige and always impressed people. It was nice being able to say she was an associate after four years there. It had a distinguished ring.

"The serious stuff," he acknowledged, and she nodded. "You're young to be an associate, aren't you?"

"I'm older than I look." But clearly not by much—she had her long blond hair loose down her back and was wearing jeans and a sweatshirt. She was twenty-five and admittedly the youngest associate at the gallery. But she had earned the position through diligence, long hours, and hard work.

"Collin Stone." He shook her hand properly, impressing his name on her again. "This is quite an event."

"For a very good cause," she said demurely.

"Do you have a personal interest in it?" He wasn't afraid to ask questions, and was curious about her. She was a very pretty young woman.

"My mother died of breast cancer when I was three. I never really knew her. That was a long time ago, and there have been a lot of improvements in treatments since then, but I don't want other little girls to lose their mothers. She was only thirty-three when she died."

"My mother had it but beat it five years ago. So you're right, treatments are better now, and effective. Thank you again for improving my booth."

"Happy to help. See you tomorrow night," she said, although she knew she probably wouldn't. The event would be a zoo, and the only people she expected to see there were her colleagues and the gallery's clients at the two tables the gallery had taken. Theirs were platinum tables too, like Collin Stone's clients from Las Vegas.

"Good luck with the event." He flashed her a smile.

"Thank you for donating work for us to sell." She waved and walked away as she answered a call on her walkie-talkie. One of the two women was calling to inquire how it had worked out with him. "It's fine. He's happy. I gave him the booth that just freed up."

"Thank God for you. He looks like a saint, but acts like a devil."

"He's just full of himself and wants to look good to his clients flying in from LA and Vegas. We're going to have all kinds here tomorrow night."

She managed to get a break at dinnertime, and took

a cab to the gallery to check the messages on her desk, before going back to Lincoln Center for the rest of the night, to watch the booths get finished. As soon as she walked into her office, she saw two dozen long-stemmed roses in a vase on her desk and thought they might be from Putnam to wish her luck, since he had been so supportive and proud of what she was doing.

She opened the card, expecting to see his name, and instead the card read, "Thanks for helping me out. You're an angel. Good luck! Collin Stone." It was a nice gesture, although the two women who had put up with his arguments before she got there deserved them more than she did. She jotted down some notes, called two of her best clients who had just gotten to town, grabbed a yogurt and a piece of fruit from the fridge in the gallery kitchen, and rushed back to Lincoln Center to lend a hand wherever she could.

As she expected, she got home at two A.M. Maeve was asleep on the second twin bed in Theo's room, snoring softly. She kissed Theo and tucked her in and tiptoed into her own room, in the pleasant apartment Putnam had provided for them the last four years. The apartment was cozy more than handsome, and Isabelle had added enough touches to make it feel like a home and not just an apartment. She fell into her own bed as soon as she took her clothes off and was asleep in five minutes.

*

The day of the event was predictably insane, but considering all the moving parts they were dealing with, everything went smoothly. She was there on time to help greet the guests as they came in, in glittering evening gowns with lots of jewels. All of the New York social set was there, along with heavy hitters from the art world. Isabelle looked quietly elegant in her plain black dress with the string of pearls Putnam had given her when Theo was born. He had called to wish her luck that morning, knowing she'd be too busy to talk after that, and he made her promise to send all the newspaper clippings about the event. He had given her permission to buy a painting for him if she saw anything she thought he'd like, up to twenty-five thousand dollars, since it was a charitable event, and she thanked him profusely. She had already seen one or two that were his taste by artists he liked, and she said she'd be pleased to bid on them for him.

They had sponsors for the event, and had already received sizable donations from people who weren't able to attend. She was sure they'd make their goal, and probably do even better. She greeted whoever she knew in the crowd, although there were many people she didn't recognize, clients of other galleries and socialites she had never met. She was wearing a badge that identified her as a committee member, and directed people to the booths they were looking for when they asked her. She was observing the scene when Collin Stone walked past her, and stopped as soon as he saw her.

"Thank you for the lovely roses," she said when he approached. "I really don't deserve them."

"Yes, you do. I'd rather take you to dinner. I'm flying back to LA in two days. How about dinner tomorrow?"

"I'll be dead on my feet by then. I've been here every night for a week. Maybe next time." She didn't want to encourage him. He was handsome, but pushy and arrogant.

"I don't come to New York that often," he said, looking innocent and incapable of making the kind of scene he'd made the day before. He was a man who expected to get what he wanted, and wouldn't take no for an answer. "I'll call you tomorrow and see how you feel." He looked dashing in black tie, in an impeccably tailored dinner jacket, which made her wonder how Putnam would look in evening clothes. Undoubtedly aristocratic and handsome. There was something very LA about Collin Stone. He was well dressed, perfectly groomed, and had a great haircut. He had shining dark hair and dark eyes, and stood just a little too close when he talked to her, as though they already had an intimate relationship. Isabelle hadn't dated in the five years since she'd met Putnam and had been a student before that, dating boys her own age. She didn't feel ready for Collin, nor interested. She guessed him to be in his mid to late thirties. She was just happy to be out, enjoying a glamorous evening and watching people. She didn't need to pick up an art dealer from LA, no matter how charming he was. He was a powerhouse, and she felt out of her league when she was with him. He looked like someone who dated a lot, maybe movie stars or starlets. She was just a gallery associate, whose nights out consisted of pizza with her four-year-old daughter. She was sure Collin would have been bored to extinction by her and her real life.

She saw him sitting at one of the platinum tables with his guests when the auction began, and she noticed that they looked a lot like he did, slick and racy. The women all had amazing figures poured into skintight shimmering dresses, and had big hair and flashy jewels. The men looked rich and older, and very LA compared to the crowd from New York. The people at his second table looked even showier, and she guessed they were his guests from Las Vegas. Then she got distracted by the auction.

She bid on a painting for Putnam, for eighteen thousand dollars, under his limit, and attributed the purchase to Putnam Armstrong. The showstopper of the evening was a painting that sold for five hundred thousand dollars, donated by a gallery in Palm Beach. It had an impeccable provenance from an important collector who had owned it before, and was a recent acquisition for the gallery that donated it. The proceeds from the auction came to seven million dollars and the evening was a huge success. Isabelle noticed that only one of the pieces Collin's gallery had donated sold in the auction, and went for ten thousand dollars. It was by an unknown artist, and Collin looked pleased. He invited her to dance almost as soon as the band started, and she didn't want to be rude and decline, so she walked onto the floor with him, and he swept her around expertly as he congratulated her on the success of the evening.

"It was a huge team effort," she said modestly. "I was only a tiny cog in the machine."

"Don't be so humble," he said, looking down at her as though he knew her better than he did. "Do you have a husband here somewhere?" he asked and she shook her head, wishing she had had the sense to nod instead. There was something about Collin Stone that unnerved her. He was so forceful and direct, and wasn't afraid to go after what he wanted. He was the opposite of Putnam, who was so gentlemanly and subtle—everything that Collin wasn't. But there was no denying that Collin had a certain powerful charm of his own, like a heady fragrance, along with his good looks and sex appeal.

"I'm divorced," she said, lying to him, as she did to everyone, to explain Theo.

He looked surprised at that. "You must have been very young when you married."

"I was twenty. I spent my junior year abroad, in France. My ex-husband lives there. I have a four-year-old daughter." He was even more surprised at that. She didn't look old enough to have all those encumbrances, an ex-husband and a child.

"You're lucky. I've been looking for the right woman to settle down with since I turned thirty. No luck so far. I'm thirty-five. I want a wife and kids. I think I may have set the bar too high. I'm hoping to find the perfect mother for my children. You might just be it," he said glibly as he smiled down at her, and she had no idea how to respond to anything so direct and intimate, even if he was just kidding. But he looked like he meant it. "I have a great nose for people. You're a very special woman, Isabelle. I knew it from the first moment I saw you." He wanted to sweep her off her feet, and she was trying to keep them planted firmly on the ground.

"How do you know I'm not an axe murderer?" she teased him.

"You don't look strong enough to pick up an axe, let alone swing it. You'll have to shoot me with a very small pistol, not chop me up in little pieces. And you're not a widow, so you obviously didn't kill your ex-husband."

"No, I didn't. We've stayed very close, for my daughter's sake."

"That's what I mean. You're an unusual woman and a nice person." He seemed sincere, and she felt dazed when he led her back to the table and returned to his guests. Two of them had bought very expensive paintings, and Collin had paid two hundred thousand dollars for the tables, so she knew he must be doing well. They'd known that some of the paintings sold that night wouldn't be paid for or collected, and were just show-off gestures by the people who bid on them. But almost every sale they'd made had been bona fide, and the bidders had shown up with their credit cards right after the auction. A major part of what they'd spent would be tax deductible.

She wasn't on the breakdown committee, so she didn't have to stay to see the dismantling of the event, and went home at a reasonable hour, exhausted but thrilled with the results. She was in her office early the next morning to catch up, when Collin called to remind her of his invitation to dinner. "La Grenouille at eight o'clock?" he asked, trying to tempt her with one of the best restaurants in New York.

"I really can't, my sitter is exhausted, and I promised her she could go home tonight."

"Chinese takeout then? I want to meet your daughter." He was clearly a full-service date, willing to meet the children. She knew Putnam would have shied away at that, but Collin flinched at nothing. There was something very bold about him, which was at the same time frightening and appealing, and he made it difficult to turn him down. He was so insistent that she finally agreed to let him come to dinner, and said she would cook.

"That defeats the whole point. I want to spoil you, Isabelle. I know how hard you've been working on last night's event."

"Fine. Then bring pizza. Theo will love you."

"That's better." He sounded pleased.

When Collin showed up at the apartment, he was wearing a well-cut dark suit that looked Italian, and a white shirt with no tie, and quickly took off his coat and rolled up his sleeves. He was carrying two pizza boxes and another package, from which emerged a tin of caviar on ice with all the fixings, a bottle of champagne for them, and an ice-cream cake that looked like a clown for Theo. She clapped her hands the minute she saw it, and broke through her usual reserve to smile broadly at him, after Isabelle had introduced them. It made her slightly nervous to have him suddenly in the heart of her private life, and meeting Theo, but he chatted easily with her, as though children were no mystery to him. He read her a story, while Isabelle set the table and put out dinner. And Theo was enjoying the attention.

The conversation during the meal was easy and light, and he stayed while she put Theo to bed. Then they sat on the couch and drank champagne, while he commented on the rave reviews they'd had in the press for the breast cancer event.

"You were a star last night," he said, smiling gently at her. He seemed more low key than he had when she'd first met him. His private side seemed much less strident than when he was in the guise of art dealer trying to impress his clients. "How did you get into the art world?" he asked her.

"I grew up around it, and my father used to be a curator at the Boston Museum of Fine Arts."

"Is that where you grew up? In Boston?"

"Only until I was five. Then we moved to Newport, Rhode Island. I lived there until I graduated from college, and then I came here to find a job."

"Very fancy," he commented about Newport, but she didn't want to give him the wrong impression, and her apartment wasn't showy or luxurious.

"Not as fancy as it sounds." She didn't want to tell him about the Vanderbilt estate or her father's job. Collin had a way of walking into private spaces and exploring whatever he wanted, and he seemed like someone who had no secrets of his own. Everything about him was wide open. "What about you? How did you get into selling contemporary art?" She deflected the conversation back to him.

"It's where the money is these days. Big money for some people. I want a piece of that." He was undeniably ambitious and made no attempt to hide it. "My father made a killing in real estate and the stock market. He was a very smart guy, and then he lost everything with a slew of bad investments. So not so smart in the end.

For a while my mother and I had everything we wanted, and then one day, bingo, it was over when he lost it all, and we had nothing. It destroyed their marriage and my mother divorced him. I want to get back on top with the art market, if I sell to the right people. I don't want to wind up where my father did, living in a fleabag motel, selling insurance and eventually driving a limo. He died without a penny. I figure I've got ten or fifteen years to make it really big, and I intend to." She didn't doubt for a minute that he would. He had the kind of drive and determination to make it happen. He was a born winner, and he was hell-bent on making a fortune.

"The art market is a hard way to do it, especially with contemporary work. You can't always predict what will turn out to be a good investment," she said sensibly.

"I know that, but you'd be astounded what some people are willing to pay for new work, and as the dealer, I get fifty percent of every sale. There's a fortune to be made with what I'm doing, particularly in LA. The art market there is huge, and I've just recently started exploring Vegas. My clients may not be as polished and blue-blooded as yours, Isabelle, but their money smells just as good to me." He was blunt about what he wanted, which was foreign to her, but in some ways intriguing. One had to admire him for working so hard at climbing the ladder to success. She had never been as ambitious, and was satisfied to build her career more slowly. She had her eye on the big picture and a respectable career, not instant money. "What do you want to be when you grow up?" She smiled at the question.

"An art consultant, dealing in Old Masters and Impressionists. It's what I know best. I want to help people put together important collections. I get satisfaction from that. It's like matchmaking in a way."

"I don't have your patience, or your knowledge," he said honestly, and she liked that about him too. He hid nothing, and she was enjoying him much more than she had expected she would. "With a woman like you at my side, I could move mountains," he said dreamily.

"I have the feeling you can do that on your own," she said as she finished her glass of champagne and he poured her another. She was feeling slightly tipsy, which she didn't like when she was alone with Theo, but Theo was fast asleep, and Isabelle knew she would be soon too, after Collin left, so what they were doing didn't seem dangerous. Just this once.

"My life has no meaning without a wife and kids," he said softly as he looked at her longingly. "Success is only half of it. The rest is what really matters." She knew that too, but for her the lesson had been hard won. "I just have to meet the right one. And, Isabelle, I really think you're it. I knew it from the moment I saw you." His saying it was premature and embarrassed her, but with the help of the champagne it didn't seem quite so shocking, nor did it when he kissed her a moment later. He tried to lay her down on the couch, but she wouldn't let him.

"My daughter's in the next room," she reminded him sternly.

"And if she weren't," he whispered, "would that make a difference?" She didn't know what to say to him. She hadn't slept with anyone since Putnam, and it had been three years since she'd been physically involved with him. She was twenty-five, and Collin was fatally attractive. He had a hand on her breast, which she knew shouldn't be there, but she didn't want him to remove it. "I know this sounds crazy, but I think I'm falling in love with you. You're everything I've ever wanted. Beautiful, smart, sexy, a good person, and a wonderful mother."

"You don't know anything about me," she said, feeling sober again and a little frightened. He was moving very quickly. Much *too* quickly, and building a fantasy about her.

"I know everything I need to know about you." And she knew nothing about him, except what he had told her. "If you married me tomorrow, I know it would work."

"Well, fortunately, neither of us are crazy enough to do that." She finally moved her leg away and put down her glass of champagne.

"When can I see you again, Isabelle? I can come to New York whenever you want me. I'm seeing a client here in two weeks. He's flying in from Moscow to meet me. I have to go to Hong Kong after that."

"You lead a much more interesting life than I do." It was hard not to be impressed by what he was saying, and how enterprising he was. He was someone who made things happen. He didn't wait for life to happen to him.

"Then share my life with me. You can come with me whenever you want."

"I have a daughter and a job," she said, smiling at him, "and both are important to me."

"I want to be important to you. I want to have children with you." It was crazy talk, but the way he looked at her, coupled with what he said, was mesmerizing.

"Beware of what you wish for," she said softly.

"You would be my dream come true, Isabelle. I want to see you again, as soon as possible. I'll be back in two weeks. Make time for me. Would you go away for a weekend with me? Can you get a sitter for Theo?"

"Yes, about the sitter. But I won't go away with you until I know you a whole lot better. If you really want to spend time with me, let's do it more sensibly than this. I don't want to rush into anything. I've already made one mistake, I don't want to make another." He nodded, willing to slow down if it would help him win her. "And I don't want to lie to you, Collin. I'm not divorced. I wasn't married to Theo's father. I loved him deeply, and still do in many ways, and he's a wonderful father to her. But I was hasty about throwing myself into a relationship with him. I don't regret it because of Theo. But the next time I fall in love, I want to be sensible about what I'm doing. I was twenty then. I don't have that excuse now." He was impressed by her honesty and understood her caution.

"I'll try not to rush you, but I know what I want." He was so determined—it still puzzled her. They hardly knew each other. Why her, and why now?

"I've already seen that side of you," she said, smiling at him, and he kissed her tantalizingly on the lips. If she had let herself throw caution to the winds, she would have gone to bed with him, but she knew she shouldn't, and wasn't going to until she was more sure about what she was doing, and who he was.

He got up to leave then. He had said enough. He'd put his stake in the ground and wasn't going to let her get away, or let fear keep her from doing what he wanted. Once Collin made up his mind to do something, nothing could stop him.

"We could work together one day, if you wanted to," he suggested as she walked him to the door.

"I think I'm better where I am. It's what I was trained for." He nodded, willing to accept a rejection on that front and no other. "Thank you for the caviar and champagne."

"That's the life I want to share with the woman I love. Caviar and champagne forever. I'm working toward that now." But riches and luxuries had never been motivators for her, and she didn't love Putnam for what he had. Collin had no way of knowing who Theo's father was. He thought Isabelle was a bright young woman with a good job, in a modest apartment. He didn't understand that this was all she wanted, until she could do more for herself. She wasn't looking for a man to support her. She only needed some help for her daughter, and Putnam took care of that.

She thought about Collin that night as she lay in bed, slightly unnerved by the evening and how brazen he was, and at the same time flattered and aroused by it. He was a hard man to resist, and she wondered if he would pursue her now, or lose interest and move on to someone else.

He called her the next morning before he left the city, and from LA that night, where he was seeing clients. She heard from him again from Palm Springs and Newport Beach, and Las Vegas. He was just as besotted by her as ever. When he came back to New York to meet his Russian client, he invited her to dinner with them, but she declined. He took her out to dinner after his client left. Collin said the Russian had bought a million dollars' worth of paintings from him, which meant he had just made half a million for himself. She congratulated him on the sale. She dealt with even larger amounts at the gallery where she worked, but the big commissions were for the house and not for her. She made a set percentage on her sales, which was a respectable amount, but nothing like what Collin had just made. He was on a fast track to the big time, which was where he wanted to be, and he wasn't shy about it. He said the client he was meeting in Hong Kong was even bigger, and he was vague about who that was. He said he had others in Dubai, which was a burgeoning new market, and a hotbed of international money, much of it recently made.

Collin seemed desperate to tell her about everything he was doing to impress her and make her feel like she was part of his life. She'd been alone for a long time, which made her vulnerable to him, but she was determined not to get into a relationship she couldn't handle with a man she didn't know.

He tried to get her to go back to his hotel with him after dinner, but she wouldn't. He was still moving too fast for her. She had enjoyed the evening with him and was trying not to be overwhelmed by him. He kissed her longingly in the cab when he dropped her off at her apartment and she wouldn't let him come upstairs. Her resisting him and insisting on their taking their time was driving him insane. He had never waited for a woman before, but said she was worth the wait.

She mentioned him to her father on Thanksgiving when she and Theo spent the holiday with him. She and Collin had been dating for almost three months by then. She described what he did as a personal art dealer, and that he'd managed to come to New York two or three times a month to see her, which meant she had seen him about eight times since they'd met.

"He sounds interesting, but be careful, Isabelle. You do need to get out more, but it seems like he's on a fast track to somewhere. Just be sure it's where you want to go." She agreed with him, but was thinking about Collin more and more. He called her constantly from all over the country and all over the world. She'd grown more comfortable with him, and he hadn't wavered about the fact that he was in love with her, which still was somewhat hard to believe.

Collin came to see her a week before Christmas, before she and Theo left for Newport again. He had begged her to spend the holidays with him, but she said she couldn't let her father down. He asked her to come to the Turks and Caicos with him on New Year's Eve, and this time she agreed. She couldn't put him off any longer and didn't want to. It was harder and harder to find reasons not to make love with him. It was what she wanted now too. She had been sensible for long enough. And she thought a trip might help them get to know each other better. There were still things about him she didn't know. There were pieces of the puzzle missing that he didn't volunteer or explain.

Maeve stayed with Theo and they left on the thirtieth on a plane he had chartered for her. He had rented a fully staffed villa near the beach, with a swimming pool off their bedroom. They had barely arrived when he picked her up and carried her to bed, and they didn't leave their bedroom and the private pool for two days. She had never in her life had such an exotic experience or known such an exciting man. On New Year's Eve, he got down on one knee at midnight and proposed. She knelt down in front of him and kissed him and whispered, "I love you, Collin. But let's not get married yet. It's too soon. Let's wait." He was disappointed by her response and wanted her to keep the ring he'd bought, but she refused and said she needed longer to get to know him. He looked like a child who'd been told that Santa Claus had been delayed, and she asked him to keep the ring. She wasn't ready to promise him the rest of her life yet. He had swept her off her feet, but she wanted to be sure it would last.

She was curious about his home in Newport Beach, and the gallery, but it seemed as if he was never there. She met him in Aspen instead, Palm Beach and Miami, where he was seeing clients. They went skiing in Vermont, she slept with him at his hotel room in New York, and in April they went to Saint Bart's. He proposed again, and this time, she said yes. They'd been dating for seven months, and she agreed that they both needed to settle down, and stop meeting in other cities. The pace of their relationship had been frantic since they'd met. It seemed to be Collin's style. He was a shooting star, while telling her constantly that he wanted to slow down. But there was no evidence of it yet. And when she asked him where they would live, he answered New York. He respected her job, traveled everywhere to see his clients, and said he wanted to close the gallery in Newport Beach. His business had outgrown it and meeting clients in their homes around the globe was more profitable, with no overhead. He was prepared to make New York his home base, with her. He wanted them to get a bigger apartment in the city, and told her to start looking. But she didn't want to rush into it. She liked the one Putnam provided and it was big enough for the three of them.

He cried when she agreed to marry him, and after some discussion, they decided to get married in Newport in June with only her father and Theo present. Collin had no relatives other than his mother, who was in an assisted-living facility in San Diego, with Alzheimer's. He said she wasn't up to the trip and wouldn't enjoy the wedding. She was too confused.

Isabelle called to tell her father about getting married, and he said he was happy for her, that Collin sounded like an ambitious, hardworking man, and he hoped it would be everything she wanted. He was slightly reserved about it, and wanted only his daughter's happiness with the right man.

Collin made a big effort to woo his father-in-law when

he met him in Newport the day before the ceremony. Isabelle hadn't wanted a wedding, just a simple ceremony at their local church. She'd lost touch with her old school friends, and Theo was her life. She looked radiant when they exchanged their vows and he slipped a diamond band on her finger with the engagement ring she'd finally accepted. The only thing she was uncomfortable about was that she hadn't told Putnam about Collin yet. She wanted to tell him in person in August. Collin said he'd be traveling all summer to see clients, meeting them on their yachts and in their summer homes. He didn't see why she should stop visiting Putnam for the month as she always did. She was grateful he had no objection, and he had no problem with her keeping her job, although he said he wanted babies right away.

They postponed their honeymoon for the time being since he was traveling so much, and went back to New York after the weekend as man and wife.

For the next two months, Collin was gone almost constantly, making deals and seeing clients, mainly in Las Vegas and abroad, and she didn't see him for weeks before she was due to leave for Normandy with Theo at the end of July. Isabelle was somewhat disappointed that she had seen so little of Collin ever since their wedding. He had warned her that it would be that way, and he had apologized for it in advance. But his clients were demanding and expected him to show up wherever they were for the summer, given the amount of money they were willing to spend on the paintings he sold them. He tried to make it up to Isabelle in the days, here and there, that he managed to spend with her between trips, but basically he was a no-show, as he had feared, and he didn't expect to be in New York for more than a few days until September. He was relieved to know that Putnam would have Isabelle and Theo with him in August in France. Instead of being jealous, he was grateful to him, and from Isabelle's description of him, he sounded like a wonderful man. They had no plans to meet but Collin said he'd like to at a convenient time.

Isabelle was concerned too that Collin's traveling had cooled his ardor. Whenever she saw him, he was exhausted and jet-lagged. Their passionate love life had slowed down almost as soon as they had exchanged their vows. His traveling so much hadn't affected him before, but it did now. Isabelle left for France feeling like a wife, but not a bride.

*

She told Putnam about Collin the first night at dinner. She didn't like keeping secrets from him. He was startled at first, but liked the fact that Collin was supportive of Isabelle and Theo's summer visit and had no desire to interfere or interrupt them. Putnam was elated to see them both when they arrived. She could tell how lonely he had been by how anxious he was for Theo's company. He wanted to show her everything new on the estate, including two lambs. Theo wanted to take them to New York with her, but her father explained that they wouldn't be happy in an apartment. She had just turned five in May and was an enchanting child with impeccable manners and a kind heart. She was as shy as ever, except when she was with her father, and then they chattered incessantly, and Theo seemed to blossom, as did her father.

When they had time alone, Putnam questioned her intensely about Collin and the nature of his business. Isabelle was as vague about it as Collin was himself, and she didn't fully understand the scope of his business except that he sold high-priced contemporary art privately, and had a small gallery on the West Coast which he intended to close in the fall. He didn't need it anymore, and was planning to switch his base of operations to New York. And so far, he hadn't had time to show her his gallery in Newport Beach.

"You're sure he's on the up-and-up?" Putnam said, concerned, when she explained Collin's private art sales to him. "It's not a money-laundering operation, is it?" She laughed at the idea.

"Not at all. He's just a very ambitious guy, and is after big money. His father lost everything when he was a child. I think it traumatized him. He wants to settle down."

"I just want you to be happy, Isabelle. That's all. You deserve it." It was what her father said too. Putnam wanted Collin to do what he couldn't and knew he should have done for her. In some ways Putnam was relieved that she was in love with Collin. He didn't need to feel guilty toward her anymore and could focus on his daughter, who gave him endless joy.

Collin called Isabelle every few days in Normandy, and told her how much he missed her. She slept a lot and read on the terrace while Putnam went on adventures with Theo. She trusted him with her completely. He was an attentive and responsible father, even if only for one month a year. She was still in Normandy when she realized that she was pregnant, and must have conceived in June the weekend of their wedding. She didn't tell Putnam. She wanted to tell Collin first, when she saw him in New York when they got home. All his dreams had finally come true. It was exactly what he had wanted—a wife and a baby. And now he would have both. The future looked very bright to Isabelle too.

Chapter Five

Leaving Putnam at the end of August was as bittersweet as it always was. All three of them cried, and Putnam promised to write and call often. He took Theo to say goodbye to the lambs the morning they left.

Collin got back to New York a week after Isabelle and Theo, and when she told him about the baby, he was thrilled. It was due in March, and he said he wanted to stop traveling so much, but admitted that for the next three or four months he had some important trips scheduled. He promised to stay home with her in New York after the first of the year.

She was busy herself for the next few months, at work and with Theo, so she missed him but had lots to do. They talked about moving again, but for the first few months they were going to put the baby in Theo's room, so there was no rush, and Theo was excited at the prospect of a baby brother or sister when they told her.

Isabelle was upset when Collin missed Thanksgiving with them at her father's in Newport. He was in Las Vegas. He swore he'd make it to Newport for Christmas.

He had been in LA and Hong Kong for three weeks when he called Isabelle on the morning of Christmas Eve. He was supposed to be on a plane to Boston by then, from the West Coast.

"Don't tell me you missed your flight," she said, sounding exasperated. His constant traveling to see clients was starting to bother her and hadn't slowed down at all.

"Not exactly," Collin said in a grim voice. "I'm still in LA."

"What time are you catching your flight?" She sounded tense when she asked him. Her father had been questioning her about why he was away all the time, and it was getting harder to explain, even to herself. He always had an excuse.

"Isabelle . . . I don't know how to say this to you," Collin said in a hoarse voice, filled with emotion. "I'm not going to make my flight."

"Why not?" Her voice filled with anger and her eyes with tears. "Where are you?" He sounded strange, with voices behind him, and an echo that sounded like he was at the bottom of a well.

"I'm in a federal jail, in LA," he said in a choked voice. "The charges are bogus, I can explain everything to you when I get home. I have to make bail first, and they won't set bail till I'm arraigned." She could hear a tinge of panic as he said it, and the bottom fell out of her world.

"You're spending Christmas in jail? What are the charges against you?" She suddenly felt ice cold and was shaking.

"Multiple counts of money laundering and tax evasion. It's all bullshit. I sold some paintings to a guy in Las Vegas who's had trouble with the Feds recently." She sat down on a stool in her father's kitchen as she listened, and thought she was going to faint for a moment. She was six months pregnant by a man who might be going to prison. Her husband. And she suddenly wondered if she had ever known him at all. Why had he married her? Was he just a con man? Had he used her as a front? Was it all lies? She suddenly remembered Putnam's question to her that summer about whether Collin was laundering money. She had laughed and thought it was absurd. It was all too real now. "Isabelle, don't go crazy over this. These things happen, I'll get out of it. They can't make the charges stick."

"And what if they do? 'These things' *don't* happen, not to normal people, unless you commit a crime." She was crying as she spoke to him. She had trusted him and felt like an idiot now. She loved him. But who was he?

"I have friends in high places who can get me out of it. I'll be back in a few days, just sit tight till then. I'm sorry to miss Christmas with you. How are you feeling, by the way?"

"It's none of your goddam business." They told him

he had to end the call then, and he hung up seconds later as she sat staring out the window in her father's kitchen, feeling as though her whole world had just collapsed. Her father walked in a minute later and looked at her, worried. She was devastated.

"Are you okay?" She started to say yes and then shook her head and wound up sobbing in his arms. She told him what had happened, and his jaw clenched as he listened. "It doesn't sound good," he said quietly, and it didn't to her either. They sat at the kitchen table talking about it. She didn't know enough about the charges to discuss them intelligently with him, but it sounded like a terrible situation. Collin Stone was a charming con man, and despite her initial reserve about him and determination to be cautious and get to know him, she had been totally taken in. He was a pro.

He hadn't bilked money out of her, just used her as a respectable front, like some kind of game. But it was her life. And Theo's and their baby's were on the line too. She wondered how she could have been such a fool and believed everything he said.

She waited until three A.M. to call Putnam at a decent hour in Normandy, and he wished her a Merry Christmas as soon as he heard her voice.

"It's not exactly merry," she said and he realized then what time it was for her. She told him what had happened, sobbing.

"I don't know who this guy really is, but if I were you, I would get out of it as fast as I can," Putnam advised her. "You don't want to be tied to a criminal. And God knows what else he's done." Putnam had wondered about him from the beginning, but hadn't wanted to be critical or overly suspicious or upset her, if it turned out that he was all right. It had sounded smoky to him from the start, and now the house was on fire. That was what she had been thinking all night. But she was married to him, and pregnant with his baby. But that hadn't kept Collin from a life of crime. Putnam suggested that he have him checked out, although it was a little late for that, and Isabelle agreed. She had already been married to him when she told Putnam about him, or he would have done it sooner. And she'd been so sure he was honest.

She went back to New York after Christmas with a heavy heart, not sure what to do. She wanted to see Collin before she made any decision, and hear from Putnam about his investigation. It was ten days later when he came home.

Collin had been accused of sixteen counts of money laundering, and eight counts of tax evasion. They weren't dropping the charges, and he said he needed a federal defense attorney immediately. One of his Vegas friends had put up the bail.

"I don't have the money to pay for a lawyer," he said with pleading eyes, and he hesitated before he asked the next question, knowing she couldn't afford his legal fees either. "Do you think you could ask Theo's dad to float me a loan for a while? I'm her stepfather after all. I'm sure he wouldn't want me to go to jail." On the contrary, he thought Collin belonged there, and she was beginning to think so too. Collin knew who Putnam was by then, that Theo would be provided for for the rest of her life and was his only heir.

"Are you serious?" Isabelle stared at him. "You want Putnam to pay your legal fees for money laundering and tax evasion? You think I would ask him to do that?"

"You'd better, baby, or I'm going to jail," he said harshly, and she stared at him like the stranger he had become, and always had been. She just didn't know it. She had fallen in love with the illusion he had created, but she realized now that none of it was real. Whoever she had fallen in love with didn't exist. She had married a criminal, and she had no intention of staying with him after hearing what he had to say. None of his explanations rang true or made sense. She believed him guilty of all of it, and she wanted to get as far away from him as she could. Whatever she had felt for him had been struck dead when he called her from jail.

He tried to tell her he had made most of the deals for large sums of money with a silent partner, and was taking the fall for him. She didn't believe a word of it. And Putnam confirmed her worst fears. Collin had been selling worthless paintings for millions. Some were forgeries, others were simply fraudulently represented as to their value and provenance, some were stolen, and Collin hadn't paid income tax for years. It had been a very simple operation which relied on his clients' ignorance and innocence, and he'd earned millions and been stashing it away in tax havens. Apparently two of his clients suspected it and turned him in, and all their accusations had turned out to be true. Putnam said there probably wouldn't even be a trial, as there was too much evidence against him. He would have to plead guilty and try to make a deal with the Feds to lighten his sentence. Putnam's investigator had said there was no doubt he was going to prison. He had been charged with scams before, but not on this scale, and there hadn't been enough evidence to convict him. This time they had all they needed, and undoubtedly others among his clients would discover their fraudulent dealings with him too. Putnam advised her to divorce him as fast as she could.

The day after he came home, she told Collin he had to leave. "You can't stay here," she said in a raw voice. "You've lied to me from the beginning." She was crying when she said it, for herself more than for him. And their baby, who didn't deserve a father like this. No one did. She wondered now if the stories about his own father were true. Or if he'd been a crook too, and not just a failure.

"Great. I have a little problem, and you bail at the first

sign of trouble. What kind of woman are you? You're having my baby, Isabelle, or are you going to get rid of that too?" It was far too late for that, and she would never have done it. She couldn't imagine now why he had wanted a baby. He was a sociopath.

"You don't have a little problem, Collin. You have a huge one. You're a crook, you always were. I see that now. And I don't want to be any part of this. I want you out of here. Let me know your address and I'll send your things." He had moved very little into the apartment, and said most of what he owned was still in Newport Beach. She didn't know if that was true either. He left without an argument, and without telling her where he was going. He didn't even say goodbye to Theo, who looked worried when she saw her mother crying.

Three days later, his indictment hit the papers, both in the art section and on the front page. He had been using his fraudulent art business to launder money for several years. It had never dawned on her in the beginning that he was a crook. He was so smooth and so adoring, seemed so ambitious and hardworking, that she hadn't doubted him for a minute. She realized now that she should have. He was a total sham, and had used her to feign some kind of respectability. She suspected that she and even their baby meant nothing to him. They were just toys he had played with, or pawns in his game, not people he loved. He loved no one.

She filed for divorce in January, and learned that Collin was back in California by then. She sent his clothes and belongings to the address she had in Newport Beach. It turned out to be the home of an ex-girlfriend, not a gallery. He'd been paying her to store stolen paintings, and she was arrested too. The whole story was sordid, and she felt like a fool. And her job at Acker Johnson probably lent him some credibility by association.

Two months after she filed for divorce, Xela was born in a snowstorm in March. Maeve came to stay with Theo, and Isabelle was alone when her second daughter was born. The birth was easier than Theo's had been, but she cried all through her labor, wishing she hadn't gotten pregnant. The last thing she wanted was Collin's child. She didn't say a word when they told her it was a girl, and the baby hadn't stopped screaming from the moment she was born until Isabelle took her in her arms and looked down at her. She was beautiful, as dark as Theo was fair, and she had an angry expression, as though she were mad at the world.

"She has a big voice," one of the nurses said, but she was peaceful as her mother held her. Eventually the little furrowed brow relaxed, she hiccupped, closed her eyes, and went to sleep.

Isabelle called Maeve and her father when they took the baby to the nursery. She had already decided to put her own last name on the birth certificate. She didn't want to tie this innocent child to a criminal. And she had no way to notify Collin of his daughter's birth. She had no idea where he was and assumed he was in jail, or maybe still out on bail if he hadn't pleaded guilty yet. She wasn't even sure he would care about the baby with all the trouble he was in, or if he ever would have. She doubted everything he'd said now, about wanting to settle down and have children with her. It was all part of his act, which she had believed, while he pursued his criminal activities.

Isabelle had started using his name when they were married, and had switched back to her own when she filed for divorce after his arrest in LA. There had been murmurs at work, but no one had dared to ask her the details. She notified them when the baby was born, and they sent her flowers at the hospital and a teddy bear for the baby. They felt sorry for her. All Isabelle wanted to do was to forget she had ever known Collin Stone, but now she had the baby to remind her of him constantly. She had picked Xela's name on her own—she'd read it somewhere and liked it.

For the first few weeks, Xela cried whenever she was awake—she would ball up her fists and scream. Maeve said she was colicky. Theo stood next to her bassinet and watched her curiously.

"Why does she cry all the time, Mommy?"

"She has a tummyache," Isabelle explained.

"Will she be better soon?" Theo asked innocently.

"I hope so." Isabelle was just as eager for the baby to stop screaming. It wore on her nerves. It was as though Xela knew she had come into the world in bad circumstances, far worse than Theo's, who had a father who adored her, and a trust that would provide for her and her children, and their children one day. Her parents weren't married, but they loved each other. Isabelle hated Collin for his lies and for having duped her.

Isabelle had nothing but contempt for Collin now and deeply regretted having married him, and ever having met him. Their marriage had been as fraudulent as everything else he did. It was as though Xela knew it, and was railing against the fates that had given her to parents who were so undeserving: a father who was likely to spend years in prison, and a mother who didn't want her, because she was a reminder of the man who had lied to her. Isabelle had to force herself to spend time with Xela, and instead spent most of her time with Theo, who was learning to read in kindergarten and could sit quietly for hours poring over the words and looking at the pictures.

Eventually, Xela stopped screaming, and seemed to make peace with her existence. She was fascinated by Theo and watched her every move. Collin had contacted Isabelle by then. He was in California preparing to enter a guilty plea, and negotiating for a deal to shorten his sentence. He didn't want to see the baby, which was a relief, and he wanted to give up his parental rights. He said he was in no position to be responsible for a baby. His lawyer said there was a good chance he would do ten or twenty years. Isabelle didn't even feel sorry for him. She felt nothing for him.

The papers relinquishing his parental rights to Xela arrived a few weeks later. He had signed in all the appropriate places, and so did she. She wanted no contact with him in the future, and little by little she adjusted to having a second baby. Xela was much more difficult than Theo. The baby had a fierce temper whenever she was hungry or uncomfortable, and sometimes she still screamed herself to sleep.

"Poor little thing," Maeve said, trying to rock her to sleep one night, to no avail. "It's almost as if she knows she didn't get a fair deal right from the beginning, with a father who's a con man and caused you so much grief." Isabelle smiled at what she said. Xela was a pretty baby, in a dark, exotic way, with almost jet black hair and dark eyes, just like Collin. She hoped his criminal bent wasn't hereditary. Sometimes those things ran in families, but her father insisted that was a myth when Isabelle suggested it to him with a fearful look.

"She's only a baby, she'll grow up with you and Theo and be a lovely little girl one day." He felt sorry for Xela and for Isabelle having made such a shocking mistake.

It had shaken her faith in her own judgment, and Jeremy insisted that anyone would have been taken in by him. Collin Stone was a practiced sociopath.

Xela was five months old, and Theo had turned six, when they left for Normandy that summer. Putnam said he was happy to have Xela too. From the moment they arrived, Theo was glued to her father's side, as she always was. They spent hours together, without even talking sometimes. They were two peas in a pod. Marcel, the old butler, saw it too.

Their adventures together gave Isabelle more time to bond with the baby. She had gone back to work four weeks after she was born, and Xela wasn't screaming anymore but she was a restless child who seemed to want to be in motion all the time. Isabelle roamed all over the property with her, in the pram they had used for Theo. It took her forever to fall asleep.

Their time in Normandy was healing for Isabelle. She and Putnam talked late into the night, and she went over and over in her head how she had fallen for Collin and why she had believed him. He was exciting and dangerous. She felt foolish and gullible and couldn't imagine trusting any man again.

"He's one man, Isabelle," Putnam said sensibly. "We can all make mistakes." She had been young and trusting and wanted to believe him. "Sociopaths are ingenious people. I'm sure he was good at what he did. Wiser people than you and I have been fooled. You have to put it behind you and go on now." And then he thought of something else. "What are you going to tell Xela about who her father was?"

"I'm not sure," she said thoughtfully. "What can I say? That he was a criminal and went to prison?" It seemed a hard blow for a child. "I'll probably have to wait until she grows up to say anything." He entered a guilty plea while they were in Normandy, and there was no publicity. The press had lost interest in him. He was just another criminal going to prison. Putnam was able to find out that he was sentenced to ten years in federal prison instead of twenty. She never heard from him again and never wanted to. The waters closed over him, as though their marriage had never existed, and she was left with her regrets at having met and fallen in love with him.

In time, Xela seemed unrelated to him. She and Theo were both Isabelle's daughters, however different they were. She concentrated on both of them. Xela was always jealous of her older sister, and Theo was patient with her. When Xela got too rambunctious, Theo would retreat to her room to read a book, just as Putnam would have. Isabelle could only hope that Collin's genes weren't as strong in his daughter. Xela was a bright, enterprising child, always getting into mischief. Isabelle said she loved them both equally and silently wished that it were true.

Theo was easier to love with her quiet, serious ways.

Xela was the cyclone in their midst every day. She particularly loved torturing her sister in every way she could, taking her toys and dolls, and tearing out pages in her books. She wanted everything that Theo had, and what Theo wouldn't give her, Xela took and hid somewhere in the room they shared. But as time went on, and as the memory of Collin faded, Isabelle did come to love them both equally. After all, regardless of Collin, Xela was her daughter too.

Chapter Six

Until Theo was eight and Xela three, Isabelle concentrated only on her children, as she had done after Theo was born. She had no interest in dating, and couldn't imagine trusting a man again. Her father had given up saying anything to her about it, and Putnam had tried to reason with her too, to no avail.

"You're a young woman, Isabelle," he insisted.

"Not as young as I used to be," she said, sounding tired when she got to Normandy that summer with the girls. She was twenty-nine years old.

She was the senior consultant and salesperson at the gallery now, and working very hard. She still dreamed of being an independent art consultant, but needed the handsome salary they paid her. She was living in the same apartment, and saved money wherever she could. It always felt good to get to Normandy in the summer and relax. Theo and her father would disappear all day. He took her out in his sailboat in a life jacket, with Isabelle's permission. But Xela was too young, and she was a hellion. Even at three, she hid in the bushes, loved to play hide-and-seek and climb trees. She kept her mother busy every day. And Theo loved having a break to spend time with her father, without having her sister tag along.

"Why can't I go too?" Xela would complain to her mother.

"Because I'd be too lonely without you. You have to keep me company." They visited the chickens and collected the eggs, watched the farmer at the château's farm milk the cows, and Putnam led her around the riding ring on a pony he had bought for Theo, and Xela clamored loudly that she wanted one too. Putnam promised that in a few years he'd get her one, and Theo, as always, was patient about sharing her pony with her sister. She was long-suffering and kind.

The month always flew by in the peaceful French countryside, and when they went back to New York, Isabelle felt restored. Both girls had had a wonderful visit with Putnam, and they talked about it for months. Xela wanted to take the pony home with them, but Putnam said the pony would be unhappy in New York and needed to stay there. Both girls were always sad when they left, and Putnam the saddest of all. He and their grandfather were the only male figures in their lives, and Isabelle assured Put that wasn't going to change.

"You never know. You may meet someone who suits you perfectly one of these days. You don't have to look for it, it will find you."

"If it does, I'm locking the door and calling the police," she said and he laughed. Collin had been in prison for more than two years by then, and she still shuddered at the memory. All she ever said about him was that getting involved had been a terrible mistake, and neither Putnam nor her father could disagree. She blamed herself for how gullible she'd been.

"When it's right, it will just happen and it will be easy," Putnam said philosophically, which was exactly how she met Declan Donahue. He came to the opening of an exhibition of Impressionists at the gallery with his law partner, Tom Kelly, a collector who had bought from them before. Declan didn't appear to be in the market for any paintings, but enjoyed looking around and stopped to chat with Isabelle before they left. They talked for a few minutes, and he commented on how beautiful the paintings were, and managed not to say she was even more so. He thought she was the most graceful, charming woman he had ever seen, and he had enjoyed her even more than the art. His partner was considering three paintings, and hadn't made a decision yet.

"It's a lovely show," Declan said, as they chatted, and she thanked him. He was tall and thin and athletic-looking. He talked about his recent trip to Paris, and she said she had gone to school there for a year, at the Sorbonne. The conversation was brief, casual, and easy, and then they left. By some odd coincidence, she ran into him when she bought groceries in her neighborhood the next day. She almost ran him down with her cart, and was startled when she looked up and saw him.

"Do you have a license for that thing?" he asked her, laughing. "You must have learned to drive in France. Do you live around here?" He was curious about her. Her cart was full of things that children would like—cereal, cookies, ice-cream cones, pancake mix—none of it food that someone with her figure would indulge in.

"I live a block away," she answered.

"I take it you have children," he said, indicating the contents of the cart.

"Two girls, three and nine. You too?"

He pointed to the dog food in his. "A golden retriever named Harvey." They stood in the checkout line together and chatted, and then went their separate ways.

She saw him again three weeks later, as they nearly collided when they both ran for a cab in the pouring rain, and he got there first. He was about to yield it to her when he saw who it was.

"That's the second time you almost knocked me down," he commented with a grin.

"I'm sorry," she said, looking contrite. They were both getting soaked in the autumn storm.

"I was about to give it to you. Why don't we share? Where are you going?"

"Downtown, to meet a client about a painting."

"I'll drop you off. I'm going to the Village." She gave him the address, and they talked easily in the traffic on the way downtown, and then he dropped her off. He called her at the gallery the next day and invited her to dinner, but she gracefully declined, saying she was busy. Her tone was cool and light—she didn't want to encourage him, or have him ask her a second time.

He switched the invitation to lunch the following week, and she turned him down again. He had his law partner check to see if she was married, and he reported back that she wasn't. He tried four more times and got nowhere, and finally asked her bluntly.

"Is it me, or do you have a boyfriend? I don't want to be a nuisance."

"I don't date," she said simply on the phone.

"Ever?" He sounded shocked. She was gorgeous.

"Not recently, or not for the last three years, closer to four actually."

"Can I ask why not? Are you planning to enter a religious order?"

She laughed at the question. "No. Shit judgment. I lost my dating privileges and decided not to renew them."

"That sounds much too intriguing to just let it slip by. Have lunch with me once at least, and tell me about it." He suspected a bad divorce since she had two children, but she was amazingly firm with her refusals.

"It's not a very interesting story, and talking about it might give me indigestion."

"Then have lunch with me anyway. That's not a date. It's just eating. Nothing big ever happens over lunch. Lunch is for mothers and daughters, fathers and sons, and old school friends." She smiled at what he said and finally weakened.

"Okay. Once. After that we meet in the supermarket, where I try to run you down."

"You sound dangerous."

"I'm not," she assured him. She met him on a Saturday at a deli halfway between their apartments and shared a humongous turkey sandwich with him.

"Okay, so tell me the horror story that led you to give up dating."

"One isn't a horror story, just an error of judgment. The other is more unpleasant. Which do you want first?" He was easy to talk to, and she liked him. He seemed like he'd make a nice friend.

"The nice one."

"I fell in love with a recluse, an American living in France, when I was twenty. He's a wonderful person, and we're best friends to this day. My children and I spend a month with him in Normandy every summer."

"Where's the problem there?" He looked puzzled.

"I got pregnant by mistake and had the baby. We never married. He's a terrific father, one month a year."

"Ah. Okay. I can see that might be a problem, but at least he sounds like a nice guy."

"He is. A great guy. And I love him dearly."

"Are you still in love with him?"

"No, I'm not," she said simply, although it had taken a long time.

"And the bad story?"

"A super handsome guy, a total charmer, a sociopath, in retrospect. I fell for all his bullshit, hook, line, and sinker, all lies I discovered later. We got married nine months after I met him, I got pregnant on our wedding night. Fast-forward to when I'm six months pregnant. He gets indicted for money laundering and tax evasion, and goes to prison for ten years. He's still there. Totally shit judgment on my part to have married him in the first place. I filed for divorce three weeks after he got arrested. I had the baby two months later. He relinquished his parental rights by his own choice. End of story. I figured I should retire after that one."

"Why?" He looked unimpressed. "Granted, being married to a guy in prison for ten years doesn't sound like a lot of fun, but you got out of it, pretty fast it sounds like. And you got two great kids out of it. Doesn't sound like a horror story to me."

"Maybe not. The con man rattled me because I believed him."

"If I gave up dating every time a woman lied to me

and I believed her, I'd have had to become a priest twenty years ago. My grandmother would have liked that but my parents wouldn't. They retired and moved back to Ireland a couple of years ago, but they're very progressive. Women have lied to me all my life. I expect it," he said, and she smiled at him. "Some people are liars, some are cheats, some are good people, some aren't. It takes all kinds. You can't give up after a couple of mistakes. We'd never have landed on the moon if the boys at NASA felt that way. And Einstein wouldn't have discovered the theory of relativity. You have to keep trying until you get it right. You will one of these days."

"So what's your story? Divorced? Single?" She turned the focus on him.

"Single. Two long relationships, ten and eight years. In the end they went nowhere. I never knew when to give up and go home. So suddenly I'm thirty-eight and living with a golden called Harvey. He's pretty good company. And I haven't given up dating, even when women turn me down five or six times. It's the Irish in me. I'm stubborn, or 'thick' as they say there." She laughed. "I figure I'll get it right sooner or later and find a woman who adores me . . . and Harvey, of course. We come as a pair. Do your kids like dogs?"

"More or less. We've never had one."

"Maybe we could go for a walk in the park sometime. Harvey's good with children. Or is that off your list too?

Walking a golden retriever is *not* a date." She smiled again. She liked him. But she didn't want to.

"No, it isn't." He walked her back to her apartment after that, and said he'd call her some weekend to take Harvey and her daughters to the park.

He called two weeks later, and they walked to Central Park and had a great time. Xela loved the big friendly dog. As usual, Theo was more reserved, but she threw a ball for him when they got to the park.

"They're sweet kids," Declan complimented her on the way home. "Do you suppose they'd want to come up to my place to make s'mores and popcorn? It's all I know how to cook." They went with him and the girls loved it. Harvey was jubilant to have company, and Isabelle enjoyed watching Declan with her children. He handed her a s'more, and she got the marshmallows and chocolate all over her mouth, and he helped her get it off and said in a soft voice, "S'mores and popcorn. *Not* a date." He had the faintest Irish accent, and she discovered that he had grown up in Dublin, and came to the States when he was thirteen.

She finally agreed to have dinner with him, at an Italian restaurant near her apartment. Just as friends. "*Not* a date." Everything they did together was low key and normal. He wasn't trying to impress her, or run her life. He waited a long time to be romantic with her, and when she finally trusted him, which took time, they went away for a weekend in Connecticut. It felt as if they had always known each other. They dated for almost a year, until she left for Normandy with the girls, and she talked to Putnam about him. He had become her mentor and advisor on all subjects, almost like a second father to her.

"He sounds great, so what's the problem?"

"He wants to get married and have kids one day. I've already done that. I don't want to try again. He should be free to find the right person to marry and have babies with."

"Why can't you have another child?"

"I don't want to. I do an okay job with the two I have. Three is too many."

"Not if you have a husband. You've never had a real one."

"I shudder at the word."

"You sound like me now," he scolded her. "Don't be such a coward. You're thirty years old. Don't waste your life bound to the past."

"The last time you told me that, I married a con man."

"Declan doesn't sound like one to me," Putnam said.

"He isn't. Do you want to meet him?"

"I might. Here? Is he in France?"

"He's visiting his parents in Ireland and offered to come by on the way home. I think he knows he needs your stamp of approval."

"I like him already," Putnam said, smiling at her. He was fifty-seven years old, and Isabelle had noticed that he had aged considerably in the past year. She saw that Marcel was concerned about him too. Putnam was very pale and had been eating very little, and he seemed tired.

Isabelle called Declan the next morning, and he offered to come for a day at the end of August. He didn't want to intrude but he wanted to meet the man who meant so much to her.

He flew to Paris, rented a car, and planned to leave that night and go back to Dublin. He and Putnam hit it off immediately. They went for a long walk together and a short sail in Putnam's boat, and Declan understood perfectly why she loved him. Putnam was an honorable man, and a kind one, a gentle soul, and he loved her like a beloved sister and wanted only the best for her.

Declan left at eleven o'clock that night, and Putnam told her after he'd gone that he heartily approved.

"He's a fantastic person. I think you should grab him before someone else does."

"I'm not doing any grabbing," she said primly, but Putnam was insistent and brought it up again before she and the girls left for New York.

"I want to know you're in safe harbor, Isabelle. You can't stay alone for the rest of your life. You need someone to take care of you, and I won't be here forever." A shadow crossed his eyes as he said it, and Isabelle felt panic ripple through her, like a finger running the wrong way up her spine.

"Don't say that. You have another forty years left in you and I'll be a grandmother by then."

"I'm serious," he said quietly, and she didn't pursue the subject. But she was still worried about him when they left a few days later, and she whispered to Marcel to call her if Monsieur had any problems or fell ill. It was the first time she'd said it, and Marcel nodded. He was as concerned as she. Putnam didn't look well.

She and Declan went back to dating after that, but she remembered what Put had said to her about grabbing him before someone else did. And in October Putnam called her and said what she had never expected to hear from him.

"I'm sick, Isabelle. I knew it when you were here, but I thought I'd have longer than I do. I have pancreatic cancer. I'd like you and Theo to come over sometime between now and Christmas." Theo was only ten years old, too young to lose her father. And Isabelle felt no more ready to face it at thirty, but she agreed to come back in the next two months, and spoke to the gallery to arrange it. The hardest part would be preparing Theo to see her father for the last time. Isabelle couldn't bear thinking of it. They made the trip in early November, and left Xela at home with Maeve.

Normandy was bleak at that time of year, and the

château looked dark and gloomy. Putnam had lost a shocking amount of weight in the last three months and tears sprang to Isabelle's eyes the moment she saw him, which she concealed from him.

They spent a week with him and said everything they needed to. Seeing him as he was, Isabelle doubted he would live until Christmas. It was wrenching when they said goodbye to him, and he made Theo promise that she would do good things for unfortunate people as soon as she was old enough to do so, and she said she would. She clung to her mother all the way back to the airport, and they both cried in the car. Putnam had held Isabelle for a long moment before she left him, and whispered to her, "I have always loved you, my beloved girl, and always will. Thank you for Theo." She had to gulp back sobs as she walked to the car.

Ten days after they got back to New York, Marcel called Isabelle. Putnam had died peacefully in his sleep, and he'd been happy ever since they'd been there. Marcel was crying when he called her. He had worked for Putnam for thirty-two years, and had been as much a friend as a valet and butler to the man he admired so much. He had always said Putnam was a man of honor.

The hardest part was telling Theo, who cried great wracking sobs when her mother told her. Isabelle left the next day and flew to France alone for Putnam's funeral. She thought it would be too upsetting for Theo, so she left her in New York. He had wanted to be buried in the small cemetery on the estate that had become not only his home but his entire world for the thirty-two years he'd lived there. Walking through the house without him was a painful journey.

She met with his French banker and attorney who told her that because of Theo's age, Putnam had said the house should be sold. It made no sense to maintain it until she was old enough to use it or live there. And keeping it for one month in the summer didn't make financial sense.

The proceeds of the sale were to go into Theo's trust, but Putnam's world as they had known it was about to disappear forever. And in some ways, although it saddened her greatly, Isabelle thought it might be better. It would be too painful to be there without him, and she thought that Put had made the right decision.

There were only a handful of his employees and Isabelle at the funeral. At his request, there was no religious service, and he had left a letter for her, and one for Theo, telling them how much he loved them and how much joy they had given him.

Leaving Marcel was almost like leaving Put again. They clung to each other and sobbed at the airport, and she told him to stay in touch. She had never expected Putnam to die so young, but his lonely life had taken something from him, like a flower in winter. He lacked the warmth and sunshine he needed to truly flourish. And their brief visits hadn't really been enough to sustain him. Marcel said that Put was sad without them for most of the year.

She looked devastated when she got back to New York and had lunch with Declan the next day. He felt terrible for her, but he was glad he had met Putnam.

"I don't need to ask you how it was, I can see it."

"They're selling the château," she said bleakly. "Theo will inherit everything. She doesn't understand what that means yet." And in some ways Isabelle didn't either, and she was genuinely shocked when his lawyers sent her a copy of the will. Putnam had left her a bequest which would allow her to buy a house of her own and start her own business. He had calculated it as generously as he did everything, and he had prefaced it by saying that Isabelle had never wanted anything from him, but he wanted her to be secure in her own home, and to help make her dream come true about her work.

She called her father and told him about the bequest, with tears streaming down her cheeks. It was what he had wanted for her, but could never give her. He had never met Putnam but had come to respect him over the years, and now more than ever. He had always resented his not marrying Isabelle, but in the face of his gift to her, it was easier to forgive him.

"He loved you, Isabelle. Of that I'm certain."

"I know, Dad," she said and then hung up the phone,

unable to believe that the man who had meant so much to her and always would had disappeared forever. Her life and Theo's without him would never be the same again.

Chapter Seven

Isabelle stumbled through the days after Putnam's death, trying to be a support to Theo. Declan came to have dinner with them, and played with Xela. She had no real understanding of what it meant that Putnam had died. As always, she was boisterous and demanding, constantly teasing and annoying Theo, but for once it was a good distraction.

They went to Newport for Thanksgiving, and Isabelle invited Declan. He was in awe of the remarkable estate where they lived and she had grown up. They gave him a tour of the grounds and inside the house, and he treated it with reverence. He took long walks with Jeremy. He was glad that he had finally met him, and he realized that Isabelle was slowly opening up to him. They had known each other for just over a year by then. But two days after they left Newport, she got a call she had never expected. The stablemaster was on the line. He told her that her father had collapsed in the stable that morning and died instantly of a heart attack. He had been in good health, and there had been no warning. He said the paramedics had arrived quickly but had been unable to revive him.

"I'm sorry, Isabelle. I guess he just ran out of time." He was sixty-five years old, which was much too early to lose him. In two weeks she had lost the two men who were so important in her life. Putnam and her father. She was in shock when she sat down after the call. She had promised to come to Newport that night to make the arrangements, and Declan called her shortly after. She broke down in sobs when she told him, and hadn't told the children yet.

"Oh my God, I'm so sorry. Can I come over?"

"Yes." The word was barely more than a croak and he was there five minutes later. She hadn't left for work yet, nor he for the office.

"Do you want me to come with you?" he asked about the trip to Newport. She didn't want to lean on him unduly, but she needed him. She had no one to turn to. She was responsible now for everything in her life.

"Would you mind terribly?" She looked innocent and broken.

"Of course not." Declan was a strong presence to lean on.

She told the girls when Maeve brought them home from school, and they both cried. Death had visited them too often recently. She had told the gallery what had happened and that she'd be gone for a few days.

That night she and Declan caught a flight to Boston. He rented a car at the airport, and they drove to Newport and let themselves into her father's house on the grounds. The Vanderbilts had already sent a message of condolence and said they were devastated, after twenty-five years of loyal service.

Declan never left her side while she made the arrangements. Unlike Putnam's funeral, the church was crowded with her father's friends and people he had worked with. It was the same church where she had married Collin, and she tried not to think about that. She had decided not to bring the children, it was just too sad. She and Declan arranged to have his body taken back to Boston, for burial next to her mother. It was a painful, mournful day, and Isabelle told Declan she couldn't have gotten through it without him, and it was true. These had been the worst weeks of her entire life.

She still had to come back and clean out his house, but the Vanderbilts had insisted there was no hurry, and Declan said he would come back with her.

He took her home to New York and put her to bed that night, and he sat with her until she fell asleep, wishing there was more that he could do for her, but he knew there wasn't. She just had to live through it and pick up the threads of her life again, but she had lost so much in such a short time.

The next day, Saturday, when she woke up with the

weight of the world on her chest, she could hardly breathe thinking about her father's funeral the day before, and Putnam's two weeks earlier. And thanks to him, she had other things to think of now. Putnam had given her the ability to buy a house and start her business as an art consultant. She wasn't ready to do either yet, but she had that to look forward to. There were big changes ahead. All she wanted to do now was get through Christmas with her girls. After the holidays she would look to the future, the future Putnam had given her.

Christmas was a small, pitiful affair at her apartment with the girls. She didn't even want to see Declan. On New Year's Day, Declan came to see her, and she talked about the house and the business. He looked at her hesitantly then, as though there was something he wanted to say, but wasn't sure if he should.

"There's something I've been meaning to talk to you about, although this probably isn't the right time." He paused, looking at her. She appeared to have no idea what was on his mind, and he felt awkward broaching it with her.

"What is it?" Her eyes looked dead, with dark circles beneath them. She was having trouble sleeping.

"Someday I want to marry you, whenever you think it's the right time, if it ever is," he said carefully.

"Are you serious?" She looked shocked.

"No, I'm kidding. Of course I'm serious. I want to take

care of you, and be your husband, and have babies with you, if you're willing."

She groaned at that. "I know you should have children of your own. But I'm not sure there's enough of me to give to another child. The two I have are a handful. Theo is always closing in on herself and trying to shut out the world, like her father. And Xela is a time bomb waiting to explode. She's always having a fit about something. How would I manage another one?"

"With a husband who loves you and your children. You've brought both of them up alone. And with all due respect to Putnam, it takes more than money. I want to be here with you, to lighten the load for you, and share my life with you."

"That's what Put said I needed when he told me I should marry you." She smiled at him.

"You never told me that." Declan looked pleased to hear it. "I'm not trying to rush you, but I'm turning forty this year, and it might be nice to get married before that." She was thirty-one, and Theo and Xela ten and almost five.

"And you really want another child?"

"It's not a deal-breaker. I'm sure in time I'll come to love Theo and Xela like my own. It might just be nice to have one of ours, to kind of cement the deal." He smiled and put his arms around her. "You don't have to decide right now. You've just been through a tough couple of months."

"When would you want to get married?"

"Yesterday . . . last week . . . I love being with you, and how peaceful and easy our life is together."

"I feel that way too. Do you want a big wedding?" she asked him, considering the whole question. It was a lot to think about, and her losses were still fresh.

"No, just us and the kids. And Harvey maybe."

"I love the idea, Declan," she said as she snuggled next to him. "Let's do it soon. And we can look for a house together." He was surprised by her answer, and jubilant.

They told the children the next day, and both girls were happy about it. On a Saturday in January, they got married in a neighborhood church, with a few of their friends present, his law partner, Tom Kelly, and Bert Acker, the owner of the gallery where she worked. He didn't know yet that she was leaving. They went to an Italian restaurant for lunch afterward. Isabelle felt as though her life had finally landed in the right place. She was home at last.

Everything happened quickly after that. In February they found a beautiful house on East Seventy-Fourth Street between Fifth and Madison. It was in perfect condition, and she could afford it thanks to Putnam's bequest. They moved into it in March, two days after they found out that she was pregnant. The baby was due in November, and Declan was wildly excited about it. Isabelle loved the idea now too. He was right. Their child would close the circle and they would be a family.

She gave notice at the gallery in June, and planned to open her art consultancy after she had the baby and the holidays were over. She was going to start her business in January, and take some time off first to enjoy Declan and the baby. She hadn't had a break in ten years, not since she'd graduated from college. They rented a house in Connecticut for the summer. It was going to be a big change from Normandy, but they were starting new traditions, and Declan said that one day he'd like to buy a country house too.

They had a peaceful summer and came back to the city at the end of August to get the girls ready for school. Xela was starting kindergarten, and Declan asked Isabelle if she minded his spending the Labor Day weekend in New Hampshire with Tom Kelly, his law partner, and half a dozen male friends. They wanted to go fishing. She told him to go and have fun. He hadn't left her side for a minute all summer. She was six months pregnant and had never felt better. Happiness agreed with her. Declan was everything she had hoped he would be. Their life together was idyllic, and she finally had what Putnam had wished for her—a safe harbor, with a good man at her side to take care of her.

She and the girls bought school supplies that weekend, and new uniform shoes. They went to a movie and baked cookies on Sunday for Declan when he got home. The doorbell rang at six o'clock and she thought he might have forgotten his keys. She went to open it and found Tom Kelly standing in front of her in his fishing clothes. He had driven straight down from New Hampshire. She assumed Declan was parking the car as Tom stood staring at her.

"Isabelle . . ." Something about the way he said it terrified her. And there was no way to tell her except exactly what had happened.

"Harvey got swept away in the current and Declan went after him. He couldn't get to him in time. Harvey went over the falls, and Declan after him. Neither of them survived it," he said, reaching out to her. She looked as though she was about to faint in his arms.

"That's not possible," she said, looking confused. "He couldn't have . . . he was captain of the swim team in college." She looked up at Tom with eyes that said he was robbing her of every dream she'd ever had. "It can't be," she said as he led her inside, sat her down in the kitchen, and gave her a glass of water.

"I'm so sorry," he said with tears on his cheeks. They'd gone to college and law school together and were best friends. "He went after the dog before anyone could stop him."

"Where are they?" she asked, looking blank and confused.

"At the coroner's office in New Hampshire, until you decide what you want to do." She nodded and started to sob then as Tom held her, which was all he could do. They had been married for seven months, and their baby was due in three.

Tom held her for what seemed like hours. When Theo saw her mother, she knew, and took Xela to her room.

It didn't seem possible that something like this had happened. Everything about their life had been so perfect and so happy, and now Declan was gone too.

*

In the days afterward, Isabelle went through all the motions that were so familiar to her now. They held the funeral in the church where they were married. His father had a heart condition and couldn't come from Ireland, while Declan's mother didn't want to leave him and didn't think she could face it. His two brothers who were priests came and said the funeral mass. Isabelle had to pick a plot at the cemetery to bury him. Everything had an unreal quality to it, like a terrible movie, or a nightmare she was having and couldn't wake up from.

Her girls stood next to her in church at the funeral. Tom Kelly took them home. Declan's brothers went back to Ireland after seeing New York for the first time. They'd both been in the seminary when their parents lived there. And then it was over, and Isabelle was alone again with her children.

The girls started school, and Isabelle sat alone in the

house every day, waiting for Declan to come home, as the baby grew in her belly. Maeve watched over her like a mother hen, and brought her Irish tea and things to eat, but Isabelle felt like a zombie for the next three months. She couldn't manage living again without him. She just couldn't do it. She remembered what she'd said to him in the beginning about having shit judgment. And it turned out that she hadn't had poor judgment at all. Just shit luck this time. The worst possible luck imaginable.

She still looked dazed when she went into labor. The girls were in school, and Maeve took her to the hospital and stayed with her. She howled with grief more than pain when she felt the baby coming. She didn't want to see it without him. How could she have this baby now with him gone? What cruel turn of fate had done this?

The baby came even faster than her sisters, after a shorter, harder labor, but Isabelle didn't care—she was in so much anguish without him that the physical pain of giving birth was almost a relief. And then after pushing for what seemed like hours, there was silence in the delivery room, and for a moment Isabelle thought she might have died, and that his baby had died too. It suddenly woke her up. They had told her it was a girl, and then she had heard nothing.

"What happened?" she asked, craning to see. "How is she? Is she okay? Is something wrong? Is she breathing?"

She hadn't given a wail, or screamed like Xela. Instead the baby gave a gurgle that was almost like a giggle, and sounded like she was laughing. They rubbed her back and she cried a little, and gazed around the room as though she was delighted to see them. And just as Isabelle had hoped, she looked like Declan, and had his happy-go-lucky nature. They put the baby in her mother's arms, and she looked up at her and cooed.

"I've never seen a baby do that when she was born," the doctor commented. "I think she was laughing at us. Does she have a name yet?" Isabelle nodded. She and Declan had picked it.

"Oona." She was the happiest baby they had ever seen, and she looked right at home in her new surroundings. Isabelle had a feeling that was how it always would be, just like Declan. "Welcome home, Oona," Isabelle whispered as the baby crinkled up her eyes and looked like she was laughing at her. She was happy to be there. A little piece of Declan had come back to Isabelle with Oona.

Chapter Eight

It was harder to adjust to Declan's death than she had expected. They hadn't been married long, but they had all come to depend on him in the two years they'd known him. He took care of everything, more than Isabelle realized, and suddenly they were all lost without him.

Theo had been quieter than ever since her own father's death almost exactly a year before, and with each passing year Xela got angrier and more argumentative and picked more fights with Theo. Declan had been the only one who could talk her out of it and be the peacemaker. The ray of sunshine in their midst once she arrived was Oona. She was always happy, smiling, and gurgling, and had everyone laughing from the moment she came home from the hospital.

At thirty-nine, Declan hadn't expected to die and had left no will. What he had went to Oona, but he had very little, just some meager savings. He owned no property. He'd made a decent living as an attorney, but had spent it as quickly as he had made it.

The only one with real means and a substantial

inheritance was Theo, and it was well safeguarded for her until she was old enough to manage it.

Isabelle wanted to start her business as an art consultant, but waited almost a year after Oona's birth to set it up. She was too upset by Declan's death to do it before that. But once she established her business, it took off. She had solid clients, and the business grew exponentially over the years. She was one of the most respected art consultants in New York, just as Putnam had hoped when he left her the money in his will.

Isabelle concentrated solely on work and her daughters while they were growing up. Each of them had so many traits of their respective fathers. They were almost like an experiment in genetics. Isabelle sometimes wondered if her genetic contribution had even mattered. Theo looked like Put and acted like him so much of the time, retreating to her room as a child, studying subjects that interested her. And a trip to India when she graduated from college changed her life forever. The world she had dreamed of had been waiting for her. In the years since, at thirty-seven, she had built villages, paid to construct dams and lay sewer pipes, brought electricity into the darkness, built hospitals and provided medical assistance, and good and fresh water for remote parts of India and Africa, although India was where she preferred to be most of the time. She lived in a bubble where only the people she was assisting mattered. She had observed surgeries, tended sick children in epidemics, and walked for miles carrying dying newborns to hospitals hoping to save them. Her family was of far less interest to her, given what she saw around her every day. She had put her father's money to good use for the past fifteen years. Xela always said, with some irritation, that being with Theo was like being with a modern-day saint.

Isabelle heard from her infrequently and admired what she was doing. As far as she knew there had been no serious romances in her life. She was astonishingly like Putnam, and although she was in the world, she was never really part of it, and had trouble connecting with anyone at a personal level. She came to New York once a year to see her mother, and her father's bankers in Boston, but she had little in common with the rest of the family or her sisters, other than the fact that they had the same mother, which seemed like a very thin bond to her.

Xela's war with the human race and eternal anger, particularly with her older sister, had continued into her teen years and thereafter. She liked to say that Theo had dedicated herself to emptying the ocean of human misery with a thimble and was about as effective, dismissing all of Theo's acts of compassion and kindness. For every hundred people she fed or saved, there were thousands more right behind them who were going to die anyway, no matter how much of her money she spent.

Xela had nothing in common with Theo and found

her fatally annoying. Xela felt that she rose above every comment and occasion, and poured money into a thirst she could never quench, instead of doing something more sensible with it.

Xela had a remarkable head for business, with her father's creativity and mother's integrity, which was a winning combination. Isabelle's passion for art didn't interest her, but she had real entrepreneurial talent and a Harvard MBA. But she never had the money to fund her projects, and spent her life wrestling with venture capitalists who wanted majority control of her companies, which she didn't want to relinquish. She knew she could make a fortune with some of her ideas, but she needed the investors first. She had never asked Theo to help her, and was sure she wouldn't have anyway. She wasn't saving lives, she was doing business and trying to take her latest venture public without giving up control to the VCs who wanted to invest. Her work life was a constant struggle, and her personal relationships were more of the same. She'd been involved with married men and narcissists, sociopaths like her father, or men who wanted to control her or dismissed her impressive talents as second rate.

At almost thirty-two, she hadn't had a successful relationship or business venture yet. She had announced at thirty that she was giving up on romance and focusing only on work. And she didn't seem any happier for it.

Isabelle was sorry for her and wished she could give her the money she needed, but she couldn't afford the kind of funding the venture capitalists could give her. Theo could have, but she had no interest in business, and the two sisters had never been close, and even less so once they grew up.

The one in their midst who was always happy, and had been all her life, was Oona, just like Declan. The glass was half full to her, or better. She made compromises, found the positive solutions, and made things work. She had no interest in business or art, and had none of Theo's grandiose plans to improve the world. She had spent her junior year in Florence, where she fell in love with an Italian aristocrat who owned a farm in Tuscany, near a town called Castellina in Chianti. She had left school and married Gregorio at twenty-one, despite Isabelle's reservations. Five years later at twenty-six, nearly twenty-seven, she had three sons and was expecting twins.

Oona loved Gregorio's family, and cooked lunch and dinner for her husband and children every day from recipes her mother-in-law had taught her, and she loved living on their farm. Gregorio controlled everything in their world, and lived in the dark ages in terms of modern relationships, but Oona didn't seem to mind. She loved everything about her life, including her charming, macho, old-world, domineering husband. There was no denying that she was happy and had the life she wanted. She hadn't been back to New York since she'd married him. Isabelle visited her in Tuscany once or twice a year, where Gregorio's father openly flirted with her in front of his wife. It was another culture and not what Isabelle would have wanted, but it suited Oona. She was undaunted by the prospect of having twins. She would soon be the mother of five at twenty-six. All she ever wanted was for everyone to be happy.

Visiting her was always a joy, because she was so content with her children, her marriage, and her life. She had Declan's easygoing disposition and positive view of the world. She loved both of her sisters, who she thought were talented and remarkable, although she hadn't seen Theo in several years. Theo never went to Italy, and Africa and India were not in Oona's travel plans. Gregorio would have had a fit if she went so far away to visit her sister.

Neither Theo nor Xela seemed interested in marriage or having children of their own. Theo was too much of a dreamer and felt obligated to save the world. And Xela was somewhat self-centered, and wanted to make her mark in business before focusing on anything else.

Isabelle couldn't imagine three more different women, or three more different fathers. Each man had left a mark on his child, even though the girls had hardly known them, or didn't remember them at all. Sadly neither Xela nor Oona remembered Putnam or Declan, who had been the good men in their mother's life.

Theo remembered some of her father's words to her, though her memories of him were fading now, twenty-seven years after his death. But she was carrying out the mission he had given her, to use his money, once it was hers, to change the world, and she had.

Isabelle was the bridge between them and had her own regrets. She couldn't boast a successful romantic life, from her own perspective. Having Theo had been a bold thing to do, with a man who was so unable to function in the world, and yet he had protected her in many ways, and she had loved him until his death.

And Declan had been the joy in her life, the normalcy she had always longed for and never found until him. Luck had been cruel to them when he died. She wondered sometimes if she'd only been destined to be happy for a short time. A few months with Putnam, and with Declan. And Collin had remained a terrible mistake. She had told Xela the truth about him when she'd turned eighteen, that her father had been a criminal and had gone to prison. Xela had searched for stories about him on the Internet and had discovered that he had gone to prison for a second time, after he got out, for a major credit card scam. She was deeply ashamed of it, and had said she hated him for a while. She hadn't mentioned him in years.

*

Isabelle loved all of her daughters. She had tried to give each of them what they needed, and wasn't sure if she had succeeded. She had attempted to give Theo a more realistic view of the world than her entirely altruistic one, working with people who had no intimate connection to her life. She didn't want her to end up like her father, unable to function outside his own world, beyond his walls, even with his child for more than a few weeks a year. He had deprived himself of the love and bonding that might have made him happier. Theo had somehow taken the torch from his hand and was carrying it for him, trying to atone for what he thought of as his sins.

Xela was always trying to scale tall walls and resented everyone for what they had and she didn't—a father, a fortune, a birthright. She focused much of her bitterness and anger on her older sister. She had been jealous of Theo all her life, whether she admitted it or not.

Only Oona was satisfied with the life she had chosen, but Isabelle wondered if it was enough, to be dictated to and controlled by Gregorio, as though she had no mind of her own and was incapable of thinking for herself.

It led Isabelle to consider the men she had chosen: a recluse unable to take responsibility for their child, although he had loved them both; a criminal who had duped her; and the kind man she should have met and married from the first, if she had waited for him to turn up. Instead she had fallen prey to the fascination Putnam represented to her, and the excitement of Collin, who was all glitter and flash, smoke and mirrors and nothing real. She had been leery of him at first, but not enough. Declan would have been worth the wait until he came along, but she was too young to know that then. She had tried to impart that to her girls, that exciting men were never the right ones in the end. The fireworks always burned out quickly.

She had never tried again after Declan died. She was too shattered at first, and too busy with her children and her career after that. There was always something more important to do than trying to meet someone, or give them a chance when she did. She always had an excuse not to get involved, just as Theo and Xela were doing now. Only Oona had embraced love wholeheartedly, whether Isabelle fully approved of Gregorio or not. She just wished he would be more respectful of Oona's intelligence. As a result, Oona assumed that she would be incapable of doing anything without him, even though she helped him run the farm, cooked his meals, brought up his children, and had loved him passionately for five years. As far as Isabelle was concerned, he was a lucky man. But her daughter thought she was the fortunate one, and Isabelle was willing to concede now that maybe that was enough. If you believed yourself lucky, maybe you were. And who was she to expect more for her daughter, or even herself?

She often worried that she had somehow taught Theo and Xela to be afraid of love and the risk it represented, because her relationships with their fathers hadn't worked out. And Xela's harsh criticism of Theo bothered Isabelle too. Theo deserved their respect for the remarkable feats she had accomplished. She had carried out her father's wishes more than he could ever have hoped. He would have been proud of her, and Isabelle was too.

All Isabelle wanted was for her children to be happy. The only real happiness she had known as an adult was with Declan, but it was for so brief a time. She had been afraid she'd be disappointed if she tried to meet someone like him after he died. She had had no desire to try again for twenty-six years, and at fifty-eight, had decided that it was too late. She wasn't old, and she didn't look her age. Her business was thriving, but she was lonely now without the girls. With Theo in India, Oona in Tuscany, and Xela involved in her own life, she was alone almost all the time. Even that hadn't given her the courage to try again. She just worked harder to fill the void. She went to exhibits and art auctions, met with new clients, and did research on paintings on the market until late at night, but her house was quiet, her weekends were deadly, and she went to bed alone. There were times, too many of them, when it didn't seem like enough.

She glanced at her watch just after two o'clock. She had an appointment downtown at three. She needed new glasses, and had finally admitted it to herself when she hadn't noticed how close she was to the bookcase and banged her arm badly the week before. She still had a nasty bruise from it. Twice she had almost missed a step going down the stairs. It was time to get stronger glasses before she fell. And who would hear her or help her if she did? She lived alone. She wasn't old enough to need assistance. All she needed were new glasses, she reminded herself. It wasn't a tragedy, just a practical issue.

At two-thirty, she put on her coat, picked up her bag, turned off the lights, set the alarm, and left the house. She was a self-sufficient woman and intended to stay that way for many years. The last thing her children needed was her becoming dependent on them or injuring herself in some foolish way.

She was careful when she stepped off the curb as she waved an arm to hail a cab. When it stopped, she got in and gave the driver the address. She hoped the visit to the eye doctor wouldn't take long. She had a new client coming to meet with her at six o'clock. He had been referred by another client. The new one wanted an entire art collection assembled, purchased, and installed in his new home and on his yacht. She was looking forward to meeting him. He was going to keep her busy for months.

Her work was still her passion and brought her joy. She loved the people she met and the works of art she found for them. The new client would be fun. He was an innocent, admitted he knew little about art, and wanted her to educate him. He had lots of money to spend, as did most of her clients. She would help him build a collection tastefully, as they gathered the pieces he wanted to impress his friends and show off his wealth.

*

The cab stopped at the address she had given him. It was a medical building with mostly dentists, X-ray labs, and a few physicians, her eye doctor among them. She hadn't been to see him in three years, and her eyes had seemed fine until now. It was only in the last few months she had begun bumping into things.

She gave her name to the receptionist, and thumbed through an art magazine she'd brought with her, still thinking about the man she was meeting at six. They'd only spoken over the phone and never met.

Twenty minutes later, a nurse called her in and asked some questions to update her chart—same address, phone number, job, next of kin. She always listed Xela since she was the only one in New York, but hoped they'd never have reason to call her since she was the least nurturing of her children, and the least responsive.

The doctor came in shortly after, Dr. Phillip Calvin, a pleasant-looking man with a nondescript face. He glanced at Isabelle's chart and got started with the exam.

She had read the eye charts that appeared in the machine that felt like looking through binoculars, and he asked her which was best, left or right, near or far. It was all routine. And then he asked her a number of other questions she didn't recall his asking her before, but they were all fairly mundane. He asked her about recent problems with her vision, and she told him matter-of-factly that she had bumped into a few things, which told her it was time to come in and get stronger glasses. She said she had missed a step once or twice on the stairs, and reminded him that she didn't want bifocals, or even progressive lenses. She'd tried them before and she found them awkward, and they made her feel sick. He jotted some notes on her chart and continued the exam, and then looked at her carefully when he finished.

"Ms. McAvoy," she had reverted to her own name after her brief marriage to Declan, "we have a problem. It's called macular degeneration, which can progressively dim your central vision and reduce it to a very narrow field. It can also affect your peripheral vision."

"Can or will?" She interrupted him with a sharp look.

"That depends," he said honestly, "on how severe it is, how rapidly it advances, and how responsive to treatment. We can slow it down considerably, although we can't restore you to perfect vision. There are two kinds of macular degeneration, wet and dry. We can effect considerable improvement with treatment for wet.

There's nothing we can do for dry." It sounded like a death sentence to her as she listened.

"Which kind do I have?"

"You're lucky, you have wet macular degeneration, in both eyes." It didn't sound "lucky" to her.

"What's the worst that can happen?" she asked, looking him straight in the eye. She had never been cowardly about anything in her life, and met her challenges head-on.

"At the very worst, you could go blind," he said cautiously. "We'll try not to let that happen." His words hit her like a bomb. She was at risk of going blind and he called that luck? But at least she didn't have the kind that couldn't be treated.

"What do the treatments entail?" She imagined painful surgery with patches on both eyes for months, like something in a bad movie, while she stumbled around her house.

"Injections in your eyes." He answered her question and she winced. It sounded ghastly to her, but blindness was unquestionably worse.

"Painful?"

"Uncomfortable. We use anesthetic drops to numb your cornea." He used the medical word she hated most, "uncomfortable," which was almost always a lie, a euphemism for unbearable agony he didn't want her to know about in advance.

"I'm an art consultant, Doctor, I can't afford to go blind."

"We'll do everything we can to improve the situation, for as long as we can. And you may never go blind. That's at the far end of the spectrum. You asked me about the worst case. I don't expect it to get to such an extreme degree if we deal with it now. You'll have to be reliable about coming in for treatment." She nodded. Obviously, she didn't want to go blind, no matter how "uncomfortable" the treatments were.

"I'm going to give you some drops I want you to use several times a day. Do you have anyone to help you administer them?" he asked kindly, and she shook her head.

"No, I don't."

"You can manage it yourself. It's just easier if someone helps."

"So is life," she said cynically. "Things don't always work out that way." He glanced at her chart and saw that she had checked off "widowed." She was an attractive woman and looked younger than her age, although there was something faintly austere about her, and she was visibly shocked by what he'd said. It was a hard diagnosis to hear. There was a strong chance she wouldn't go blind, but it was always a possibility, and he didn't want to lie to her about the seriousness of the disease.

"Why don't you make an appointment next week for your first treatment? I'd like to get started," he told her, and she stood up out of the chair and felt like her legs were going to buckle under her.

"Do I need glasses too?" She had forgotten all about them till then, in the face of what he'd said.

"I'll have them ready for you next week. You can pick frames on the way out, if you want to get them here."

"Thank you," she said in a soft voice, and a moment later, she stood staring at the vitrine full of eyeglasses as her vision blurred with tears. She knew that going blind was not a sure thing, but even the remote possibility of it was terrifying. If she did, how would she take care of herself? She made an instant decision not to tell her children. They didn't need to know about it yet, or maybe ever. She wanted to see how the treatment worked first. She didn't like them knowing about her frailties. They had always seen her as a tower of strength they could rely on. The idea of being helpless or vulnerable was not the image she wanted her children to have of her. She had always thought that would be far down the road, not in the near future. She wanted to be strong and in good health until a great age, working until the end. And what would happen to her work if she went blind? What would she do if she could no longer see the art she selected for her clients? Her whole world had turned upside down in a matter of moments.

She selected two of the eyeglass frames without even looking at them and handed them to the nurse. And five minutes later, she was back on the sidewalk, after making an appointment for the following week. She wanted to begin the injections quickly. She didn't have a moment to lose.

She felt as though she'd been in the doctor's office for a week. She got jostled by people on the sidewalk and nearly stumbled when she stepped off the curb to hail a cab.

"Steady," she said out loud to herself as a yellow cab stopped and she got in and gave him her address. She was silent on the drive uptown, trying to absorb what had happened. It was five-fifteen, and half an hour later, when she got home. She walked into her house and turned off the alarm. She didn't have a minute to waste before the appointment with the new client. She tossed her coat on a hall chair and rushed upstairs to her office to lay out the files and catalogues on her desk and two art books. She was forcing herself to concentrate on the meeting and not what the doctor had said.

William Casey, her new client, arrived five minutes early. She opened the door and offered him a drink when he came in. She directed him upstairs, and followed three minutes later with the scotch on the rocks he'd asked for. She set it down carefully on a table next to him, cautious not to miss the table, and paying close attention not to release the glass until she knew she'd set it down on the hard surface.

Bill Casey was large, red-faced, overweight, expensively dressed, and somewhere in his mid-fifties, she guessed. There was an innocence about him as he asked for Isabelle's advice. She began to show him the catalogues and art books she had set out, to give him an idea of the kind of artists she had in mind for him, and she wanted to know how he liked them. He loved everything she had marked with Post-its, and she explained patiently and clearly why the various works fit well together and would be the foundation for a cohesive collection. It was what she envisioned for both his home on Long Island, and the two-hundred-foot sailboat he kept in the Caribbean. He showed her photographs of the yacht and its interior. It was a magnificent sailboat he'd had built by Perini in Italy.

He mentioned that he'd had lucky oil ventures in Oklahoma and Louisiana, and she admired and praised him for wanting to use some of it to buy important art. She liked working with him. He was so grateful for her help, and eager to learn.

He stayed until seven-thirty, and she sent him home with the catalogues. If he was interested, there were two paintings she hoped to bid on for him in the next sale at Christie's. She thought they would be the perfect cornerstone for his collection, and a great starting point. He agreed and said that he wanted to show his wife, but made it clear that the final choices would be his. His wife didn't know anything about art, and neither did he, but Mrs. Casey found the whole project daunting, and was trusting him to create the collection with Isabelle's advice.

She came back to her office as soon as he left, sat down at her desk, and dropped her face in her hands. For a brief time she had almost forgotten what the doctor had told her, and it all came rushing back like a tape playing in her head as the word "blind" kept going round and round in her mind . . . *blind* . . . she couldn't even imagine what it would be like and didn't want to, as her shoulders shook and her whole body was seized with wracking sobs.

The phone rang on her desk but she didn't answer it. All she could think about now was that she might be going blind. When, if, how soon were questions there was no answer to . . . She had no idea how long it would take to lose her sight, if she did. She had never expected this in a million years . . . and then she remembered the word he'd used, "lucky" that they had caught it early, but she sure didn't feel lucky now. She felt doomed as she continued to cry for several hours, and finally, feeling totally drained, she went to bed.

Chapter Nine

Bill Casey called her the next morning to say he wanted her to bid on the two paintings at Christie's, to start his collection. His wife had liked them too, when he showed her the images. They established a maximum price she could bid up to. He sounded very excited, and she was happy for him. This was a major step, and a big investment.

She called Christie's afterward, to let them know she wanted to participate in the live bidding on the phone. She knew everyone in the department. And then she sat staring out the window for a long time, wondering how it would feel if one day she could no longer work. She couldn't be an art consultant if she lost her sight. She couldn't even imagine it. Forcing the thought from her mind, she went downstairs to the kitchen to make coffee, stumbled on a step, and almost fell. She caught herself just in time before she did, and felt shaken when she walked into the kitchen. Her hands were trembling when she sat down with her coffee.

She wondered if she should hire an assistant. She had

a woman who came in twice a month to update her books and send out bills for her, but she didn't like having anyone underfoot, and hadn't needed it. She considered waiting to hire someone if her vision began failing severely, and couldn't decide whether it would be smarter to try to find someone now and break them in, so they would already know how she ran her business before her sight got any worse, or to wait. In some ways, the former option seemed more reasonable, but it made her feel vulnerable again, which was the last thing she wanted to be, and even thinking about it made her feel queasy and filled her with dread.

She called the employment agency at noon to see what they would suggest. She'd had girl Fridays from them occasionally for short-term projects, and they'd always sent good people. She described what she thought she needed—a business assistant to help her with research and client meetings—and they said they'd check their current listings.

The woman at the agency called her back two hours later to say that she had a candidate for her, a woman who said she was knowledgeable about art and had worked at a gallery when she was younger. The agency faxed her CV to Isabelle, who read it carefully. There was nothing distinguished or exciting about her, but she seemed to have good solid business and computer skills, which would be useful. She was coming to try out the next day. Isabelle still didn't like the idea of someone hanging around when she didn't need her yet, and wasn't sold on the idea.

When Margaret Wimbledon showed up the next day, she looked prim and older than Isabelle expected. She was wearing high heels and a black suit, and Isabelle was in sneakers and jeans. She didn't know what she'd expected an assistant to wear, but the woman seemed overdressed, with perfectly coiffed white hair. She didn't smile when Isabelle explained her duties to her. She gave her some filing to do, a stack of bills to get ready for the accountant, and asked her to mark auction catalogues with tags for clients she'd bought paintings for. It was all she could think of to give her. Margaret had it all in good order before noon. She was definitely efficient, but had an air of disapproval about her, and her mouth was set in a thin line when Isabelle sat at her desk writing some letters and asked her to bring her a cup of tea.

"I don't do food service," she said with an angry look.

"Sorry," Isabelle said, watching her retreat to the table where she was working. A cup of tea hadn't seemed like a lot to ask, but it reminded her that she needed to define the job. For the moment, her notion of what she would need from an assistant was still vague.

Margaret announced she was going out to lunch a few minutes later, and came back punctually in an hour, ready for her next assignment. Isabelle gave her some research to do. She wasn't sure why, but she didn't like her. She wasn't pleasant to have around. There was an aura of tension about her, and she made Isabelle uncomfortable. It seemed easier to do the work herself, but that was now, while she could still see.

After Margaret did the research, Isabelle let her go at four o'clock.

"Should I come back tomorrow?" she asked before she left.

"I'll call the agency and let them know," Isabelle said vaguely, but the thought of having her around again depressed her. There had been no friendly exchange all day. She seemed more like a secretary for the director of a gallery or a CEO. It made Isabelle realize that she wanted someone more casual and flexible, who would say a pleasant word or two and wouldn't balk at making a cup of tea. Margaret acted as though the entire job was beneath her, and her refusal to make tea made her seem inflexible, even hostile.

Isabelle tried to explain it to the agency when she called them at five o'clock. She had been thinking about Margaret for the last hour, was unenthusiastic about her, and told them she wasn't right for the job.

"There's nothing wrong with her, and she's very efficient. I just don't think I have enough work for her right now. I want to wing it for a while, with someone a little more adaptable, while I figure out what I need."

The woman at the agency sounded pensive for a minute, as she riffled through some papers on her desk. "We signed a candidate up yesterday. He has no training or experience in art, but he has an interesting history as a kind of jack-of-all-trades, mostly in communications and sports. I wouldn't have suggested him for you, but he may be more flexible than someone like Margaret, who wants a more high-level job. I don't think she would have worked out." She had already called to complain about the boring day she'd spent. She had expected Isabelle to be more high powered, and she wanted to be involved with clients, not just do research and filing. And as in any job, not every day would be exciting. "The man I'm referring to is Jack Bailey, he was on a sports radio show for several years, worked at a TV network as an assistant producer, also in sports. He has been a DJ and a sports announcer. He's been in PR. Most of his jobs have been sports-related, but his references say he's great with people, very personable, can repair anything, which could come in handy. He worked in the office of a senator in Washington, doing special events, and traveled with him as a personal assistant during his campaign, and the senator gave him a glowing reference. He left because he has a sick sister in New York, and he takes care of her. He came in again this morning, and he presents very well. He's looking for a job as a personal assistant. I didn't know if you'd want a man."

"Either one." But he had no work history at all that involved art. And she didn't need a DJ or a sports announcer, and had no special events for him to plan.

"I was going to send him to NBC to a producer who's looking for a PA. I could send him to you first."

"He might be bored. I basically have clerical work right now, but he could sit in on client meetings with me. I've always done them one-on-one with the client, but if he's willing, I can try him out. It's not as exciting as working for a senator, to say the least." She felt slightly foolish interviewing people who had had better jobs. She was thinking more of a young woman fresh out of college who didn't have grandiose ideas, and wouldn't get her back up over making a cup of tea. And if her sight became a serious problem, whoever she hired would have to help her with a multitude of things. She had recently noticed that working on her computer strained her eyes more than it used to, which was one of the reasons she had thought she needed new glasses.

"Could you see him at ten o'clock tomorrow? I'm sending him to NBC at noon. I do think he'd be flexible, he's got a varied background. He's willing to travel, but needs advance notice, so he can make arrangements for his sister."

"How sick is she?" Isabelle inquired, concerned.

"I think she has MS. He said she can manage on her own when he's at work, and a neighbor looks in on her during the day, but he stays with her at night. He has no other encumbrances, no wife or kids—he volunteered that himself, since I can't ask." Isabelle wondered how old he was, but couldn't ask that either. She'd have to guess from how he looked. "I'll email you his CV, with his references." She did so twenty minutes later, and it confirmed everything she had said. Isabelle noticed when he had graduated from the University of Washington, and calculated that he was about forty-six, which seemed a good age to be energetic, but not so immature he'd leave in a few months. She saw that he'd stayed with the senator for five years, which in the current job market was a long time, and he'd only left the job in the last six months. She emailed the woman at the agency to tell her she'd see him at ten the next morning.

That night, she thought about her visit to the doctor again. The full impact of what he'd told her hadn't sunk in yet, and she wanted to talk to her daughters, just to hear their voices, not tell them the bad news, but she didn't want them to guess that she was upset. It was almost impossible to reach Theo, currently in India helping to set up a hospital she was financing, and it was the middle of the night in Italy, so she couldn't call Oona. It was hard to find a good time to call her anyway—she was always busy with Gregorio and the boys, cooking lunch or dinner, or overseeing the planting of some new garden on their farm. She never had time to talk for long.

Isabelle missed both of them, and Xela was even harder to reach even though she lived in New York. She was either in meetings, on a conference call, or at the gym at six in the morning. Isabelle's calls to her always went straight to voice mail since she never picked up, and sometimes it took Xela days to call her mother back. Her entire life and contact with the world was run by text.

Isabelle finally fell asleep at four A.M., and could have called Oona by then, but she drifted off to sleep for four hours, and woke up at eight. She was showered and dressed in jeans and a sweater in time for the interview.

Jack Bailey arrived on the dot of ten and rang the doorbell. Isabelle was startled when she saw him. He was very tall and she looked up into a well-lined face with a cleft chin. He had gray hair, and warm brown eyes. He smiled at the look on her face—his height always took people by surprise. He was just over six feet six, slim with broad shoulders and strong arms. She asked him to come in, and he followed her upstairs to the room she used as her office, which was partly a sitting room, where she met clients. He sat down in a big upholstered chair with his long legs stretched out ahead of him. He was wearing gray slacks and a blazer and she noticed that his shoes were shined, and thought he looked nice.

"I don't know anything about art," he confessed immediately. "I've mostly worked in radio and sports TV. I had fun as a DJ for a couple of years, and I worked in PR, on male or sports-oriented accounts, Nike, L.L.Bean, *GQ,* a fishing magazine we represented, and *Road & Track.* I've done just about everything on my jobs, including picking up dry cleaning and walking the dog for the senator." He smiled at her. "Do you have pets?"

"No, I don't," she smiled back at him, "and my dry cleaner delivers. I might need help with clients, but not at the moment." She was looking toward a possibly bleak future as she said it. "I bid for art at auctions, mostly on the phone. And I could use some help with the computer, with research. I travel to visit my daughters, but it's planned well in advance."

"Where do they live?"

"My oldest in India, my youngest in Tuscany." He looked startled when she said it.

"That should be interesting. I've never been to India, and I haven't been to Europe in a long time. Do you have other children in New York?" He was watching her closely, and paid attention to everything she said.

"One, my middle daughter," she answered. "To be honest with you, I haven't fully figured out the job yet, and exactly what my needs are. I want some help, but maybe not enough to occupy you in a meaningful way at first. You've got a lot of experience in areas that don't relate to what I do."

"I'm good with repairs, and happy to fix things around

the house. And I've got all the usual computer skills." He rattled them off and she nodded. "Would you want me to travel with you?"

She thought about it for a minute and nodded again. "I probably would." Especially if what the doctor said was true. Even if she didn't lose her sight completely, it would be reassuring to travel with someone, although she never had before. "Would that be a problem for you?"

"Not at all. I live with my sister, who needs assistance, but I can make arrangements for her if I know ahead of time. And I don't mind filling in where you need me to. I liked being a personal assistant to the senator. It was different every day. And I enjoy making people's lives run smoothly, whatever it takes."

"I travel to see my clients' homes too, or to install a painting, mostly in the United States, in California or on the East Coast. Occasionally on a boat, usually in the Caribbean. But most of the time, we'll be here in New York."

"It sounds great to me." He smiled pleasantly. "I don't mind buying groceries, or serving lunch if you have a client here." He seemed accommodating and willing to do anything she needed, however menial, unlike Margaret the day before.

She showed him around the house, and he seemed totally at ease. He said he spoke a little Spanish, which she didn't need. He was just an all-around easygoing guy, who was willing to do whatever she needed on any given day, and said he liked the variety of being a personal assistant, and not being confined to a corporate office, which he admitted he had never really enjoyed. She asked him about driving, because the doctor had said that could become a problem for her. She had a car in a garage nearby but she rarely used it. And he said he would be willing to drive her. He seemed to be tailor-made for the position, however the degeneration of her vision progressed, or even if it didn't. She wasn't used to anyone helping her to that degree, or at all.

She ended the interview at eleven and said she'd call the agency. He had to duck his head as he went through the front door but he was used to it. She called the woman at the agency immediately.

"He's perfect for the job," Isabelle said, sounding hopeful. "He's exactly what I need, and willing to do anything."

"I like that about him too," the agent said, pleased that it had gone well. He was an unusual candidate for any job, because of his varied experience, and Isabelle thought the salary he wanted was reasonable.

"I hope he doesn't take the job at NBC." Isabelle was suddenly worried about it.

"He won't. It's an office job, in sports, and he thought it sounded too confining and too limited, but he was an obvious candidate for it so I sent him. I'll let you know as soon as I hear." She called Isabelle back ten minutes later and said that Jack had just called her, and unless NBC offered him a fortune, which they wouldn't for the opening they had, he wanted to work for Isabelle. He had liked her a lot, and the fact that he'd be a PA again. He had enjoyed what he had learned with the senator about being a personal assistant, having a real bond with an employer and making their life easier.

She called again at one o'clock as Isabelle was eating a yogurt at her desk and waiting for an auction call, so she couldn't stay on long.

"He wants the job with you," she said, sounding pleased about it, and so was Isabelle.

"That's great news. When can he start?"

"Tomorrow, if you want him to."

"I think that will work out just fine. I have a client coming tomorrow, he can sit in on the meeting, to see what I do."

"I'll tell him. Coat and tie?" It was more formal than she needed, although he would look nice in a suit.

"More like jeans and a blazer, or something along those lines. He doesn't need to wear a tie. I'm very pleased." She had a feeling that he would be helpful to have around, and unobtrusive. She had a desk in the kitchen she was going to have him use, so he would be nearby, but not close enough to be intrusive.

"He really does seem like the right fit for the job." She

liked it when that happened. Isabelle's auction call came in then, and she had to get off quickly.

She did well in the auction for a client in Palm Beach. She called Xela afterward, who returned the call that night, while Isabelle was getting ready for bed. Jack had emailed her earlier about how pleased he was to get the job. His email was short, friendly, and polite.

"I hired an assistant today," she told Xela, almost forgetting the somber reason why she had hired him. He seemed like such a stroke of good luck.

"You did?" Xela was surprised. She'd never had one before, but she took it as a positive. "Business must be good."

"I'm busy, and I thought I needed some help. How are you doing with your investors?" They always talked about her business, it was all that mattered to her.

"They're driving me crazy. The venture capital guys are sharks." Her startup centered around delivery services in several cities, and her dream was to make it nation-wide, and she needed their money for that, and to take it public eventually. Ultimately, she wanted to sell the business for big money. She wanted her Harvard MBA to pay off and to make a fortune of her own one day. She knew she'd never have as much as Theo, but she had dreams of being a millionaire in her own right and a self-made woman, and she was willing to do anything she had to to get there. She already owned her own apartment in SoHo, but her mother had been the guarantor on the mortgage. She didn't want her help in the future. She wanted to make it on her own and was extremely proud and independent.

"What's she like?" Xela asked her about the new assistant.

"Who?" Isabelle didn't know who she was talking about.

"The assistant?"

Her mother laughed in answer. "She's a guy, and about ten feet tall. He had to stoop over to get through the front door."

"Sounds scary," Xela said with no further interest.

"And don't forget, you said you'd be here for lunch on Thanksgiving. Theo will be home for it."

"Saint Theo," Xela said in an acid tone that her mother was used to but didn't like. "I'm surprised she's coming all the way from India."

"She has meetings with the bank in Boston, to get the hospital up and running. And I don't want any trouble between you two. She's coming a long way to be here, and I don't want either of you ruining Thanksgiving. I want you to respect that, Xela." She knew her middle daughter well and the tension between the two sisters and what it led to.

"I will," she said grudgingly. Theo tried to avoid the arguments, but Xela had a way of making it happen. She couldn't be in the same room with her older sister without being resentful about something, and making barbed comments.

"I'm counting on you both," Isabelle said in a firm tone. She didn't want either of them spoiling the day. The holidays meant a lot to her and she saw too little of them to have it go badly.

"I can hardly wait to meet the new assistant," Xela said, changing the subject. "What's his name?"

"Jack."

"As in Jack and the Beanstalk? He sounds like a giant."

"He seems like a nice guy. I'm sure he'll help me a lot." She felt wistful after she hung up. She would have liked to have been able to tell her daughter that she was terrified of what the doctor had told her. It would have been comforting to be open with her. But she never liked to show signs of weakness to her children. They counted on her to be strong for them. She always had been. But she wondered how long she would be able to do that. She intended to fight this battle alone. With Jack Bailey's help, even though he didn't know it was why he was there, and she wasn't going to tell him either. At least not yet, and hopefully not for a long time.

Chapter Ten

Jack showed up for his first day of work as promptly as he had for the interview. He had gotten up at five A.M. to get things ready for his sister, prepare food for her and leave it in the refrigerator. He'd showered, shaved, and dressed carefully, and helped her to the couch where she liked to spend the day, dozing and watching television. Her condition had worsened dramatically in the last year, which was why he had moved back from Washington. She could get around the apartment with the walker, and he took her out in a wheelchair on weekends.

"Play nice at school," Sandy admonished him gently as she looked him over. She was forty-nine years old, had two children, and was divorced. Her son had moved to Sweden after college and was married there, and her daughter had married a somewhat difficult commercial fisherman in Alaska. She didn't want to live with either of them and be a burden. She couldn't afford a nurse. And Jack had seen clearly how hard it was for her to manage. With great regret, he had given up the job in Washington and moved in with her.

Living together reminded them both of their childhood in Seattle. Things hadn't turned out the way they'd planned for either of them. Her husband had left her when her kids were very young, and she'd been struggling ever since, and lived on disability payments now. And Jack's romance with his high-school sweetheart evaporated when his promising career ended in an instant, and several dead-end relationships had left him childless and unmarried at forty-six. But he felt it had worked out for the best since it left him able to take care of his sister, and he had always found good jobs he liked, which also allowed him to help her financially. He didn't like to think about what would happen when her condition worsened, which it would inevitably. She was starting to talk about moving to a nursing home, so she didn't become too big a burden on him. She was thrilled for him about the new job, and grateful to him for living with her.

"You look very handsome. I hope this woman knows how lucky she is to have you. You could probably run her business blindfolded," she said with total faith in him, which wasn't entirely unjustified. He had done well at every job he'd had, and had become essential to all his employers. He had a wonderful way about him and was a caring person. Sandy knew just how lucky she was to have him with her and the sacrifices he made.

"Hardly. I don't know a damn thing about art," he

confessed nervously. "I'd better do some boning up. Maybe we should go to a museum this weekend, so I can tell the difference between a Picasso and a Rembrandt. I read about her online, and she has some major league clients, and some very big-deal art."

"You'll do fine. You've never had a job where they didn't love you."

"Thank God for biased older sisters. I should have asked you for a reference." He had gotten the job on his own merits, and his serious, straightforward demeanor and willingness and flexibility in the interview. Everything about him had felt right to Isabelle. He had asked her all the right questions about the job, and she'd figured that a man his age dedicated to taking care of a sick sister had to be a good guy. And she liked that he was single and had no kids, which gave him more spare time than if he had a family. She knew from her years at the gallery that employees with young children were always a problem, and their childcare arrangements were never as fail-safe as they said.

He took the subway to work from their apartment downtown near the Bowery. It was an old rent-stabilized building and there was no doorman, but the Puerto Rican super was a kind person, and he let himself into the apartment to check on Sandy from time to time when he knew Jack was out.

Isabelle had just finished coffee and a piece of toast

when he rang the bell. She went to let him in, and led him back to the kitchen, where she'd been reading *The Wall Street Journal,* and he noticed a magnifying glass on the table. Reading it online made her eyes burn from the strain. She saw him notice the magnifying glass and said she was waiting for new glasses and had been to the eye doctor a few days before.

She showed him where the coffee machine was, told him there were several delis and small restaurants nearby for lunch on Lexington Avenue, led him upstairs to her office, and sat down at her desk.

"I have a client coming in this afternoon," she said easily, "and calls to make this morning. You're welcome to sit in on the meeting to see what I do. We're going to go over photographs of Mary Cassatt paintings with the client. He wants to buy one for his wife for their anniversary, and we're trying to pick one from what's currently on the market, either at auction, or in galleries here and in Europe." She took a book out of her bookcase then, about Mary Cassatt, and handed it to him. "She's an American Impressionist and was a remarkable artist. She painted mostly women and children. Have you ever seen her work?" It was a straight question and not meant to embarrass him, and he answered honestly.

"Not that I know of. Unless she was in women's basketball, I don't know her." She laughed.

"That's a little more recent than her body of work."

He looked grateful for the book. He was willing to do homework to learn the job. "And I'm putting together a collection for a man from Tulsa, who just bought a house here, and has a yacht in Antigua. I got the first two pieces for him yesterday from a Christie's auction. We have a lot to buy for him."

"You sound busy." He still wasn't sure exactly how he fit in. Neither was she. "Will you want me to deal with clients?" he asked her, nervous about it since he knew nothing about the art world.

"Not unless you're with me, not on your own. But you can make notes during the meeting, and I'll need you to do research. I'm sure you're a lot better on the computer than I am. Just when I find what I want, I hit the wrong button and it disappears." He smiled. "There are two spotlights burned out in the living room if you don't mind replacing them, and I want to send some catalogues to the man we're doing the collection for." She pointed to a stack on her desk. "I have a FedEx account, just call and they'll pick up. The boxes are in the pantry closet." It all sounded easy so far, and interesting. And very different from the multitude of tasks he'd done for the senator.

"What kind of paintings do you put on a yacht?" He was curious about it.

"I suggested contemporary, but he wants Old Masters, and he fell in love with a Turner, and he loves some scenes of Venice by Felix Ziem that I showed him." She stood up and handed him two more books. "Basically, paintings with boats in them." She smiled at Jack.

"Makes sense, even to me." He picked up the stack of catalogues, and then he turned to her. "Do you like sports? I still have some connections for tickets, at the network where I worked." The senator had loved that, and was a huge baseball and football fan. Isabelle smiled hesitantly at him.

"I know as much about sports as you do about art. Maybe we can trade information sometime. My last husband died twenty-six years ago, and I have three daughters. I've been to the US Open and Wimbledon, but that's about it. And that reminds me, if we have time later, I want to pull out the Thanksgiving decorations today. My daughter is coming home from India for a few days, and I want to get out the things for the table. They're on a high shelf I can't get to."

"That's right up my alley." He grinned at her from his considerable height. "And thank you for lending me the books." He went to find the FedEx boxes for the catalogues, and Isabelle spent the morning making calls about various paintings, while Jack read the books, sitting in the kitchen. He showed up with a cup of coffee for her on a tray with cream and sugar halfway through the morning. She smiled and nodded her thanks while deep in conversation on the phone, and he discreetly disappeared again, and let her know when he left for lunch. The morning had gone well.

He was back in less than an hour, and had taken a brisk walk after he ate a turkey sandwich and a cup of soup at a deli. She showed him where the box of Thanksgiving ornaments was. He didn't need a ladder to get to them, which she would have, and they unpacked them together. There were some silver birds from Asprey in London, and a brightly colored porcelain turkey as the centerpiece, and some smaller things that would make the table look festive and autumnal, some of which were relics of when the kids were younger. She was holding a small ceramic turkey Theo had made at school, and Isabelle smiled as she held it and set it down on the table. But she missed the surface by several inches and it fell on the floor. Luckily it didn't break. She bent to pick it up and set it down in the center of the table as he watched her, having noticed that she had dropped it in midair, but he didn't comment. He volunteered to polish the silver pieces to cover the awkward moment, which had clearly upset her. She went back upstairs a few minutes later.

He set out the decorations on the dining room table, after he polished the silver birds. And a little while later, the client who wanted the Mary Cassatt for his wife arrived. He was a distinguished-looking man in his late sixties or early seventies, and Jack had had a few minutes to glance through the Cassatt book by then. He was quiet during the meeting, but the few comments he made were intelligent, and he made careful notes of what happened, typed them up on his computer afterward, and handed them to Isabelle. She looked surprised.

"That was fast." She had just called the gallery that had the painting of a mother and child the client wanted.

"It wasn't very complicated," Jack said, smiling at her as she looked at the pages he had handed her, and she paused for a moment.

"Can I ask you a favor? Would you print these again just a little bit larger? The font is very small." It wasn't, but he didn't argue with her, and suspected she had a problem with her eyes, or was overdue for the glasses she was waiting for that she had mentioned earlier. He assumed that was the problem.

"That's easy. I'll be back in a minute." He had it in her hands five minutes later, and she was impressed when she read his notes. They were concise and clear and listed the essence of the meeting with bullet points.

"You do a great job, Jack," she said, praising him honestly. "I wasn't sure I needed an assistant, but you've convinced me in a single day that I've been depriving myself."

"What made you change your mind and decide to hire someone?" He had a feeling that there was some bigger reason behind his getting the job, but he could sense how private she was and assumed she wouldn't tell him. And sooner or later, he'd figure it out.

"I can't do it all. And it's nice having some help. The woman I have to do my billing twice a month isn't enough. You're going to spoil me very quickly." The senator had said as much to him many times.

"Will your daughter be staying here when she's in town? Do I need to make any arrangements for her?" he volunteered, assuming it was part of his job. He liked to think ahead, and Isabelle noticed that too. "Airport pickup? Flowers in her room? Hair appointment?" He had done all that and more for the senator's wife.

"The airport pickup and flowers would be nice. No need for hair." Isabelle was slightly in awe of him. He thought of everything. "I'll give you her flight details," she said, riffling through a stack of papers on her desk, and handing him a page. "She's coming in the night before Thanksgiving and leaving for Boston on Monday morning."

"Will she come back here after Boston?" he asked, being curious more than organized.

"No, she won't. She's flying to London, and back to Delhi from there. She's meeting with a doctor in London who is putting a team together to visit the hospital she's trying to enlarge. She's a very enterprising young woman, our very own Mother Teresa," she said proudly, but he could see sadness in her eyes too. He deduced easily that

Isabelle missed her and wondered if it was something more. For a woman with three children, she seemed very much alone. But so was his sister, Sandy, with hers too. Children had a way of moving on. It was why he had never longed for any of his own. They were part of your life for such a short time, it seemed very brief and ephemeral to him, but he didn't say that to her.

"I'll order a car for her for Wednesday when she arrives, and Monday."

"She may balk at the one on Monday. She believes in living a very Spartan life. She's not given to extravagances," Isabelle said and he nodded. "And just a small bouquet of flowers in her room, nothing lavish. She has lived with poverty and its ravages for sixteen years, she doesn't approve of the way any of us live."

"That's interesting," he said thoughtfully. "Are the others that way?"

"Not at all. They're all different. My daughter Xela, who lives here, has an MBA and has established a struggling startup she wants to make into a nationwide success. She is the embodiment of capitalism and the American Dream. My youngest daughter, Oona, is married to an Italian count from a very old family, and lives on a farm in Tuscany. She grows her own vegetables, but has a comfortable lifestyle. She has three children, soon to be five. She's expecting twins. She's twenty-six. Theo, who lives in India, is very ethereal and removed from the world we live in. Her father was like that too. He lived in France." She sounded like she had had an interesting life, but he didn't want to ask too many questions and seem like he was prying. But the few details she'd just given him intrigued him, and he had the feeling she'd been married more than once. He wondered what her daughters were like. He liked their mother so far, and the open, direct way she communicated with him, neither too personal nor patronizing. There was nothing snobbish or grand about her, and he could tell she worked hard.

He stayed until six, although they had agreed his workday would end at five-thirty, but he wanted to finish up a few loose ends, and Isabelle came down to the kitchen before he left. It was immaculate and in good order, although he'd used it as an office all day.

"Is there anything else I can do for you before I go?" he offered, and she shook her head with a smile.

"You've managed to spoil me already. I don't know how I got along without you until now."

"Very well, I suspect." She seemed to have her life very much in hand. And it struck him again that she seemed youthful and energetic, although he had correctly guessed her age from things she said and how old her daughters were. She didn't look it. "See you tomorrow, then," he said, picking up his coat, and left a few minutes later to go home.

Isabelle walked around the kitchen after he left. Everything he had used was back where it belonged, the FedEx packages had been sent, the notes from the meeting were on her desk in a larger font. And she noticed that he had taken the books with him, to do his "homework" to learn more about the artists they'd discussed, for two of her clients. She was vastly impressed. The house seemed strangely quiet once he was gone. He wasn't intrusive, but he filled the space in a pleasant way. She glanced into the dining room and saw the decorations gleaming on the table. She went to pick up the little ceramic turkey Theo had made and was glad she hadn't broken it when she dropped it. The years when the girls were young had been the best of her life.

*

"How was your first day at school?" Sandy asked him with a grin when he walked in, took off his coat, and sat down next to her in the small living room. She could see that he looked pleased. "Did the kids all talk to you? Was the food good? Do you like your teacher?" She smiled at him.

"I had a turkey sandwich at a deli nearby. And I really enjoyed the day. She's an interesting woman. Her kids are grown up and she doesn't complain, but she seems lonely," he said, and Sandy nodded. She understood that only too well. She missed hers too. "I think there's some underlying reason for why she hired me, but she didn't say it. I just have a feeling about it. I sat in on a meeting, polished silver, sent FedExes, and I have some books to read about three artists. Mary Cassatt, Turner, and Felix Ziem."

"They're all big deals." Sandy read a lot and lived on the Internet, where she learned a multitude of things. "It sounds like fun." She was happy for him—he deserved it, and she still felt bad about the job he'd given up for her.

"It is. It's different from the senator. He was more of a hard hitter, and there were constantly people trying to get to him I had to keep away. She lives in a very enclosed, orderly, controlled world. She has it very much together, and her clients are varied. We saw an Englishman today who lives in Connecticut. She's putting a whole collection together for some oilman from Oklahoma, for his yacht."

"It sounds like the fast lane to me."

"It is. But I'm not sure she's part of it. She seems to live a quiet life. And her kids sound intriguing too. A saint in India, a businesswoman in New York working on a startup, and her youngest is married to a count in Italy, lives on a farm, and has five kids."

"You learned a lot in one day." Sandy looked amused. She thought her brother seemed a little dazzled by his new employer and she wondered if he had a crush on her, which wasn't like him. He never got involved with women where he worked, or never had. "Is she good-looking?"

"Don't start sounding like a big sister. She's in her fifties and she's my boss."

"Stranger things have happened," Sandy said with a knowing smile.

"Just shut up. What do you want for dinner?"

"I've been dreaming of Chinese food all day," she said.

"Your wish is my command," he said, and headed for the kitchen phone to order Chinese takeout from the menu they kept there. He called in their dinner order to be delivered, came back, sat down, and switched on the TV. "There's a basketball game tonight," he said as he wound down and stretched out his legs. He smiled at his sister and turned to the evening news. He liked living with her and having someone to talk to. It filled a void for both of them. He hadn't expected to wind up living with Sandy at their ages. But life never turned out as you expected, for better or worse.

And in the house on Seventy-Fourth Street, Isabelle was eating a leftover salad she'd bought at the deli the day before, and turned on her favorite TV series, while Jack watched NBA basketball downtown. She was pleased with how the day had gone. Having an assistant was turning out to be a good idea, whatever the reason for it.

Chapter Eleven

Isabelle had had two injections in her eyes by Thanksgiving week, and it was traumatic more than painful. She was quiet when she got back from the treatments, and grateful for Jack's help. In a short time, he was proving to be invaluable, with clients, in meetings, helping her organize things, and just doing small tasks and projects and repairs for her. And he frequently brought her a cup of tea or coffee even before she asked for it. She was happy to have him, and he helped her set the Thanksgiving table with the things they had unpacked and the silver he had polished the evening Theo was due home, the day before Thanksgiving.

He had noticed that Isabelle looked stressed, and she had said she had a doctor's appointment the day before. She had had her new glasses for a week, but she still liked her emails printed in larger font, and kept her magnifying glass close at hand. Twice he had seen her nearly stumble on the stairs and almost miss a step. He wasn't sure if she was distracted, or something else was going on, and she squinted as she looked at the dining room table once they'd set it.

He decided to be bold with her and see what happened. "You seem nervous, are you okay?"

She hesitated for a moment and nodded. "I am nervous. Theo and Xela don't always get along—to be honest, they never do. It's been that way since Xela was old enough to talk. She has a knack for starting arguments with her sister, and I don't want that happening on Thanksgiving. Theo is only going to be here for four days. I hardly ever see her. She's a difficult person to get close to, geographically and emotionally. Her father was very reclusive, and she isolates herself in her own way, surrounding herself with strangers thousands of miles away, while she does good deeds. And when she finally does come home and I can see her, Xela starts a fight with her. It doesn't make coming back here very appealing to her. And I miss her."

"Have you told them how you feel about it?" This was all new to him, and he hadn't met either of them, but he could see how tense Isabelle was about it, and had been for several days.

"For about thirty years," she answered his question. "It doesn't stop either of them. Theo used to fight back when she was younger, although she always tried to be kind to her baby sister. But Xela isn't a baby anymore and she hits hard, usually below the belt if she can arrange it. Theo just leaves and flies away again. She's out of reach now, which drives Xela crazy."

"Families are never as easy as they appear from the outside. Sandy and I tried to kill each other as children. It wasn't until after our parents died that we realized we really needed each other. And then she got sick, which brought us closer too. I couldn't let her go through that alone after her husband left her. Were any of your girls close to each other at all as kids?" he asked, still curious about her. There was something faintly mysterious about Isabelle, truths that he knew she wasn't revealing.

"Sometimes. They both love Oona. She's the easy one, the peacemaker. They both consider her their baby. And she gets along with everyone. She could be best friends with Godzilla and Frankenstein. She's an intrinsically happy person. She makes it all look easy, even her macho Italian husband." Isabelle knew she personally would have strangled him in two minutes, and his family, who were involved in everything Oona and Gregorio did. They told Oona how to cook the meals, treat her husband, and bring up the children, and she turned a deaf ear to their criticism and went on her merry way, happy and not even resentful.

"It's amazing how kids can grow up in the same house with the same parents, and come away so different," he said as he helped her set the table.

"That's the thing," she said, looking at him. "They didn't. Same mother, different fathers. They each have a different father, and genetics are a powerful force. They all have a lot of their fathers in them."

"You were married three times?" He looked surprised and cautiously asked the question.

"Twice," she corrected him, which raised another question but he didn't ask it since she had already said that the three girls each had a different father, and he didn't want to offend her.

"You've had an interesting life." She nodded and didn't comment. Theo was arriving at the house at six, and Jack was leaving early. She wanted to be alone with her that night, before they added Xela to the mix the next day. Jack was making Thanksgiving dinner for his sister, and had ordered a turkey. He said he had a lot to be grateful for this year. He was loving his new job.

He stopped in to see her in her office before he left. She was answering emails and turned to smile at him, standing on the other side of her desk. He looked seven feet tall instead of 6'6" when she was sitting down.

"Have a wonderful Thanksgiving, Jack," she said warmly.

"You too. Thank you for everything. I'm grateful for you this year."

"It's an even trade. You help me more than I ever knew someone could." And she meant it.

"Have fun with your daughters. I hope they behave."

"Me too."

She sat quietly in her office after she heard the front door close, and then went to check Theo's bedroom. She had put a vase of white roses in it. The bed was freshly made. The house looked perfect. They were going to have a light meal that night, before Thanksgiving lunch the next day. When they were all together, they'd call Oona. There was no Thanksgiving holiday in Italy, but Oona always made a turkey anyway, and told her children what her Thanksgiving was like when she was a little girl. It was one of her favorite holidays.

Isabelle had promised to visit her at Christmas. She was too pregnant to travel, especially with twins, and Gregorio wouldn't leave his family at Christmas anyway. Theo would be back in India, and Xela had rented a ski house in Vermont with friends. So Christmas in Tuscany sounded good to Isabelle, with her daughter and three grandsons. They didn't know the sex of the twins yet. Gregorio wanted them to be surprised, although Oona wanted to know. As usual, Gregorio's wishes ruled the day.

Isabelle went back to her own room to lie down, while she waited for Theo, and at last the doorbell rang. She hurried down the stairs, mindful of the steps, opened the door, and stood looking at Theo, who was the image of Putnam, and pulled her daughter gently into her arms. She was no bigger than a waif, and still looked like a teenager at thirty-seven, although there were fine lines around her eyes. She was as fair as her mother, with huge blue eyes. She was dressed for the cold weather, but put on a sari for dinner with her mother. She found them more comfortable than Western clothes, except when she was doing hard manual labor, and she looked beautiful with her long blond hair loose down her back.

She told Isabelle all about the hospital over dinner in the kitchen, which Isabelle had cooked. Theo had convinced a group of British doctors to come out and help them, and was meeting them in London the following week.

"I have to transfer some more money first and sell some investments," she said simply, and Isabelle was certain it was a sizable amount. She had been funding similar projects for years, and could well afford it. She had followed her father's instructions to the letter, and was making a difference in the world. "When are you going to Italy?" she asked her mother.

"Right before Christmas. Oona says she's huge."

Theo smiled at the image of her sister. "She sent me a picture. She looks like she's having triplets. Do you think this will be it?"

"Probably not. Gregorio's one of seven children. He probably wants half a dozen more." But Oona was happy, her babies were beautiful, and they had a good life on the farm. It wasn't the life Isabelle had expected for her either, but it seemed to be working well for her. "I'm taking my new assistant with me, and giving him time off when I'm with Oona. And then we're going to Paris for a couple of auctions, and to see some work being sold privately. I haven't been to Paris in a while." She was afraid of falling if she traveled and had asked Jack to come along. He had arranged for a nurse to come in at night for his sister, and was delighted at the opportunity. He was planning to spend Christmas with an old friend in Rome. He said his life had suddenly become very glamorous, although Isabelle didn't see it that way.

Theo went to bed early that night, and was wearing a beautiful sky-blue sari when her mother found her in the kitchen the next morning. Isabelle had already put the turkey in the oven, hours earlier, and Xela was due at noon. They were planning to have their traditional meal at two o'clock, and could eat leftovers that night. Xela arrived half an hour late, kissed her mother at the front door, and raised an eyebrow when she saw her sister in the living room.

"You've gone native?" were the first words she said to her. Theo had changed into a rust-colored sari trimmed in gold with a short taffeta blouse beneath it in pale green, and gold shoes.

"The colors are perfect for Thanksgiving," Isabelle said to cover the awkward moment, while praying silently that Xela would kiss her sister and bury the hatchet at least until the end of lunch. Theo was the first to make a move and hugged Xela, who looked stiff and uncomfortable. She was wearing a red sweater and jeans, and

Isabelle was wearing a dressy black sweater and black velvet slacks. The turkey was almost ready and smelled delicious. The fragrance wafted throughout the house.

"How's your business going?" Theo asked her politely, looking more than ever like her father, as Isabelle came and went to the kitchen to check on the food. She was glad she'd had the previous evening alone with Theo, before things got tense the moment Xela arrived. She had a knot in her stomach as Xela told Theo about the problems she was having with potential investors. It was the only thing she cared about, and Isabelle couldn't help remembering Collin while she talked endlessly about getting her business off the ground. But Xela was an ambitious, earnest young entrepreneur, not a crook. She had her father's ingenuity and creativity for business, but her mother's honesty and integrity, which was a better combination.

"I'm making a big investment in the hospital I'm working on now too," Theo said quietly in her peaceful, otherworldly way.

"The big difference between us is that you can afford to, with your own money. I have to run around begging people to invest who want to skin me alive. It's not exactly the same thing." But she wasn't saving lives either, which no one pointed out.

They sat down to lunch after that, and the conversation was strained, despite Isabelle's efforts to keep it light. The turkey was delicious, as were all the vegetables and stuffing she'd made to go with it. It was her annual tour de force in the kitchen, which she avoided for the rest of the year. The table looked beautiful. The only mishap was when she set a bowl of peas down after passing it around. She put it too close to the edge of the table and it fell, spilling peas everywhere. Isabelle rushed to clean them up, and Theo helped her. No one seemed shocked by it. It seemed like an ordinary accident to them.

"Sorry, I wasn't paying attention," Isabelle said, looking embarrassed. Neither of her daughters read it as a sign that something was wrong with their mother. They had begun to relax by then, and talked about how enormous Oona was and how incredible it was to think she was going to have five children soon, and was turning twenty-seven shortly.

"It couldn't happen to me," Xela said, sounding sarcastic about Oona. "I don't have time for men and babies. I want to get this startup going and make some real money," she continued single-mindedly, and then looked cynically at her older sister. "And you're too busy saving the world to have kids. It'll probably take you your whole life to give it all away." Her jealousy came through her pores, and Theo didn't answer for a minute, and then answered her sister with a small smile.

"There's still enough left," she said, sufficiently irked by her to rub it in intentionally. The temptation was hard to resist, although Theo rarely reacted to her sister, but she knew what annoyed her.

"I'll bet there is," Xela said tartly. She resented Theo for never offering to invest in her business. Theo had no interest in commercial ventures, only philanthropic ones. "You are definitely the Number One member of the Lucky Sperm Club. If Mom hadn't had an affair with your father when she was practically a kid, you'd be working your ass off like me on less noble projects, or have a job you hate like the rest of the world." It drove her crazy that Theo was exempt from the stresses she lived with and could rise above it all.

"Girls!" Isabelle said sharply, looking straight at Xela. "It's Thanksgiving. Let's be grateful for what we have, not angry because of what someone else has. And by the way, I don't hate my job."

"Neither do I," Xela said. "I just want to make a heap of money out of it, so I can play saint like Theo."

"I don't play saint, Xela, I love what I do," Theo stated quietly. "Just like you do. You would hate what I do every day."

"Damn right I would. Sick babies and starving people are not my thing."

"Have you met Mom's new assistant?" Theo asked her, changing the subject. She could see how uncomfortable their mother was at the turn the conversation had taken.

"He's not here at night when I come by. He sounds

like the Boy Wonder," Xela said about Jack, irritable about him too.

"He certainly is," Isabelle added, grateful they had moved on to a more neutral topic. "He's learning very quickly."

"What did he do before he worked for you?" Theo asked her, to be polite.

"He worked for a senator in Washington as a personal assistant. And on sports radio and TV and in PR before that."

"That's quite a leap to art, isn't it?" Xela asked skeptically.

"He's supporting a sick sister who has MS."

"Oh God, not another saint." Xela rolled her eyes as she said it, and Theo didn't comment. The conversation limped along until they had tried all the pies, with ice cream and homemade whipped cream. She always bought their favorites, pumpkin, apple, and mince, so they could have a thin slice of each. And pecan, which was Oona's preference, although she wasn't there. They had coffee in the living room. Isabelle almost spilled Xela's when she set it down, and she looked at her mother with a raised eyebrow.

"You've got the dropsies, Mom. You need more practice than just cooking once a year."

"I suppose I do." It never dawned on Xela or even Theo with her altruistic nature that there might be another reason for it. They both lived in their own worlds, totally absorbed in their own doings, and no one else's, with no concern for their mother, whom they considered competent in the extreme. She had been the role model for all of them. And Oona was just as capable at being a wife and mother as they were in their jobs. They were four superwomen, each in her own way.

It was hard for Isabelle to remember now what it had been like to cook for children and a husband. She had been married to Collin so briefly, and he was never there. She had never lived with Putnam. She and Declan had shared the cooking, but he died when they'd only been married for seven months. Despite three men and three children, she had never had a long-term full-time relationship. It felt strange to admit, even to herself.

"I guess none of us are good at relationships," Xela said later in the conversation, referring to herself, her mother, and her older sister, and they all knew she wasn't entirely wrong.

"I've been doing other things that are more important to me right now," Theo defended herself.

"I can't help what happened to your father, Xela," Isabelle said quietly. Collin had never tried to contact his daughter, and when Xela had researched him later on, she discovered that he had gone to prison again after the first time, and for all she knew he was still there. She no longer wanted to know. "And Declan died before Oona was even born. I didn't kill him," she said sadly. He was the only normal relationship she'd ever had.

"But you never tried again either," Xela reminded her.

"I didn't have time," Isabelle said coolly, "and by the time you all grew up, I was too old."

"You were fifty when Oona left for college, Mom," Xela persisted. "That's not too old, and you're not too old now. You just don't want a man in your life. Neither do Theo and I. We have bigger plans."

"You can have your careers and a man," her mother pointed out.

"I'm not so sure," Xela said. "I work eighteen-hour days."

"I work twenty-four sometimes," Theo added. "Besides, I never meet anyone where I am. No one I'd want to marry, or even date, and that's not what I'm there for."

"No cute doctors?" Xela challenged her. "I'll bet there are some." But Isabelle knew how much Theo was like her father. She could only focus on one thing at a time, and her life in India was her way of not engaging in the world, just as Putnam hadn't. They were emotionally frightened people, and in her own way Xela was too. She hid behind her startup so she didn't have to meet a man. Isabelle wondered if she was afraid to fail at both.

"Maybe I set a bad example for you all by being alone for so long. Most of the men I met weren't eager to take on three children, and I was more interested in being with you than running around dating." She had ended up alone as a result. She didn't regret it. She had known true love at least twice, with Putnam and Declan. She didn't count Collin, since everything that had happened with him had been a fraud, except for Xela, who was all too real.

"Well, we're all doing fine," Xela confirmed. "I have my business, Saint Theo has her hospital, Oona has Gregorio and her seven million children. And you seem happy to me, Mom."

"I am," she said peacefully.

"And now you have your assistant to help with the practical stuff. You don't need a man." Xela had it all figured out for everyone. She tossed a few more barbs at her sister, and at seven o'clock she left, having spent the whole afternoon with them. Isabelle was grateful there had been no major explosions, and Theo looked exhausted as her sister left. They had hugged at the front door, and Xela was going away for the weekend with friends the next day. There was snow in New Hampshire and they were going to check it out and hoped to do some skiing.

"God, she wears me out," Theo said with a sigh after Xela left. "She hates me, she has all my life." Isabelle looked aggrieved to hear her say it. It pained her for both of them.

"She doesn't hate you. She resents what you have and she doesn't."

"That's not my fault," Theo complained. "You should have slept with three equally rich men, then we wouldn't have this problem," Theo teased her.

"Sorry. I never thought of it. His money had nothing to do with why I loved your father. And Declan had almost nothing. I've always been careful to support myself, even when I was involved with your father. I didn't want to depend on him, or anyone else. I needed to know I could take care of myself. And I have."

"It's so unpleasant that Xela is so focused on the money. She doesn't see me as a person. She never has."

"That's why she wants to make a lot of money one day. To compete with you, I think." They both knew it was true. "She'll never have what your father left you. Neither will I."

"The difference is that you don't think about it and don't care. She thinks about nothing else," Theo said reasonably.

"It's sad for her," Isabelle said. "She's never content. It's why she drives herself so hard."

They went to tidy up the kitchen then and load the dishwasher. It took a long time. They had used Isabelle's good china, which had belonged to her parents. The kitchen was spotless when they finished. Theo was good at scrubbing up. Xela hadn't stayed to help. She never did.

They both went to bed early, tired after the day. It had

been a good Thanksgiving, better than Isabelle had dared to hope. There had been no major explosions, and no one had left the table.

The next day they got up and walked around the neighborhood. Theo had a few errands to do before she left on Monday. She wanted to buy underwear for some of the children who had never had any, and some American medicines she couldn't get in India. She bought a pair of hiking boots for herself, and some small presents for the children, and a huge bag of lollipops she squeezed into her suitcase.

The weekend flew by too quickly, and Isabelle felt the same ache in her soul she always felt when Theo left. It was as though she was slipping through her fingers. It was the same sensation she had always had when she'd left Putnam at the end of August and knew she wouldn't see him for another eleven months. With Theo, she never knew when she would see her again either. And just as they began to get close after a few days, Theo was gone. She was the butterfly one couldn't hang on to. The bird that always flew away.

Isabelle was looking sad when Jack came to work on Monday morning, and found her in the kitchen. He had the feeling she'd been crying but didn't want to ask.

"How was Thanksgiving?" he inquired, making coffee for both of them, and setting hers down on the table in front of her just the way she liked it. No sugar and a splash of milk. By now, he knew her habits. "I thought about you all weekend, but I didn't want to call and intrude."

"It was nice." She smiled as he sat down across from her, his legs stretched out a mile. "Maybe too nice. It makes it harder when they leave."

"No fights?"

"Some skirmishes and caustic comments from the usual source. Nothing serious. No major casualties for a change. I just never know when I'll see them again."

"My sister feels that way too. Your children live so far away. We should go to India sometime to visit Theo," he suggested.

"She's too busy. I've been there but I always feel like a nuisance when I visit. How was your Thanksgiving?"

"Easy. Pleasant. I cooked a decent meal. Lots of football after that. Thanksgiving isn't really about being grateful, it's about food and football." He smiled at her. He was excited that they were leaving for Italy in three weeks. Sandy was happy for him too. She never wanted to hold him back.

They worked together that morning, and Theo called in the afternoon. She'd done everything she needed to, and Isabelle wanted to beg her to come back to New York so she could see her one more time, but she had changed her ticket and was flying to London that night. She was well versed in being the mother of adults, and particularly

Danielle Steel

someone like Theo, so Isabelle didn't ask her when she would see her again. It was enough for now that she had come home for four days, just as a month in the summer with Put was all she'd known she'd ever get. They weren't capable of more.

*

She had another session with her doctor the next day, and came home rattled and exhausted after the shots. It was too soon to see any improvement, and she was so tired when she got home, she tripped over the carpet when she walked into her office and almost fell. Jack shot a hand out instinctively and caught her.

"Good reflexes," she complimented him with a tired smile. The corner of the rug had been folded back, and she hadn't seen it.

"You do that a lot, don't you?" he asked hesitantly, out of concern not curiosity.

"Not really. Just clumsy and distracted." He didn't comment but, not for the first time, he wondered if she had MS like Sandy. She fell a lot in the beginning too. But she wound up flat on the ground when she lost her balance. Isabelle bumped into things she didn't see, or misjudged distances. He never pressed her about it, but had kept her from falling several times. Sometimes he wondered if that was why he was there. But she was involving him in her business too. She introduced him to clients, let him sit in on meetings, and lent him more books, in order to educate him in her field. He enjoyed what he was learning and told his sister about it at night.

"Maybe you'll be an art dealer when you grow up," she teased him.

"Not likely. I blew it when I gave up being a DJ. They make a fortune these days. They didn't then, or I might have stuck with it."

"You can always do that at night." She smiled. She liked seeing him look happy and enjoying his job. Coming to New York for her had worked out well for both of them, and had been a blessing in disguise when he got the job with Isabelle. "Just don't meet the love of your life in Italy and never come back," she warned him and he laughed.

"Not going to happen. You're stuck with me."

"You'll meet the right girl one of these days," she said.

"I'm not looking for it. I like my life the way it is now. I think I missed the boat, and I don't mind at all." She almost believed him, but not quite. She knew him better than that, despite his brave words. And she saw through him. There was a lonely man behind the smile.

Chapter Twelve

Jack and Isabelle flew from New York to Paris five days before Christmas, had a three-hour layover at Charles de Gaulle airport to switch planes, and then flew to Florence. They had both slept for most of the overnight flight from New York. Normally, she would have put him in business class, but with her new concerns about her sight, she got him a seat in first with her.

"What have I done to deserve this?" he asked her when they got to the airport and he saw the tickets. He hadn't flown first-class in twenty years, and under circumstances very different from this.

"I thought it would be a nice kickoff to the trip." She didn't want to tell him the real reason, but if her eyes failed her or tricked her, she didn't want to fall flat on her face on the plane. She was still surprised that her daughters hadn't reacted when she'd dropped the bowl of peas on Thanksgiving.

He thanked her again when they settled in their seats, and had a midnight supper that was luxurious and very French, with a four-course meal that included caviar and foie gras. And then he watched a movie while she slept, and eventually went to sleep himself, with a comforter, a mattress, and a pillow.

They spent the time between flights in Paris in the first-class lounge, and the plane to Florence left on time.

"Where exactly do they live?" he asked as the flight took off. It would take just over an hour.

"She lives about an hour south of Florence, in Tuscany. Near a little town called Castellina in Chianti, north of Siena. They have a fantastic horse race in Siena twice every summer. It's called the Palio. The jockeys ride bareback and race right around the Piazza del Campo in the center of town. But the little village close to the farm is sleepy and picturesque. Gregorio bought the property before they got married. He's kind of a gentleman farmer, but he takes the farm very seriously, and their vineyards. A nobleman in love with his land. I never thought she'd turn into a country girl after growing up in New York. But she loves it, and it's a great place for their three little boys." Jack was going to take her there, with the car and driver that picked them up. He had been directed to wait, and take Jack back to Florence for the night, and in the morning he was going to Rome to meet up with his friend, and come back for her in two weeks. They were both looking forward to the trip. "I'd have asked you to stay but you'd die of boredom." And she wanted to be alone with her family. There would be enough people around.

Gregorio's family had been established in Florence for centuries, and he had several sisters and brothers nearby. They were constantly in and out of the house, and his parents visited on weekends. It would be hard to get five minutes alone with Oona. Gregorio always had some project for her, or something he needed her to see at the far end of the property. He was as demanding as the children, who were eighteen months old, three, and four, and now the twins.

They found the driver easily at the Florence airport, and he spoke perfect English. Jack oversaw all their bags. He had brought one small rolling bag for his trip to Rome, and Isabelle had two big suitcases for her clothes, and a third one full of Christmas gifts for the children, Oona, Gregorio, and a handsome silver box for his parents. They would be at the farm for Christmas too. His mother was a charming, aristocratic woman, and his father always followed Isabelle around with lust in his eyes and a roaming hand that found her bottom or a breast at every opportunity. She did her best to avoid him, though not always successfully. He was persistent, and had pursued her with Italian perseverance for the past five years, since Oona had married Gregorio. All Isabelle hoped was that Gregorio didn't turn into his father as he got older. Gregorio made it obvious to everyone that he ran the show, which irritated Isabelle, and seemed disrespectful, although he loved Oona.

They drove for an hour in the Tuscan countryside in a light rain, as Jack admired the scenery, and Isabelle dozed for a few minutes. The sun broke through the clouds as they got there, and the car drove through the gate, and headed to the main house. It was a seventeenth-century building that had originally been a monastery. There were ancient trees bordering the driveway, pastures, a barn where they kept horses, and another larger one that housed their dairy facilities, and there were vineyards on the gently rolling hills.

"This is really wonderful," Jack said, impressed. It was a big place, and Gregorio took it all very seriously. He was very proud of their grapes and their wine.

"Oona loves it," she said almost sadly as they pulled up in front of the house. There were three big dogs outside. They began barking, and a moment later a young woman came out looking like a caricature of a pregnant woman, with a toddler on her hip. "That's Massimiano, he's a terror," she said to Jack, as Oona approached the car, beaming, with the dogs swirling around her. Two little boys shot out of the house with a young girl following them at full speed.

Isabelle got out of the car and put her arms around her daughter as all three children started shouting.

"Nonna Bella, Nonna Bella!" She kissed each of them as Jack smiled at the scene. It was total chaos, but of the very best kind. He was startled by how beautiful Oona was, and he guessed that Isabelle must have looked just like her at the same age. Her hair was a shade closer to red than her mother's, with a strawberry blond tint to it, and two of her sons were redheads. Massimiano on her hip had white-blond hair like his mother and grand-mother as children. She took him from Oona, who lumbered after the two other boys, and a minute later, all three of them greeted Jack politely and made little bows and shook his hand. He was enchanted by them, and then followed them all into the house, which had an enormous living room filled with stylish modern furniture and contemporary paintings. The place was fabulous and had twenty-foot ceilings. It looked like something in a magazine. They went to the kitchen afterward, where Oona pulled out platters of sausages and cheeses she had prepared for them.

"Gregorio will be home in a few minutes. He had to go to the village." She offered her mother and Jack wine, which they both declined, still having jet lag, and gave them apple cider from the farm instead, and a cup of espresso each. The boys scampered off to play after chattering to their grandmother in Italian, and Oona translated easily, and rattled off something in Italian to them. None of her children spoke English yet, and Isabelle hoped they would. Gregorio wanted them to learn French first, which he thought was more important.

Jack was looking around the house and the terrace

while Oona chatted with her mother, who was still stunned by the size of her daughter with the twins she was carrying.

"Are you supposed to be walking around? Shouldn't you be in bed with twins?" Oona laughed at the idea.

"Of course not. I haven't had any problems. They're not due for another two months, at the end of February. I was out on the tractor yesterday. Do you want your assistant to stay here tonight, Mom?" she offered.

"That's sweet of you. He's going back to Florence tonight, and to Rome tomorrow while I'm here. Then we're going to Paris for some auctions." He had met up with the boys by then and was having a lengthy conversation with them in pantomime. He was laughing as hard as they were.

"He seems nice. Are you that busy that you needed someone?" She had always been so averse to having anyone work for her that Oona was surprised when Xela told her their mother had hired him.

"He's actually turned out to be very good," Isabelle said casually.

"What does he do for you?"

"A little bit of everything, from changing lightbulbs to sending packages and meeting clients with me. It's been a pleasant surprise, and it really works." Oona smiled and they went back outside after a young man they had working for them carried Isabelle's bags to her room. She stood smiling as she watched her grandsons climb all over Jack. They loved how tall he was. And while they were watching, a devastatingly handsome man appeared with dark hair, green eyes, broad shoulders, and long legs, in a black turtleneck sweater, jeans, and riding boots. He was fatally sexy-looking, and Oona looked as though she would melt as soon as she saw him. She was as in love with her husband as she had been the day they'd met.

"Ciao, Gregorio," Isabelle said warmly as he came to hug her with a broad smile.

"Ciao, Mamma." He greeted her and kissed her cheek, and then held out a hand to Jack. "Don't let my sons abuse you," he warned him, "their mother allows them to be very badly behaved." He gave Oona a scolding look, and corrected the boys in rapid Italian, and they calmed down a little. "Their mother lets them do anything."

"That's not true," she said, looking adoringly at her husband, who put an arm around her and pulled her close and then rubbed a hand across her belly.

"How do you like our *gemelli*?" he asked, referring to the twins. He spoke flawless English, and had taught Oona Italian himself. "We're hoping for two more boys. You need men on a farm." He laughed and showed perfect teeth. He looked like a movie star or a model, and together they made a striking couple.

"*You're* hoping for two more boys," his wife corrected him. "We need some girls around here."

"Next time," he said confidently, with the self-assurance that always got on his mother-in-law's nerves. He didn't doubt for an instant that he was master of the ship and his wishes were supreme. And his comment told her what they had wondered on Thanksgiving and Isabelle suspected—that he wanted more children. It seemed like a lot for Oona to deal with, but she didn't seem to mind. And her figure always bounced back the moment she had them. When she wasn't pregnant, she was lithe and as thin as her sister Theo, and until now, she had gotten pregnant every time very quickly, with ease. Gregorio believed in her nursing them until she got pregnant again. He was a very old-fashioned man, and very Italian. Independent, free-thinking women were not part of his life experience, and he and Xela had not gotten along the few times she had visited them. He thought both of Oona's sisters odd not to be married at thirty-two and thirty-seven. He had married Oona at twenty-one and was ten years older than her.

He showed Jack around after that and walked him to the barn, showed him their dairy operation, and then took him to the horse barn, which was impeccable.

"You should stay for a few days," he encouraged him and Jack looked embarrassed. He was an employee after all.

"I don't want to intrude on the family," he said discreetly.

"On the way back then, before you leave. I insist." How Isabelle might feel about it was immaterial to Gregorio. He liked Jack's look and style, and could see that he was intelligent and interesting. "I'll take you to the vineyards and our winery when you come back," he said proudly.

"I'd like that," Jack said politely and wondered when he should leave. He walked over to Isabelle, who was talking to her daughter, and spoke to her quietly. "Do you want me to get your computer set up?"

"I'd like that a lot." She smiled at him, and showed him to her room.

"This is a fantastic place," he said, getting her laptop computer out of her briefcase.

"I know, it's just so far away. I feel like she lives on another planet sometimes," she said softly and sat down on the bed. "Like Theo. They both live a million miles from New York and have such full lives where they are. I'm happy for them, but I miss them so much. I try to come here two or three times a year, so I can bond with the kids. But I don't speak much Italian, and they see Gregorio's mother several times a week. It's hard to compete with that."

"You don't have to," Jack said quietly, connecting her computer. He had gotten the WiFi code from Gregorio. "You just have to be you. I'm sure you're much more glamorous than their other grandmother."

"She's quite something," Isabelle said admiringly. "And proximity counts for a lot with kids their age. Out of sight out of mind." He felt sorry for her and she looked tired. She always felt like an outsider here, even if Oona was happy to see her. "I'm going to miss you when you're in Rome, Jack." He had only worked for her for six weeks, but she had gotten used to him rapidly, and seeing him five days a week. The weekends seemed oddly quiet now when he was off.

"I'll miss you too, but you'll be fine. Just watch out for all the little steps." He had noticed that there were many of them, and the stone floors would be unforgiving if she fell. He didn't want her to get hurt. But she'd obviously been there before, and was used to them.

"I'll try not to break anything before you get back." She smiled.

"You can always call me in Rome if you want me here earlier."

"I'll be okay. Just not as pampered as I've been lately. I may actually have to make my own cup of tea." He laughed and as soon as the computer was set up, they went back to Oona, Gregorio, and the children, and Oona invited him to stay for dinner. He hesitated, not wanting to be rude, and Gregorio insisted. Jack looked to Isabelle for approval, and she nodded, smiling at him, so he agreed to stay, and said he'd go to Florence immediately after. He didn't want to overstay.

They had dinner in the old monastery refectory, at a long sixteenth-century table they'd found in Sicily. Gregorio lit a fire in the fireplace, and the children were in bed by then. It was a warm cozy scene as the four of them had dinner like old friends. And after an unforgettable tiramisu Oona made from her mother-in-law's recipe, though not quite as well as his mother, Gregorio said, Jack got up to leave. By then, he had understood what bothered Isabelle about her son-in-law. He always had a little negative comment to make about his wife, while seeming to praise her. She never did anything quite well enough. He obviously loved her, but put her down either openly or subliminally. Jack thought she was a spectacular woman, yet Gregorio was lord and master, and Oona was his willing slave. It annoyed Jack for her too, but she seemed totally oblivious to it.

"He's a handful, isn't he," Jack said to Isabelle in a low voice, as she walked him to the car, after he thanked Gregorio and Oona for dinner.

"You noticed."

"I like him, but he must be the most macho guy I've ever met." And Oona lapped it up, which was the troubling part.

"And a huge narcissist," Isabelle added softly. "It makes me want to slap him sometimes for the things he says to her. Or her, for putting up with it. She never dishes it back to him."

"It doesn't seem to bother her," Jack commented as they stood by the car and the driver waited. The kitchen staff had given him dinner so he was content. "Take good care of yourself, and have fun here. And Merry Christmas," Jack said, smiling at her. He had helped wrap the presents she'd brought with her, and given her a beautiful book on Renaissance art he had noticed she didn't have. She had given him a warm cashmere muffler he said he loved, and Sandy had exclaimed over.

He waved to her as they drove away, and she went back into the house, feeling lonely without him for a minute. He was good company, and Gregorio raised an eyebrow as soon as she got back.

"A new lover perhaps, Mamma?" he asked her lasciviously, and she was instantly irritated by him.

"Hardly. But a very good assistant," she said dryly.

"I'm glad he's nice to you, Mom," Oona said sweetly. "Someone needs to take care of you."

"You should marry him," Gregorio said, sipping an espresso with a brandy near at hand. "A younger man is always good for a woman your age. It will keep you young." Isabelle didn't bother to comment, and a few minutes later, Oona went to their room. It had been a long day for her, and Isabelle was grateful to go to hers, have a bath, and climb into bed. She had an email from Jack, thanking her again for bringing him on the trip. She was touched by how grateful he always was. She checked some other emails, and a few minutes later she went to sleep.

And at six o'clock the next morning, two little boys woke her up jumping on her bed, and she pulled them sleepily into bed with her. They chatted to her and each other awhile in Italian, and then she went down to breakfast with them. Their babysitter was already in the kitchen with Massimiano, and Antonio and Marcello sat next to him and helped feed him.

"Two more babies are coming to live here soon," Marcello told him solemnly in Italian, and Oona translated for Isabelle. "They'll be very noisy at first. We hope they won't be girls. Girls make even more noise." Isabelle could imagine Gregorio saying it to them.

She and Oona went on long walks together and had some good time to talk. She had no secrets from her mother, and she was totally content with her Tuscan life and domineering husband. She thought the sun rose and set on him.

His parents came from Florence two days after she arrived and stayed for dinner. As always, Umberto, Gregorio's father, kissed her on both cheeks, and his hand barely grazed her breast as he did. Nothing had changed. And he did it right in front of his still quite lovely wife, who paid no attention to his flirting with Isabelle. She was used to it.

They entertained the entire family on Christmas Eve,

some of whom lived nearby, and others who came from Florence. The refectory table was crowded with relatives, parents, and children, and Isabelle always felt a little bit lost among them, but Oona introduced her to everyone and explained who they were. Isabelle had seen most of them before, with a few new additions, and half a dozen added infants since her last trip six months before. She was planning to come back in March this time, after the twins were born. She wanted to let Oona settle in with them for a few weeks first, although she would have loved to be there when they arrived. They had all liked the presents Isabelle had brought, and the days sped by like minutes. Isabelle could see how much more tired her daughter was only two weeks later. She still had six weeks left, but the doctor had warned her that twins often came early. And Isabelle had a feeling they would. Oona wanted to have them at the little clinic in the village, but Gregorio insisted they go to Florence the moment she went into labor, and for once Isabelle agreed with him. She wanted Oona at a city hospital too, for a delivery that might be complicated. But Oona didn't seem worried about it at all.

"You're happy, sweetheart? Everything's okay?" she asked her one afternoon as they walked past the orchards that produced delicious plums she had tasted before.

"I'm fine, Mom. It suits me here. I couldn't live in New York again. Sometimes it's hard for me to believe I grew up there. It seems so foreign to me now, and this is home." Isabelle could see it, and it made her sad at times. She had lost her baby to Gregorio and his family, and she wondered what Declan would have thought of it. She suspected he would have been pleased for his daughter. It was hard to imagine strong, youthful, wonderful Declan as a grandfather. But she didn't feel like a grandmother either, except when she was here, with the evidence in front of her.

Jack came back two days before she was due to leave, at Gregorio's insistence, and he took him all over the farm, in his truck, on foot, and on horseback. Gregorio was in love with his land, almost as much as with his wife and sons. A love of the earth was in his blood.

Isabelle was sad to leave—she hated to be away from Oona when she had the babies. She had been there for the first one, but not the two others. Oona and the children stood and waved, lined up outside the house, as they drove away. Isabelle's eyes were filled with tears, and instinctively, Jack reached over and touched her hand.

"You'll be back soon," he whispered and she nodded.

"I miss her so much sometimes," she said softly. "She's the sweetest of my children. I hope he appreciates her."

"I'm sure he does, he just comes from a very male-dominated world. His brothers and father are the same way." She nodded agreement, wishing that Oona had fallen in love with an American and lived closer to home.

She was quiet on the flight to Paris, and when they got to the Hotel George V, Jack was in awe of the elegance of it and the spectacular flowers in the lobby. He'd had a wonderful time in Rome too, though on a much smaller scale, and had stayed at his friend's apartment off the Piazza Navona. In Paris, Isabelle took him to galleries and auction houses and the Louvre. He had been to Paris before but not in such lavish circumstances. He learned more about art on the trip. She cheered up once she was busy in Paris, and they had several remarkable meals at wonderful restaurants. She enjoyed going with him and said that otherwise she wouldn't have gone out alone at night.

It was over much too quickly, and they were back on the plane, headed for New York. They'd been away for three weeks, and it was already mid-January.

Isabelle was quiet on the trip home, thinking of the treatments she had to resume for her eyes. The time in Europe had been a nice respite from them, but now she had to face real life again.

The recent shock she'd had about her vision had made the trip even more meaningful to her. She kept thinking how terrible it would be if she could never see her daughter again, or her grandsons, or the twins who were about to be born. Every moment was more precious now, worrying that it would never come again. She had thought about it a lot in the last three weeks and it had brought her to another decision, which she knew was long overdue. There were things she felt she had to do now to make her peace with the past. She was going to ask Jack to help her, but she didn't want to say anything to him until they were back in New York.

He took her to the house and settled her in before he went home. She was feeling very proud of herself. She hadn't fallen once at the farm, in spite of all the steps everywhere. She was more careful than she'd been previously. And it felt good now to be home, although she had loved her visit with Oona.

"You don't have to hang around," she said to Jack as he lingered. "You must be eager to get home to your sister."

"I've been calling her every few days. She's doing fine. Thanks for a great trip," he said. It had been one of the best in his life.

"I'm glad you enjoyed it. See you tomorrow," she said and heard the front door close a few minutes later. She looked around the room and thought of Oona and her children. They seemed a million miles away now. And she'd only heard from Xela and Theo on Christmas, and not in the three weeks since, and hadn't been able to reach them. But there was someone else she had to see now. It was all she could think about. She knew she should have done it sooner. And suddenly it seemed so important, before it was too late, and while she could still see him.

She went to bed, thinking about it, and woke up early the next morning, still on European time. She was already at her computer when Jack came to work. He had woken up early too, and he came in to see what she was doing. She was looking frustrated.

"Can I help?"

"I thought I could do it myself, but I can't." She concentrated very intently on the screen.

"What are you looking for?" He'd never seen her work so hard on her computer.

"A man named Charles Anderson, in Providence, Rhode Island. Except his name may not be Charles Anderson anymore. They . . . he might have changed it. If it's changed, I won't be able to find him." But she knew she had to try anyway. A force greater than her was pushing her now.

"Do you know what he might have changed it to?"

She shook her head.

"Do you know his address?" She shook her head again. "There might be a lot of them by that name." He pulled up a chair to sit next to her, and she turned the computer toward him so he could do it for her.

"I have his date of birth." She gave it to him. The man she was seeking was forty-three years old.

"Let me play with this for a minute. There are search engines to locate people, like old classmates or lost relatives, or first girlfriends. It's not that complicated." He re-entered the information, came up with nothing in Rhode Island, and broadened the search to include the Boston area, and ten minutes later, he had five of them by that name, including one with the right date of birth. He increased the size of what he was looking at to fill the full screen and turned it toward her. Charles Henry Anderson, in Danvers, Massachusetts. They were looking at his driver's license. She stared at it for a long time, leaning forward, examining his face in minute detail, without saying a word. Her whole body was tense as she looked at the image on her computer.

"Do you know him?" Jack asked, watching her. She nodded at first, and then shook her head.

"I haven't seen him in a long time." He didn't look like anyone she'd known, and he was close to Jack's age. "Thank you," she said in a whisper, and jotted down the man's information, with his address and phone number. Jack stood up to leave. He could see that it was important to her, but she didn't explain why.

She sat staring at the photograph for another hour after Jack left the room. She looked like she'd been transported to another time, another place. And then she picked up the phone on her desk and called. She had no idea what to say when he answered, or what kind of message to leave if he didn't. He might not want to talk to her after all this time. She had waited his entire lifetime to reach out to him.

Chapter Thirteen

Charles Anderson was in the garage of his home in Danvers, twenty miles out of Boston, tinkering with his car, which he loved to do on weekends. His son, Steve, answered the phone, hung out the kitchen door, and yelled to his father in the garage.

"Someone on the phone for you, Dad."

"Who is it?" His hands were covered with grease and oil. He was working on an old Mustang that was his pride and joy. He had a sixteen-year-old son, an eleven-year-old daughter, and a wife who was a teacher. Charles was a sales rep for a publishing house in Boston, and wasn't crazy about his job.

"She didn't say, it's a woman," Steve called back to him, and Charlie wiped his hands on a rag, walked up the kitchen stairs, and picked up the phone. There was silence when he answered, and he thought it was a prank and was about to hang up when she spoke.

"This call is long overdue. I'm not even sure if I should be calling you, or if you'd want me to," she said, sounding nervous. "I'm your birth mother, Charles. I've wanted to call you for forty-three years. I dreamed of this. But I didn't have the courage, and I didn't want to upset you."

He was stone-faced as he listened. "Why now?"

"Because time passes and one day we won't have the opportunity. If you don't want to talk to me, I understand. But I wanted to reach out in case you're curious about me, or there's anything you want to know." She wanted to know about him too, and if he'd had a good life without her. She had wondered that for all of her adult life.

"Yeah. A lifetime of questions in one call. Why did you give me up?" he asked, sounding hurt even forty-three years later.

"I was fifteen, a sophomore in high school, I got drunk with a senior at a dance, and he didn't want to know when I found out I was pregnant. I didn't even realize it myself for several months. He was seventeen, and he left for college in New Mexico before you were born. I never heard from him again. I couldn't bring up a baby by myself." Although in the end she had with all of them, but she'd been older then and not a child herself. "My father wouldn't let me keep you. He said he wouldn't help me if I did. I didn't have a mom, she died when I was three. I had no choice and no way to take care of you, nowhere to go. I was just a kid. So I let my father force me to give you up. He said it was the right thing to do for you. I've regretted it every day of my life ever since.

"I tried to find you once, when I turned eighteen, but

I didn't know where to look. The adoption agency wouldn't tell me where you were or even your name. I named you Charles when you were born, and I thought your new parents would change it, but I guess they didn't. A nurse in the hospital told me their last name was Anderson. That was all I knew, and your birthday. I managed to hide that I was pregnant till the end of sophomore year, my father sent me away to some nuns for the summer, and I had you at the end of August, and gave you up in the hospital. I went back to school to start junior year two weeks later. No one ever knew. I've never told anyone, but I never forgave myself."

"How did you find me?" he asked, curious in spite of himself, wanting to run away and to talk to her at the same time.

"It's easier to find people now," she said quietly. "Your driver's license, and it turns out your name is the same, which I didn't think was possible. Someone helped me with the Internet an hour ago and there you were. I should have tried years ago, but I never thought I'd find you, and I figured by now, it wouldn't matter to you, and maybe it doesn't. But I've thought of you every single day of my life since you were born." And then she asked him a question that nearly stopped his heart. "Would you like me to come to Boston and meet you sometime? I live in New York." There was no easy answer to that after all this time.

"Maybe. I need to think about it." He was angry and

excited all at once. Even all these years later, he felt shaken by hearing her, but had always wanted to and fantasized about it all his life, that one day she would just show up. And now she had. She gave him her phone number and told him to call whenever he wanted to, *if* he wanted to.

"I know I have no right to walk into your life now. And it took me a long time to feel ready to find you. I never forgot about you. I was afraid you hated me. But I thought about you every single day." It had the ring of truth to it.

"I did hate you for a long time," he said honestly. "I didn't know you were that young. My birth certificate has my adoptive parents on it, and nothing about you. I have a sixteen-year-old son, and an eleven-year-old daughter. I can't imagine either of them with a child at fifteen," he said fairly, and then wondered something. "Do you have other kids?" She almost hated to admit it to him, it seemed like such a betrayal after giving him up.

"Three girls." She had had Theo because of him. She couldn't bring herself to give another baby away, or have an abortion. She knew she would have abandoning him on her conscience forever. One was enough.

"Do they know about me?"

"No, they don't. No one does. But I'd like to tell them now. They have as much right to know they have a half-brother as you do to know about them, and meet them if you want."

"I'll have to think about that too."

"And I'd like to meet your children too," she said gently, "if you'll let me." She had two more grandchildren.

He was still shocked by her call when he went back to the garage, picked up the grease-stained rag, threw it against the wall, and burst into tears.

*

Isabelle thought about her call to him all night. She wasn't sure she would have done it if she hadn't been told she might go blind. A giant clock was ticking now, somewhere in her head. Everything mattered, more than it ever had before. She wasn't dying but she wanted to tie up the loose ends in her life. It was time, and Charles was the biggest one of all.

She couldn't sleep. She was wide awake and finally got up, and went back to her computer. She wanted to know more about him, but all Jack had found on the Internet was his driver's license. Thank God he had found that, or she could never have called him. She wanted to do something to distract herself then. She needed to calm down.

Just for the fun of it, she put Jack's name into the same search engine she had seen him use that morning, and she knew his date of birth from their employment contract. She had no idea what would turn up, probably his most recent employment with Senator Douglas, or something from when he worked as an assistant producer on TV, or the radio show. It was just an experiment to see if she could do it.

She had barely finished putting in the information when an image leapt onto her computer screen. It was the front page of the sports section of a newspaper from twenty-one years before. There was a photograph of Jack with longer hair, and he looked like a kid. It said he was twenty-five years old, and the headline made her eyes open wide. "Tragedy on the Court: NBA MVP Jack Bailey suffers compound fracture in last eight minutes of championship game." She read on past that to the descriptions of the accident when another player collided with him, hit him at just the wrong angle with his full weight, and the article said that fans were standing on seats crying as they took him away. Other sports pages flipped onto the screen after it with the same story, with photographs of him, and one of him being carried off the court on a stretcher, with the coaches running alongside crying. Another headline said "Heartbreaking End to a Brilliant Career." Tears filled Isabelle's eyes as she read the articles about him. Almost every writer called him a legend and said he had been basketball history in the making. There were other articles from several months later, mourning the seriousness of his injury and the impact on his life.

His brilliant career and future in basketball had ended that night.

There was an article ten years later, one of those grim "Where is he now?" pieces that followed his career path since, as sports radio show announcer, his assistant producer job in sports on TV. She had read it all in his CV but the vital information had been left out—that he was one of the biggest basketball stars that ever lived, drafted right out of college, and felled at the end of a championship game they'd been winning and lost in the final minutes once he was injured. His teammates had been too devastated to focus. The article lost track of him in his days as a DJ. She felt sick as she read the articles about him, and, unable to stop herself, she pressed the arrow for the video that actually showed the hideous accident. The bone was exposed in his shattered leg as he lay there, and they estimated the speed at which the other player had hit him. She felt like throwing up as she watched.

She was crying when the video ended, like the people who had seen it happen. And he had never told her he played in the NBA. It explained his height and passion for sports. She wondered if he was bitter about it, or resentful, or still cried about it. He'd been a boy then, and was a man now. But his life had never been the same again. What would it have been like if he'd been able to continue playing until he retired?

She was shocked when she finally walked away from her computer and stood staring out the window. She wondered how he had managed to get through it, get over it, and been able to go on, knowing what he had been, and could have been if fate hadn't turned against him. It made her wonder about the cruelties of life, with his leg being shattered, and her facing the possibility now that she'd go blind. It made her want to tell him how sorry she was, but she knew she couldn't. He had never said a word to her about it, and he obviously didn't want to talk about it, nor want her to know. He was a brave, proud man and didn't want her pity.

After reading all the articles, she felt as though it had just happened, and the video made her feel as though she'd been there. She wanted to put her arms around him and comfort him, but she couldn't. She wondered who had been there for him. A girlfriend? His sister, the one he was taking care of now? Her heart ached for him as she went back to bed, heartbroken over what had happened to him. If she'd been a sports fan she might have recognized his name when he came for the interview, but she wasn't. And the woman at the agency hadn't said anything either. Twenty-one years was a long time, and maybe people had forgotten.

She didn't fall asleep until the sun came up, and when she woke up four hours later, she was groggy and instantly remembered what she'd seen and read the night before. She could hear Jack downstairs in the kitchen, hammering something, and she didn't know what to say to him now. She felt hungover from the sorrow she had read of the night before, and wished she could tell him she was sorry. He didn't deserve that, no one did, to have all their dreams shattered in an instant. She remembered the sickening injury on the video.

She looked somber when she went downstairs half an hour later and walked into the kitchen, and Jack noticed it immediately.

"Are you okay? Did something happen last night?" She looked terrible and wanted to say "No, it happened twenty-one years ago and I'm sick for you about it," but she just shook her head.

"I'm just jet-lagged," she said vaguely and took a sip of the coffee he set down in front of her.

"Did you call that guy we looked up on the Internet yesterday? Did he threaten you in some way?" He'd looked a little rough in the photo, but most driver's license photos looked like mug shots. Jack thought his own did too.

"No, no, nothing like that," she reassured him. "I called him, and he was fine. How's your sister?"

"She did okay while I was gone. She missed me." He smiled. "It's nice to know someone does." She wondered if his accident was why he had never married. It had to take a toll on him psychologically, but he seemed so peaceful and kind and easygoing. Somehow he had managed to live with it, but his recovery and the early years must have been brutal, knowing what he'd lost. She sat quietly thinking about it, and then went upstairs to work, while he hammered some nails into a shelf that had gotten loose. She sat at her desk, thinking about him and her son, and then finally forced herself to concentrate on some catalogues she had to go through. She was making good headway on the collection she was putting together for the oilman.

She wasn't hungry when Jack brought her lunch. She felt completely out of whack and off-kilter, and she had to go to her eye doctor that afternoon. She called and postponed it until the next day. She couldn't face it after the revelations of the past twenty-four hours. She needed time to absorb talking to her son, and finding out about Jack's history. It was odd that she had learned about both on the same day.

She had just finished the sandwich he'd made her when he buzzed from downstairs to tell her Xela was on the phone. She hadn't spoken to her since she got home.

"Thank God you're back. I wasn't sure. I need to see you." She was speaking in staccato bursts as though she was breathless.

"Is something wrong?" Isabelle had never heard her sound like that. "Did something happen with your investors?" Nothing but a major business disaster could have shaken Xela to that extent.

"No, it's something else. Can I come over tonight?"

"Of course. Do you want to come now?" Isabelle was anxious to know what was going on.

"I can't. I have meetings all afternoon. I'll come over when I finish." She sounded like she'd been crying. "I'll be there around seven. Thank you, Mom." She was choked up and emotional, and then she got off the line, and Isabelle was worried about her for the rest of the afternoon. Jack looked calm when he picked up the tray, and she realized that she had only found out about his accident and ruined career the night before, so it was fresh for her. It was old news to him after twenty-one years. So while she looked badly shaken, he looked calm and had no idea that she knew now.

"Was Xela okay?" he asked her, concerned. "She sounded strange."

"I don't know. She's coming over around seven. She sounded terrible to me too."

"Do you want me to get some things for you to eat when she's here?"

"That might be a good idea. Thanks, Jack."

It had been an unusual two days, with the discoveries she had made. And now Xela wanting to see her. She had a headache by midafternoon, and the suspense of waiting to see Xela was killing her. She went for a walk to clear her head at the end of the day, after Jack left. It was five-thirty by then, and she had another hour and a half to wait before she saw Xela and heard what she had to say. Isabelle had a feeling of dread as she waited, as though something terrible was about to happen. It was as though learning about Jack's accident had set the tone for the day. She hoped that wouldn't be the case. She was counting the minutes until Xela would arrive. And hopefully, whatever it was wouldn't be as bad as she feared, or as bad as Xela had sounded on the phone.

Chapter Fourteen

When Isabelle opened the door to Xela that night, her daughter looked like a different person. Her shining dark hair, always in a businesslike bun, was loose and disheveled. She looked like she'd been crying, and there were dark circles under her eyes. The transformation since Isabelle had seen her only weeks before was terrifying. Isabelle hugged her tightly, and then followed her upstairs, telling herself that whatever it was, they would face it together. She knew it wasn't a problem with a man because there were none in Xela's life, just work. And knowing her priorities and single-mindedness about her career, the problem could only be about work. Isabelle was guessing that something about her fledgling business that she'd worked so hard on had failed. She wondered if she'd been embezzled by an employee, since every penny mattered and she had none to spare.

Xela took her coat off, threw it over a chair, sat down with a desperate look, and burst into tears. "I'm dying, Mom," she managed to choke out between sobs, as Isabelle sat next to her, and put an arm around her shoulders.

"Over what, sweetheart?" she said gently. "Your business?"

"No, really dying. I had a mammogram three days ago and a needle biopsy. I have breast cancer." What Xela said hit her mother like a bomb and struck fear in her heart, since her own mother had died of it.

"Oh my God, are they sure?" Xela nodded and buried her face in her mother's shoulder. "What stage?"

"It's very early," she said, taking a breath. "It's stage one, but I know what happened to your mother."

"That was a long time ago." Isabelle tried to appear calmer than she was. She was shaking like a leaf inside. This couldn't be happening, not to her child. It was devastating, for both of them. "Treatments are much better now. What did they say?"

"That we caught it early. I could have a mastectomy, even a double one, as a preventive measure, because of our family history, but that's so extreme. They suggested a lumpectomy, and a brief course of radiation, probably for a month. They won't be sure till after the surgery. But not chemo for now." Isabelle tried to gather her wits about her and not panic. Xela needed her to have a clear head and be strong.

"That sounds reasonable and conservative and not too radical."

"But what if that doesn't cure it?"

"We'll face that if it happens." Both Xela and Theo

had been having mammograms since they turned thirty, given their history, and Isabelle had been having them for years, with no problem. Now lightning had struck again, and had skipped a generation. Even Oona had been planning to start having mammograms, despite her youth, but she had been pregnant or nursing for the last five years. She had told her mother that she would have one after she stopped nursing the twins, which wouldn't be for at least a year. The women in Gregorio's family nursed for two years or even three, and he expected her to do the same.

"When do they want you to start?" Isabelle asked her, feeling her heart pound in her chest.

"They want to do the lumpectomy tomorrow morning at seven. I have to be at the hospital at six. They did the pre-op lab work today." She cried harder as she said it. "They have to decide what kind of radiation to do after they get the results of the biopsies. But it could be very mild radiation for a short time. They said I'd be exhausted. Hopefully, I'll be fine after that. But I'm so scared, Mom." She buried her face in her mother's shoulder as Isabelle stroked her hair.

"We just have to know that it will work, and you have to be diligent about checkups after this."

"I am. I'll have to have one every three months at first, and twice a year after that, if there's no recurrence."

"There won't be," she said firmly. But it had killed her

mother within a year. She tried not to think about it, but it filled her mind as Xela's sobs slowly abated.

"I'm terrified." Isabelle wanted to say "Me too," but didn't. She had to support Xela now, without wavering.

"I'll go with you tomorrow," Isabelle said firmly. Nothing could have stopped her.

"I knew you would. They scheduled it today, right before I called you." But she sounded less frightened than before, with her mother at her side to help her.

"Do you want to stay here tonight?" Isabelle offered and Xela nodded. She didn't want to be alone. Xela, the toughest and often the hardest of her daughters, had collapsed in terror like a small child and wanted her mother with her. She had no one but her mother now to support her. She had no close friends. She never had time to meet people because she worked constantly.

They talked for a long time about the procedure. The lump was so small that she hadn't detected it herself, and the surgery would be brief, under general anesthesia to minimize the trauma. She might be in the hospital for one night, and they said she would be sore for several days but could go back to work. They were going to biopsy the surrounding area, and wanted to take enough tissue to be safe, not just optimistic.

She lent Xela a nightgown and tucked her daughter into her own bed like a little girl. Xela still had her old room in the house, but she wanted to be close to her mother for the night. She was sound asleep when Isabelle got into bed and set her alarm for five A.M. She sat looking at her daughter for a long time, her ebony hair fanned out on the pillow. She looked peaceful and young. She looked angry so much of the time that it touched Isabelle to see her so peaceful, like a child again. She had been so sweet at times when she was little, and then so furious at other times. She was always railing at the fates about something, but not now. And it was shocking to see her suddenly so dependent and terrified.

Isabelle remembered Jack after she turned off the light, and got up to send him an email.

"Something came up. I'll be gone when you come in tomorrow. Will call you when I can. Leaving a stack of notes and files on my desk. Thanks, I." She heard the response arrive on her computer as she got into bed, and got up again. He was still awake.

"Is Xela okay? Are you?"

"She will be. Me too. Thanks for asking."

"Let me know if I can do anything to help," he shot back to her after she answered him, and she sent him a last "Thanks, Jack." He was a good person, and she had even more appreciation of him now that she knew what he'd been through himself and what he'd lost. He had no idea that she knew, and she saw no reason to tell him and remind him of the painful past.

She barely slept, woke up at five, and gently awakened Xela a few minutes later. Xela wasn't allowed to eat, but Isabelle drank a quick cup of coffee when she was dressed. Then they went outside and she hailed a cab at a quarter to six. They were going to New York-Presbyterian Hospital, which wasn't far and took ten minutes to get to. Xela walked into the hospital, looking like she was going to the guillotine, holding tightly to her mother's hand. She needed her now.

They went to the surgical floor, and were taken to a pre-op room where Xela changed into a surgical gown and her vital signs were checked, and a pleasant young anesthesiologist came to talk to her and explained the procedure to both of them. The surgeon had told her they were going to biopsy her lymph nodes too, to make sure it hadn't spread. They wanted to be as meticulous as possible at this early stage. He had said her chances were excellent that the disease could be stopped here, and she was lucky they'd found it early. Xela didn't look convinced. She was expecting the worst now. She had canceled her meetings for the next few days. Everything else seemed so unimportant and she was going to contact her sisters after the surgery. It was important information for them too.

They gave her a shot to relax her, before they rolled her away on a gurney. Isabelle walked alongside her to the elevator, and she was already looking drowsy. And then Isabelle left to wait for her, and pace the hallway alone. She had no one to talk to or to tell, or to lean on and reassure her, and the tears of worry and fear rolled down her cheeks once Xela left. It was a bleak wintry day without sun. At nine-thirty, her surgeon came to tell Isabelle that the procedure had gone well. Xela was in the recovery room, and would be back in her room by noon. Isabelle could leave for a short time if she wished. She couldn't see Xela yet anyway. She wasn't sure what to do, and then decided to go home for a couple of hours, which was less depressing than waiting at the hospital.

She walked home to get some air, and Jack heard her come in. He hurried out of the kitchen and their eyes met as she gazed at him bleakly.

"Everything okay?"

"More or less. I've been better." She wasn't going to tell him, out of respect for Xela, but as she sat in the kitchen, feeling like she'd been beaten, she needed someone to talk to, and he was a sympathetic ear. She told him what had happened and he looked shocked, and reached out and held her hand. She was grateful to have him there.

"I felt like that when they told Sandy she had MS."

"A lot of women survive breast cancer now," she said, more to reassure herself than him. "But why did Xela have to get it? My mother died of it." He nodded and listened.

"Catching it early, I'm sure she'll be okay, but I'm sorry anyway." He could see how hard it was on her. No matter how old her daughters were, how tough or independent, they would always be her children. His sister had said that many times about hers. He didn't understand it viscerally, but it made sense to him, and he loved his sister as much as he would have his own child. He didn't want anything to happen to her. "Why don't you lie down for a while?" he suggested gently. She looked terrible, and stumbled on the first step. He wasn't sure if it was fatigue, her eyes, or her balance.

"I canceled my doctor's appointment for today, by the way." Xela was her priority now. She wanted to take care of her first. Jack still didn't know what the appointments were for, and she didn't intend to tell him, or the girls.

"Do you want me to make another one for you?" he offered.

"I'll do it in a few days. I want to be around for Xela." Her own treatments upset her and were painful. She needed to be in the best shape she could be for her daughter, not frightened and sick herself. One drama at a time was enough. He didn't know if the reasons for her medical appointments were serious or not, but he had a suspicion that they were.

"Will she come back here tonight?" he asked quietly. He had a calming influence and was a soothing, re-assuring presence, even more than he appeared to be at first. He was a good man to have on hand in a crisis. He had been there himself, she knew now.

"She opted to stay overnight till tomorrow, in case she was sick from the anesthetic. She'll go back to her place then. We don't know when they'll start radiation, possibly immediately or in a few weeks, depending on the biopsies." He nodded. He was learning things he had hoped never to have to know, just as he had about MS. But his sister's illness had brought them closer than they'd ever been before, and he loved living with her. Sandy always said there was a blessing in everything, but he resisted seeing it that way. In his mind, multiple sclerosis was not a blessing, just as cancer wasn't in Xela's case or her mother's. It was just bad luck.

Isabelle came back downstairs at eleven, and had remembered that they were meeting with Bill Casey, the oilman, to show him images of some new paintings coming on the market she thought he should buy. The gallery where she used to work had given her an early heads-up that they were going to be sold, and they were willing to give her a good price for her client. She still dealt with them from time to time. They were one of the best in the business. Now she was too, in the private market, and she brought them good clients.

"I think you can handle the meeting without me, Jack," she said confidently. She didn't want to leave Xela.

"Are you sure?" He sounded doubtful. He loved

watching her work, and how smooth and encouraging she was with her clients. She made each of them feel important, and increased their knowledge of the subject without ever patronizing them.

"He likes you, and I can't be here. I don't want to cancel. Just show him the photos of the paintings and see what he thinks. You can tell him I had a family emergency, and I'll call him in a few days." Jack nodded, looking nervous.

"Maybe you shouldn't have that much faith in me. What if I blow the sale?"

"You won't."

"I'm better with a hammer, a coffeepot, and a boarding pass than I am as an art dealer," he said humbly and she smiled.

"Don't sell yourself short. He'll be here at five o'clock. Have a drink with him, he'll love that."

She took some things from her bedroom for Xela—a small pillow for her head, and a cashmere blanket from a chair—and headed back to the hospital a few minutes later. Jack walked her outside to hail a cab for her. He was just as worried about her as he was about her daughter. No one ever thought to help or take care of her. She was the one they leaned on, and never the reverse, he could always tell, and she took it all on herself. She had been the only parent to all three of them for all their lives.

They brought Xela back to the room a few minutes after she got there. She was still groggy and a nurse was putting heated blankets over her. She smiled at her mother.

"They said it went well, and the initial pathology reports during the surgery looked good." They had to wait for the more detailed ones which took longer, but the surgeon said he was pleased. And she still had two breasts, which was important to Xela.

She slept for most of the day, and felt nauseous from the anesthetic. Isabelle sat quietly at her bedside all day, and didn't go home until they'd given Xela a sleeping pill that night. She let herself into her house with a sigh, and noticed that Jack had forgotten to put the alarm on. She wondered how the meeting with Bill Casey had gone. She hung up her coat and gave a start when Jack came out of the kitchen.

"You're still here?" It was nine-thirty, and she was so exhausted from the tension of the day she could hardly put one foot in front of the other.

"I hope you don't mind. I figured you'd be beat when you got back. I picked up some food at the deli. Sometimes people forget to take care of the caretakers." She smiled at what he said.

"I've been doing this all their lives," she said as they walked into the kitchen and she sat down. She'd never had a man to help her—none of their fathers had been around. But at least there had been no one to argue with her about her decisions. She took comfort in that. None of their fathers had been in her life long. And she still missed Putnam and Declan at times. And her father too. He had been a kind man, despite his insistence on her giving the baby up for adoption. He had thought it was the best thing to do. And who knew, maybe he'd been right. At fifteen, it would have altered her life dramatically, but it had anyway, inevitably. You didn't give up a baby and just walk away unscathed. She had carried the guilt and the sorrow for forty-three years.

"You haven't been doing this with a daughter with cancer," Jack reminded her and brought her out of her reverie and back to the present, as he put a bowl of soup down in front of her, and some chicken.

"That's true," she admitted. "I didn't expect this. I always wondered if my heredity from my mother would catch up with me. I didn't think it would hit them. I thought I would be the buffer between generations, and instead it missed me and got Xela. It's so unfair."

"It is. But something good may come of this, you never know. It may be a wake-up call to her about how she wants to live her life. She seems very intense about her work. Maybe she'll rethink that." Isabelle smiled at what he said.

"Knowing Xela, she'll probably just work harder. That's how she copes. She stays away from emotional commitment and hides in her work. So does Theo."

"So do you," he said, daring to be honest with her, and afraid to overstep. They got along well as employee and employer, and he didn't want to spoil it.

"I didn't used to. I used to leap into the complicated emotional commitments, whatever the cost. I finally stopped after Oona's father died. Three tries and you're out. I couldn't do it again, and I haven't. We were really happy. I figured I could never duplicate that, so I didn't try. But before that, I took some big risks in my early life, and had heavy losses."

"You're never 'out' in matters of the heart. Or you don't have to be."

"What about you? You never married."

"I came close." He smiled ruefully. "If that counts." He hesitated for a moment before he went on and she took a bite of the chicken he'd put on a plate. "I had some fairly big career prospects at an early age. And a girlfriend I was crazy about, who claimed she loved me." She knew he was talking about his career as a basketball star in the NBA, but didn't let on that she knew. "My prospects came to a sudden end, and so did the relationship. She moved on to another guy just like me. I was a player in the NBA, and she married him six months later when my career was shot. It was a hell of a blow, but I dodged a bullet. They got divorced five years later, and I think he's still paying alimony. She got everything he had. There are some bad people out there, and good ones too."

"And after that, you married a wonderful woman, had ten children, and lived happily ever after," she teased him to lighten the moment for both of them.

"No, after that I was bitter and angry and scared shitless about my future for a long time. I finally got over it and stopped feeling sorry for myself. I had two long-term relationships with women who didn't want to marry me, and I didn't want to marry them in the end, but I learned a lot from both. My job-hopping for a long time didn't make me too appealing to some women. It's not a career profile that inspires marriage." It was sad to think that it came down to that, but frequently it did. Some women were looking for security more than love.

"And now?" Isabelle asked him gently. She was touched that he had admitted his history with the NBA.

"I'm taking a time-out while I take care of my sister. I'll get back in the romantic sweepstakes one of these days." He looked peaceful as he said it and she admired his courage.

"I'm too old to get back in the ring in that sense," she said with certainty. "I've had my moments of glory. I just want to see my kids happy now. Oona is, and has everything she wants. Theo and Xela haven't figured it out yet, and sometimes I'm afraid they never will. They're both scared to death of commitment and relationships, for different reasons. I think it's genetic in Theo's case. Her father was just like her, or she's like him. And she has a mission in life, which fulfills her. Xela has her own issues. And I guess I haven't been a shining example of emotional courage to them, but I was too busy to have a man in my life. Or maybe too scared. I made some pretty glaring mistakes until Oona's father."

"At least you kept trying. Maybe you gave up too soon. Maybe he was just the conduit to the next chapter. Some people are just there as guides to the next person or the next phase of our lives. They're not meant to be the whole story. And in any case, at your age, or any age, the story isn't over yet."

"What makes you so wise?" she asked, looking at him seriously.

"I made my own share of mistakes, and had some hard knocks. If they don't kill you, they teach you a lot. I lost everything for a while, everything I'd ever cared about, a career I loved, a woman to go with it. Now I love what I have and am grateful for it, a good job, a good life, good people, my sister. It's enough. The other stuff, the fireworks don't last. They're pretty in the sky for a minute, but dust at your feet in the end." He looked at her after he said it, curious about something. "Who was the guy you had me track down on the Internet the other day? Good guy or bad guy?"

She hesitated for a moment before she answered. She trusted him and they were becoming friends.

"I don't know if he's a good guy or a bad guy yet. He's

my son. I had him at fifteen and gave him up for adoption when he was born. I've never told anyone that before. My father pressured me into it, he thought it was best for me at that age, and for the baby. And maybe he was right. It has haunted me for forty-three years. He's why I had Theo. I had a wild, passionate affair in France and fell in love with a man twenty-seven years older than I was. Three months later, after I got back to the States for my senior year at NYU, I found out I was pregnant, and he wasn't ever going to marry me and told me that in the beginning. He was honest with me. But I decided to keep the baby. I couldn't do otherwise, after having given one up five years before. I couldn't have done it again."

"And you just found him for the first time?" She nodded. He was as impressed by her courage as she was with his. Hers hadn't included a compound fracture that ended a brilliant basketball career and stardom. She had just been a young girl having a baby out of wedlock, which took guts, but not like him. And she imagined he had had a long road to recovery physically. She was surprised he didn't limp. "Are you going to see him?" Jack asked her.

"I'd like to. I don't know how he feels. He's thinking about it. He has a right to that after I dumped him more than forty years ago."

"You didn't 'dump' him. I'm sure he was adopted by

respectable people who love him. I don't think your father was wrong. It would have ruined your life at fifteen."

"It almost did anyway. I never forgave myself for it, I still haven't and never will."

"You're a harsh judge of yourself. What would you have done if it happened to one of your girls at fifteen?"

"Killed them," she said, and he laughed. "My father was pretty good about it. And I know he was disappointed in me when it happened again with Theo. I should have known better by then."

"And you married Xela's and Oona's fathers?" She nodded. "Sometimes that's a mistake too." Although it hadn't been with Declan. "Are you going to tell the girls about your son?"

"I want to. I have to. I've been thinking about it. They have a right to know they have a brother, even if he doesn't want to meet us. And they have a right to know about my mistakes too. I can't pretend to be so perfect and hide my flaws from them. I want a clean slate now. Some things have happened recently that have made me rethink things. I was thinking about telling them about Charles, and then Xela got sick. I can't do that to her right now. We all have to focus on her. It's her turn, not mine. There's something else I should probably tell them too," she said thoughtfully as he watched her, and she decided to be brave again.

"About why you've been falling on the stairs and

bumping into things? Do you have MS?" he asked, looking worried, and she shook her head.

"No, I may be going blind, or eventually," she said quietly and it sent a shiver down her spine and made her feel sick just saying it out loud to him. "Or I might not. They don't know yet. I'm getting treatments. I have macular degeneration. Pretty ironic for an art consultant, don't you think?" She tried to sound glib about it, but she wasn't.

"It sounds like a shit break to me. I know about those things. It's a long story but I played basketball in the NBA until I broke my leg during a championship game. End of story, and a lot of other things. But in weird ways, there are compensations for it that you don't see at first. I hope you don't go blind, Isabelle, but even if the worst happens, other things happen that make up for it. It sounds crazy, but it's true."

"Like a blessing in disguise," she said pensively. "It sounds like small compensation to me."

"It isn't. Sometimes you win something a lot bigger. I've been thinking you had MS like my sister. I didn't realize it was your vision."

"I have some pretty nasty bruises to show for it." She smiled at him wistfully.

"Who goes to the treatments with you?" He wondered who else knew.

"No one. I haven't told the girls about it, and I'm not

going to. I'm willing to tell them about my mistakes. They don't need to know about my frailties. They count on me. I have to be strong for them. Like now, for Xela."

"You can't be strong all the time," he said gently.

"Yes, I can. They don't need a mother who's falling apart, or whining, or going blind. They need what I'm giving Xela now to keep her on her feet."

"You shouldn't have to go to the treatments alone," he said, and then thought of something. "Can I go with you? As your assistant?" She looked shocked at the suggestion. It had never occurred to her. "I think you're wrong not to tell them, they have to be there for you too, it's not just a one-way street at their ages. But if you're not going to tell them, or even if you do, I'd be happy to go with you."

"It's pretty nasty. I get injections in my eyes."

"All the more reason for me to be there. Caring for someone is about the nasty parts too. And I've got a strong stomach."

"I'll think about it," she said, moved to tears by his offer. He really was an extraordinary person. "I'm going to put the treatments on hold for now while I take care of Xela. And when I go back to it, I don't want to give up my gladiator status and be a sissy."

"Screw that. And you're not a sissy, just for the record. Having a person go with you does not make you a sissy. Gladiators are outdated. I think they all got eaten by lions about two thousand years ago." She smiled at what he said.

"Thank you, Jack." They had exchanged a lot of information and confidences and she was glad he had stayed and waited for her to come home from the hospital. And maybe he was right that there were trade-offs. If she didn't have a problem with her eyes, she wouldn't have hired an assistant and would never have met him, and he had added a lot to her life. And knowing she might be going blind had finally pushed her to try to find the baby she'd given up as barely more than a child herself. Along with the losses, there were blessings, and there had been for him too.

"You need to go to bed, or you'll be a mess tomorrow," he said, standing up. He was glad he had stayed late too. There was so much about her he admired and liked.

"If you see Xela tomorrow, don't say anything to her about the surgery today," she reminded him.

"Of course not. The code of a personal assistant—whatever you tell me goes nowhere. It's also the code of a good friend." They looked at each other and warmth passed between them.

"I guess we're friends, then," she said softly, and then remembered his meeting with the oilman. She had forgotten all about it. Jack said it had gone well and he was thinking over his options. He put her dishes in the sink, and she headed for the stairs as he watched her to make sure she didn't miss a step. "Thank you, Jack," she said as she went up to her room, and a minute later, she heard the front door close. It was after midnight, and had been an incredibly long day, for all of them, not just Xela. But she was grateful that she and Jack were friends, and glad he had told her about his career in the NBA. It brought them that much closer, and it was a relief to confide in him and lean on him while she gathered her strength.

Chapter Fifteen

Xela decided to go back to her own apartment after the surgery. She was feeling a little less frightened now that it was behind her. She still had radiation ahead of her, but she was trying not to think about it while she was recovering, and Isabelle went to visit her every day. Xela had two computers sitting on her bed, and a stack of work to do at home while she stayed in constant contact with her assistants. She had told both of her sisters about the lumpectomy and it had worried them both, for her, and for themselves.

Isabelle was working on a presentation for the Caseys of a group of paintings for their yacht. Jack's meeting with Bill Casey had gone well, and he liked the paintings Jack had shown him.

Jack walked into her office hesitantly two days later. She looked up and smiled at him. There had been an unspoken bond between them since their confessions the night of Xela's surgery. There was a solid foundation for their friendship.

"I wanted to ask you something about Xela," he said after he sat down.

"We don't have the final pathology reports yet," she said, still very worried about her, although she was in better spirits. "They'll determine when she starts radiation."

"I didn't mean that, although of course I'm concerned about that too." He knew how it would devastate Isabelle if the reports weren't good. "It's something else. Is she spiritual at all?"

"You mean like religious?" He nodded. "I'm not sure. I took them to church when they were kids, but they went their separate ways on it in their teens. Theo is more Buddhist than anything, I think. Oona got very serious about it when she married Gregorio because he's so Catholic and expects her to be too, and I think Xela's religion is her work. I don't know what her formal beliefs are, or if she has any. She doesn't talk about it. Why?" Isabelle was intrigued about what he had in mind.

"I had some pretty low moments after I left the NBA. And I couldn't sleep. I'd sit around all night watching TV, and mattress infomercials at four A.M. And one night, I saw this young preacher from Texas on TV. He was only about ten years older than I was, and the guy was amazing. No hellfire and brimstone, just an incredible amount of charisma, practical advice, and positive thinking, with a very subtle religious message behind it if you're open to it. I wasn't too sure about my beliefs either at the time, and a God who would let me break my leg at a championship game and end my career. I needed to blame someone, and God was convenient. In any case, I got hooked on the young preacher, and I swear he got me back on my feet and headed in the right direction, both physically and mentally.

"I flew to Texas to meet him and see him at his church. He's really extraordinary. He also believes that forgiveness has a lot to do with healing. He has a lot of ideas that worked for me, and still do. I saw in the paper yesterday that he's coming to New York this weekend. He packs the house with about twenty thousand people, when he does these events. It's a powerful message about what you can do. I came out of there floating when I went. I was wondering if you and Xela would like to go. You don't have to tell her I suggested it if you don't want to. She might be more impressed if it comes from you."

He looked faintly embarrassed as he described it to her, but Isabelle was intrigued. Religion was an entirely personal thing, but she liked the inspirational aspect of it, and that he felt it had led to healing in various forms. "Do you think she'd be interested?" Jack asked her. "I can buy you both tickets. It's at Madison Square Garden, this Saturday night."

"Why don't you buy them, and I'll talk to her. If she doesn't want to go, I will. It won't do me any harm either."

She still hadn't heard from Charles Anderson about meeting her, and she hoped he would. She had opened the door, but she couldn't pressure him, it wouldn't have been fair. Now it was up to him.

Jack bought her tickets online a few minutes later, and he would have liked to take Sandy, but she wasn't up to it. Her condition had deteriorated slightly recently. And her daughter in Alaska was having trouble in her marriage and Sandy was worried about her, which seemed to be making her breathing worse. She wanted to visit her, but she couldn't travel anymore, and she hated how helpless it made her feel not to be able to get on an airplane and see her daughter. Jack had mentioned it to Isabelle, and it made her realize that she was lucky Xela lived in New York, and she didn't have to go halfway around the world to help her. It would have been much harder for her if it were Theo, in India.

Jack put the tickets on her desk when he left at the end of the day, and Isabelle mentioned it to Xela when she visited her the next day. She listened without comment while her mother described the preacher and the event, from what Jack had told her. Isabelle had been reading about him.

"It sounds a little weird, doesn't it, Mom? What do you think?" Xela wasn't violently opposed, just mildly skeptical, but she didn't refuse.

"To be honest, I think whatever works is a good idea.

I think the body and the mind are very closely linked and affect each other, whatever one's religious beliefs. Mary Baker Eddy figured that out in the nineteenth century when she had a skating accident and established a religion based on healing. And whatever modern-day version has surfaced might have some merit to it. I want to go. Do you want to come with me? We've got nothing to lose. I don't have a hot date this Saturday. Do you?" She teased her and Xela grinned.

"Not exactly. I can't remember the last time I did, except with investors in town from California. I'll go with you." Her arm and her breast were still sore but she was being careful not to bump it or make it worse.

"I'll get a car and driver so we don't have to fight for a cab around Madison Square Garden on Saturday night. I'll pick you up at six-thirty. It starts at seven." She went back to the house then, and Jack had left a book on her desk by the preacher in question. Isabelle didn't put it down till she finished it late that night. She liked his message and said as much to Jack the next morning.

"It's so simple and clear. It's all about trust, honesty, and there's a lot in it about forgiveness." Just as he had told her.

"It works for me. I hope you like him," Jack said easily. "What did Xela say?"

"We're going."

"Me too, I bought myself a ticket."

"Do you want to come with us?"

"I don't want to intrude on Xela. You two should go alone." He was discreet about things like that, which she appreciated and she agreed with him.

*

On Saturday night, she picked up her daughter as promised, and they arrived at the Garden ten minutes before the event. Thousands of people were filing into the building in orderly fashion, looking good humored and excited. Once they were seated, Isabelle looked around and noticed that most of the crowd looked like them. She saw an attorney she knew ten rows down from their seats, and a congresswoman she admired. The crowd wasn't made up of freaks or religious fanatics, and she hoped they wouldn't be disappointed.

The lights dimmed after a few minutes, and a slight man with an energetic step and a handsome, youthful look in a well-cut suit walked onto the stage and smiled at them.

"I'm so glad you're here," he said, and she realized that he could be a well-rehearsed showman, but everything about him gave her the sensation that he was sincere. She was glad to be there. She reached over and held Xela's hand, and they smiled at each other. People were smiling all around the huge auditorium. He told funny stories and talked about incidents from his own life, his family, and friends, all situations that happened to everyone. People laughed and you could feel them relax and enjoy the moment. He became more somber with time, and talked about more serious issues, and illnesses. God was threaded into the conversation with a light touch, and never in an oppressive way. You could either embrace the idea of God, or simply the positive message he was offering, that you could hang in, you could prevail, you could get better, your marriage could improve, and if it didn't, you could find a way to leave it. Your job, your finances, your relationship with your kids. His message applied to everything and every problem you were facing. With the right attitude you could be healed, even of serious illnesses. Anything was possible and you began to feel that way as you listened to him. The burdens that you had brought with you seemed to lift, like they do in an evening spent with a good friend who offers great advice and believes in it.

There were tears in Isabelle's eyes as she listened, and when she turned there were tears rolling down Xela's cheeks. In the gentlest way, he had lightened the load for the people there. At the end of his message after two hours, people literally stood up and cheered. He thanked them, said a short blessing, and stayed to chat for a few more minutes, and then left the stage as discreetly as he had arrived with a warm wave. Isabelle felt as though he had hugged her when he left, and Xela looked shell-shocked. As they made their way out of the building, Isabelle realized that he and his very pretty wife were wandering through the crowd of thousands, randomly shaking hands and thanking them for coming. Isabelle felt as though something in her had changed that night. In the car, Xela was crying and laughing and smiling and singing his praises.

"He's fantastic!" she said to her mother and then looked sober. She had thought about it all through the evening. She knew what she had to do now. Whatever happened with her health, she had to repair the damage she had inflicted on people for so many years, sometimes even intentionally. Isabelle went upstairs to her apartment with her, and Xela looked at her seriously.

"I want to go see Theo and Oona. I've been angry at both of them for my whole life. I wanted to get even with them for what they had and I didn't. Theo had a father who adored her. I don't really remember him, but she has all his letters and she used to read them to me. You weren't married to him, but he couldn't have loved her more, he even loved you. And he left her his whole fortune, everything. Theo can do what she wants forever, she can make her dreams and everyone else's come true. She can save lives, feed villages, build hospitals, bring in doctors. I hated her for it. She can have and do anything she wants.

"My father was a criminal and a shit, he didn't even

want to be my father. He gave me up as soon as he went to jail. I never even heard from him growing up. He didn't care who I was or how I was and didn't want to know. I've been angry at Theo my whole life for her father, her money, the freedom she has. She's safe forever, and I have to fight for everything I have and live by my wits, and no matter how hard I work, I'll never have a father, or the money she does. It's like she won the lottery, and I didn't.

"I've been jealous of her all my life, and I've been a bitch to her because of it. Every time I see her, I want to hurt her to get even. Even you hated my father once you found out what he was, and so do I, for what he did to you, and to me. Declan was the love of your life, the perfect man, and Oona has that whole legacy of a wonderful man who was her father even if he died before she was born. She never knew him, just like I never knew mine, but she doesn't need to. Everything anyone says about him is good, that's what he left her, the legacy of his goodness. Oona is so free and happy because of it. And she doesn't care about money. She wears the same dress every time I see her, she doesn't care about running a business or having 'things.' She just wants Gregorio and all her babies. Whatever she has is enough for her. She never wants more. I *always* want more. Whatever I have is never enough, and if I live to be a thousand, I will never have what Theo does. I'll never save a life or build a hospital. I always feel like a loser when I'm with her. She won everything, the Great Father award, a ton of money, she won all the prizes, and I got none.

"And now, when I date, I pick the guys who don't want me, *every* time. It's almost as though if I find men like my father, I tell myself I can turn it around this time. But I never can. They're either losers or married or shits, or just bad guys who make a point of rejecting me. I can pick them out in any crowd.

"I wouldn't want him myself, but Oona has a guy who adores her, and children who love her. She's never been rejected by anyone in her life. Getting rejected is my stock in trade, starting with my father. And I've been a bitch to both of my sisters for what they have and I don't, whether it's a man, a father, or money." It was an incredible realization of what made Xela tick, and Isabelle was silent, absorbing it. She knew it was all true. It was a tremendous admission for Xela to acknowledge it. "I owe them both an apology," she said seriously. "I want to take some time off before I start radiation and go see them. I want to talk to them in person, not on Skype or by text or email. I have a lot to say, and a lot to make up for."

"I know they'll want to hear it," her mother said gently. "You're a big person, Xela, for wanting to make amends to them. Not everyone would do that, or even admit there was a problem. I understand why you feel the way you do, or did, but you forget your own strengths too. You have more degrees than either of them. Oona never even finished college and Theo was not a great student. You were. You have your BA and MBA from Harvard, and an incredible head for business. Neither of them could do what you do. One day, I think you'll be a very successful woman." It was gratifying to hear it, and Xela smiled at her mother's praise and faith in her. "Do you want a husband and kids someday?" Isabelle asked her. "I thought you were more interested in your career."

"I am, for now. But one day, I'd like to have both, if that's possible. I haven't figured that out yet. And there have been no decent candidates in my life. Ultimately, I'd like a good guy for me, maybe someone who works as hard as I do. Not some deadbeat who wants to mooch off me and put me down. I've had enough of those. And now it's a moot point anyway," she said as tears filled her eyes. "I have cancer and I'm probably going to die." Her voice caught on a sob as she said it, and Isabelle could see she believed it, and she took both her daughter's hands in her own.

"You are *not* going to die," she said with all the strength and faith she could muster. "Stop saying that right now. Maybe this was an opportunity for you to learn some things about yourself, like what you just told me about you and your sisters. Do you realize how big that is? If you stop expending energy on being angry at them, you'll have a lot more time for everything else. And one day, you'll have the right man, if that's what you want. Don't just hand your life over to an illness. You can't let it beat you, Xela. You are a winner, and this time you *have* to win." She said it with such energy, she surprised them both.

"Do you really think I'll beat it, Mom?" she asked, worried. She didn't look convinced. The idea that she had cancer was overwhelming.

"I *know* you will. I expect you to. You need to believe in yourself."

"I'll try," she said meekly. "And I'm serious about going to see Oona and Theo. I think I'll go to Oona before the babies come. She'll be crazed after that, and she won't have time to talk." She nursed her other three babies all the time and always had a breast in their mouth. Xela couldn't imagine what it would be like with two at once.

It would have been the perfect night for Isabelle's own confessions about the baby she had given up at fifteen, but she wanted all three of her daughters together in one place when she told them. She hadn't figured out yet when they'd all get together—probably not for a long time. Her secret had waited forty-three years to be told, so it could wait a little longer if it had to. And Isabelle still hadn't heard back from Charles about whether or not he would see her. She was still hoping he would, and preferably soon.

She and Xela both felt transformed by the evening they had experienced, and Xela's confessions had astounded her mother. She just hoped that she would continue to feel that way, and would be able to make a lasting peace with her sisters. It was important to her too.

*

Isabelle told Jack how much they had enjoyed the evening, and the preacher, when he came to work on Monday morning, and how much it had helped them both and moved them profoundly.

"It changed our lives," Isabelle said with eyes that sparkled. "Xela is going on a pilgrimage to see her sisters and apologize to them."

"Wow!" he said, impressed. "That's a shocker. But not really. He had the same effect on me when I first saw him. He got me back on my feet, literally. I'd been moping around and bitter until then. He changed everything, my whole outlook about life. I don't think I could have done it without him."

"I hope he has the same impact on Xela," Isabelle said seriously. "She's never been a happy person, even as a little kid, but now she sees it. And it wouldn't hurt Theo to listen to this man either. She's been looking for something all her life that she's never found. She doesn't realize it has to be within her, it's not external. Theo's a seeker. She does a lot of good along the way, but I don't think she's truly happy. Her father was like that. He was a tortured soul." Theo wasn't tormented as he had been, but Isabelle knew she felt empty, and could never fill the deep need within her, no matter what she did.

Xela called her mother two days later to say goodbye. She'd gotten clearance from her doctor to go on the trip.

"I'm leaving for Florence in the morning." She sounded cheerful and happy and energetic. "And I'm going from there to Delhi. I'm taking some time off, Mom."

"You're leaving already? That was fast," Isabelle said, impressed. "Have a fantastic time and kiss Oona for me when you get there. Maybe you'll be there when the twins come."

"That sounds scary. I hope not," she said and her mother laughed.

"It might be good practice for you," her mother teased her.

"Don't even say that. I'm not ready, and I'll never be ready for twins. One at a time would be fine, or maybe just one child. I'm not a baby factory like my sister." She promised to call her mother from Italy, and they both knew she had to be back in time for radiation in three or four weeks. But in the meantime, she was on a mission.

For the first time in her life, as the plane took off from New York, Xela couldn't wait to see her sisters and spend some time with them, and make amends for her past bad behavior. The preacher from Texas had done his job well.

Chapter Sixteen

Oona had sent one of their farm workers to pick Xela up at the airport. She thought it was the least she could do. She was touched that her sister was coming. She had two weeks left in her pregnancy, and she never said it to Gregorio but she was homesick for her mother and sisters, and nervous about giving birth to twins. Gregorio acted as though he were doubly virile for having produced them, but the reality of delivering two infants fell to her, and it sounded terrifying.

Her mother never wanted to intrude on them and thought it was a moment she and her husband should share. She always came a few weeks later, when things had settled down, the nursing was going smoothly, and the baby had adjusted. And Gregorio's family was overwhelming. There were so many of them, with so many opinions and loud voices, and they were always telling her what to do and expecting her to follow their advice, and Gregorio got angry with her when she didn't and had her own ideas. He was certain that only Italians knew how to do anything right, and his family had their directions straight from God. It left no room for Oona to speak up at all, or disagree, and she hardly ever did. And she never complained about it.

She would have really liked it if Theo had been there, since she had assisted with many deliveries in Africa and India, but she was even happy to see Xela, and hoped she wouldn't pick any fights with Gregorio. He thought that Theo was strange, and said openly that Xela was a bitch, and she was to him.

Oona ran out of the house when she heard the truck coming, and threw herself into Xela's arms when she got out.

"Thank you for coming!" she said gratefully, and Xela was touched. She looked so off-kilter and vulnerable, and Xela could see that she was tired. The twins were huge, the three little boys were active, and her in-laws were underfoot all the time and made themselves right at home. And with such an obviously pregnant wife as the evidence of his masculinity, Gregorio was strutting and crowing like a rooster. He acted as though Oona had had little to do with it, and was nothing more than the delivery truck for his offspring, which he assumed would both be boys again, as further evidence of his prowess. Xela managed to appear bland and almost docile when she said hello to him, which was unlike her. Oona was grateful for that too.

They sat down and chatted in the living room for a

few minutes after Xela arrived. The two sisters hadn't seen each other in a year, and Oona asked politely about her business.

"It's coming along. I think we're close to getting some venture capital money. I'm trying not to stress about it right now." Oona knew about her recent brush with breast cancer and asked how she was feeling. "I'm fine. I have to have radiation when I go back, and I hope that will be the end of it. They caught it very early. And the pathology reports are good. The perimeter was clean, and my lymph nodes aren't involved, but it scared the hell out of me when I found out, because of our grandmother."

"I know, it scares me too," Oona admitted.

"How are *you* feeling, more to the point? I'm sorry to come right before you have the babies, but I had kind of an epiphany after the surgery, and I wanted to share it with you, in person."

"I'm fine," Oona answered her, "just tired now at the end. The doctor says they can come early, any time, and I'm getting nervous. I saw a film about giving birth to twins, and I nearly fainted."

"Will Gregorio be with you?" She assumed he would be, especially with all the trumpeting and peacocking and posturing he did. She could easily imagine him standing by proudly and cutting the cord.

"He doesn't want to be," she said honestly. "He thinks

that's a woman thing. His father and none of his brothers have ever been at the births. He was there for Massimiano, but only because I had him so fast he couldn't get out of the room before the baby was born. He wants to leave it to the doctors and nurses this time. My mother-in-law and his two aunts want to be at the delivery, but I don't want them there. We fight about it every night," she said with a half smile, and Xela felt sorry for her. She was too good-natured, and Gregorio and his family took full advantage of it. She wanted to defend her little sister's interests and to protect her. "So what's the epiphany you had?"

"That I've been a bitch to you and Theo all my life, and I want to stop," she said seriously. "I'm ashamed to admit it to you, but I've been jealous of you both."

"Of me?" Oona looked startled, as Xela noticed her enormous belly shift in shape with visible movements, as though the twins were having a fistfight inside her. It had to be boys, she was sure. "Why?" she asked Xela.

"Because you and Theo had wonderful fathers who adored you. Or yours would have if he'd known you. Mom was crazy about him, and everyone talks about what an incredible man he was. And Putnam adored Theo and left her a vast fortune and a million love letters. But my father was a con artist and a shit, who went to prison and gave up his rights to me. I always felt left out, like some kind of loser whose own father didn't want her." Oona was staring at her in amazement. "Anyway, I've been a bitch to both of you. The war is over. Maybe getting cancer put some sense into me. I've had a lot of time to think, and Mom and I went to see an incredible preacher. It just all seemed so simple after we heard him. I love you, Oona. You're the sweetest person I know. I need to take lessons from you." As she said it, she walked over and hugged her younger sister, and Oona started to cry.

"You came all the way here to say that to me? That's the nicest thing you've ever done. I love you too. I was probably a pest when I was a kid. I always thought you were so cool and so smart and I wanted to be just like you, but you're way smarter than I am, so I got married and had babies instead. I could never do what you do. And maybe Mom just thinks my father was a saint because he's dead," she said, and wiped her eyes.

"I'm going to see Theo when I leave here. But I wanted to visit you first, before the twins come and all hell breaks loose. You'll be so busy." She nodded as Gregorio walked through the room and was visibly surprised to see them there, and smiled at his wife in the superior way he had.

"You're not cooking dinner tonight?" Xela didn't see why she should have to, but she held her tongue.

"Your mother sent over a pesto lasagna," Oona answered him with a loving smile. "So I'm off the hook."

"You are a very, very spoiled young woman," he said, smiling at her. "That was very nice of my mother," he said and Oona agreed with him. Xela thought she was a saint. She chased her children around all day, waited on her husband hand and foot, cooked three meals a day for them, and he expected her to make dinner two weeks before she gave birth to twins, and was "spoiled" if she got a night off from cooking dinner. It made Xela angry for her.

"The men in this family are treated like princes all their lives," Oona whispered when he left the room again.

"I'm not sure I'm cut out for marriage, in this country anyway," Xela said, smiling.

"I love our family life, though. Families here stick together. We're so spread out, it must be kind of sad to be in New York as the only one now. And I'm sure it's lonely for Mom. In Italy, families stay together forever, maybe a little too much so, but I like it. There's a mother and a father, sisters and brothers, uncles and aunts and cousins. I missed that growing up."

"I don't think I did," Xela said. "It would drive me crazy to have all those people around."

"Well, sometimes it does me too." Oona smiled. "But I'm used to it now. And Italian men are all like Gregorio. He's no worse than his brothers. They're all spoiled."

They chatted for a while, and Xela followed Oona into the kitchen and helped her set the table. A little while later, the boys came in with the babysitter, and Gregorio appeared, and offered Xela some wine from their vineyards. They sat down together, and his mother's lasagna was delicious. They had salad and cheese with it, vegetables from their gardens, and fruit salad for dessert. It was a perfect evening meal. Afterward, Oona put the boys to bed, and Xela went to her room to unpack.

Oona came to visit her when the boys were asleep and thanked her for what she had said earlier. She felt like she had a new sister. The cancer had definitely changed her, and had shaken Xela severely and woken her up. And as long as it didn't get worse, it almost seemed like a good thing.

They all went to bed early, and the next morning, Oona looked more tired than she had the day before. She got the two older boys off to school after she cooked breakfast, went out to the dairy to ask about some of their cheeses, checked on something in the barn, and got the meal started for when Gregorio and the boys came home for lunch. She was constantly in motion, and Xela was exhausted just watching her.

"Don't you ever stop?"

"Not till I go to bed at night," she said happily. "And we go to parties in Florence and Siena sometimes when I'm not this pregnant. It's a little late now."

She cooked dinner herself that night, a leg of lamb from a French cookbook, but Gregorio didn't like it, so she made him something else. He expected pasta at every meal, although it didn't show. He was very trim and athletic. After dinner, he went to visit one of his brothers. Oona sank down on the couch in the living room then stood up to get something, and as she did, she suddenly found herself standing in the middle of a lake with a startled expression.

"What is that?" Xela said quickly, looking around for what had spilled or sprung a leak. It was her sister.

"My water just broke. We'd better call Gregorio. He wants me to have the twins in Florence, and all the others came very fast." Xela looked panicked, and Oona called her husband and he came home twenty minutes later. Oona's bag was packed, and she was ready to go. "Will you come with me?" she asked Xela, who nodded, not sure what else to say. She was much more nervous than her baby sister about the birth, having never seen one, and Oona had been through it three times, though never with twins.

Oona told the nanny they were leaving, and they followed Gregorio out to his car, a four-door Maserati. Xela got into the back seat, and Oona next to her husband. Gregorio hit the gas like he was in a Grand Prix race.

"Is the baby going to come that fast?" Xela asked, hanging on for dear life in the back.

"No, he always drives like this," Oona said with a grin. "This is slower than usual for him." Gregorio ignored them, kept his foot on the accelerator, and took every curve at full speed, while Xela tried not to scream.

By the time they reached Florence just over an hour later, Oona had started having contractions. She could hardly walk when they pulled up in front of the hospital. Gregorio looked relaxed and smiled at them both. He had enjoyed the drive. They walked into the hospital together, and Gregorio said he was going to get a cup of coffee while they checked her in. A nurse offered Oona a wheelchair, and Xela followed them to an exam room while Oona undressed between contractions. They were getting significantly worse. She spoke to the nurse in Italian, and Xela could figure out that the nurse responded that the doctor would be there soon.

"I think the twins are in a hurry," Oona said to her sister as they waited alone in the room. "They're pushing really hard." But they had gotten quiet, and weren't battling with each other at least. Oona looked pale then, hobbled to the bathroom, and threw up.

"Should I ring for a nurse?" Xela asked, panicked and feeling useless.

"No, I'm okay," she said, and Xela helped her back to bed, wondering when Gregorio would return. It was a lot more dramatic than Xela was used to, but Oona was a practiced hand at this. The only thing that frightened her was delivering twins.

Xela watched her as the contractions continued to get

worse at a rapid rate, and she was visibly in agony when the nurse came in to check her and Oona asked for the doctor again. The nurse told her that he was at dinner but would be back shortly. Oona gave a little scream when the nurse checked her.

"She doesn't believe me, but I swear I'm having them now," she said to Xela through clenched teeth.

"Please don't," Xela begged her. "Wait for the doctor. I don't know how to do this. I've never even had puppies." Oona laughed despite the pain and then grimaced. And with that, Gregorio walked in, looking like the cover of a men's fashion magazine. Xela always forgot how handsome he was. He made a face as he looked around.

"My God, what an ugly room. Couldn't they give us a better one? Where's the doctor?"

"At dinner," Xela told him, and he went to the nursing desk and made a scene. Within minutes there were nurses scurrying everywhere. A young doctor came in to see Oona, who said the twins were pushing down hard. He looked, and they could see he was panicked. Oona was right.

"If this were a hotel, they'd be out of business," Gregorio said grandly. But it wasn't, Xela wanted to point out, and her sister was about to give birth. "I'm sure the food is terrible too," he added, as Oona started to cry. Gregorio finally came to his senses, and the doctor walked in, and told her not to push, and she said she had to, as Gregorio looked wild-eyed and Oona grabbed his arm.

"Don't leave me. I need you," she said, and for once Xela knew just how he felt—terrified. She didn't blame him. Everything was moving quickly. A moment later, they were pushing Oona down the hall at full speed on a gurney with Xela and Gregorio running along beside her, and he looked deathly pale.

Xela glanced over at him. "Are you okay?" He nodded and Oona looked angrily at her sister.

"Why are you asking him if he's okay? I'm having the babies," she corrected her, but Xela thought he was going to faint, and she wasn't sure that she wouldn't. Oona was a lot braver than either of them.

A nurse gave them both chairs next to Oona's head as they settled her on the delivery table, in stirrups, and the doctor tried to maneuver the babies into a better position for them to follow each other. Oona screamed at the manipulations and clutched Gregorio's arm and begged him to stop them, as all three of them cried. It was awful and much worse than Xela had expected. She hadn't planned to be there. Oona never stopped screaming as the first baby moved slowly down and the doctor had her push through the never-ending contractions. It seemed like hours, but was only about forty-five minutes of intolerable agony for Oona, and a little face appeared as they heard a cry. The doctor held the baby up, tapped him gently on the back, and it was easy to see it was a boy as Gregorio swelled with pride, and bent to kiss his wife.

"You are *fantastic* and I love you," he said through tears of pride and joy, but she only had a moment's respite as the contractions continued. She had to push again, and the second twin had shifted into a sideways position and wouldn't move. Gregorio was distracted by his newest son, and Oona screamed as they tried to edge the baby into a better position and couldn't for a long time, until the doctor finally declared victory. Gregorio was holding the first twin, and Oona was clutching Xela's hands.

"I can't . . . I can't . . . I can't . . ." she kept saying as Xela tried to get her to focus.

"Yes, you can. I know you can," they all shouted and told her to push, as the second baby, bigger than the first, finally emerged with a last scream from Oona, and tears ran down Xela's cheeks as the doctor said "It's a girl!" and both sisters grinned. There was silence from Gregorio for a moment as he looked as though someone had said the baby was Chinese.

"A girl? Are you sure?" The doctor laughed at the question.

"Quite sure." They cleaned her up, put her in a pink blanket, and handed her to her mother. Each parent was holding one of the twins, a boy and a girl. They had arrived at the hospital two hours earlier, and labor had barely started when they left Castellina in Chianti. Xela felt as though they had been there for a month. It was the hardest thing she'd ever seen, and it didn't make her long for a baby, but filled her with respect for her sister for going through so much pain, for the fourth time in five years, and this time with twins. And it hadn't been an easy delivery, even though it was fast. The nurse who had weighed them announced that they were each just over eight pounds. Oona had been carrying sixteen pounds of baby. Most twins weighed half that.

"My wife is born to have children," Gregorio said proudly and bent to kiss her again. Xela thought he owed her far more than that for what she had just gone through, but Oona looked ecstatic holding her new daughter, and gazed adoringly at her husband holding their son. Xela only hoped she didn't go through it too many more times. She couldn't imagine how she did it.

He handed the baby boy to one of the nurses a few minutes later and told Oona he was going to call his mother, which she knew meant that all his brothers and sisters and his mother would be in her room within the hour. She was familiar with all of it and didn't mind.

"You're my hero," Xela said when he left the room, and Oona looked at her, exhausted but victorious.

"I'm happy, Xellie," she reassured her. "I love him."

"You're a hero for that too," Xela said and Oona laughed.

"It'll be good for him to have a girl. She'll wrap him around her little finger."

"I hope so," Xela said and sat down, feeling weak. She had been through her own trials recently, which were a lot less joyous than twins. They called their mother on Xela's cellphone then, to tell her she had a new grandson and finally a granddaughter. It was six P.M. in New York, and Isabelle had been reading. Jack had just left. She was delighted at the news and happy to know that Xela was with her. She said it had been hard but Oona had been incredibly brave, and Isabelle couldn't believe how big the babies were.

She was up and dressed when Jack came to work the next morning and she told him the news.

"Congratulations. How was Xela?" he asked her after inquiring about Oona and the twins.

"Shocked, I think. Watching twins delivered can't be easy. But I'm glad for Oona that she was there. It's nice knowing the girls are together. I'll go over in a few weeks, when Oona is back on her feet and it's less chaotic. She has enough to deal with, with his family." Isabelle went back upstairs to work then, and Jack joined her a little while later. He had seen the appointment on her calendar. She was going to the eye doctor that day, since Xela was away and she had time.

"Am I coming with you?" he asked her pointedly, and she hesitated.

"Do you really want to?"

"Yes. I don't see why you should go alone. I want to be there."

"That's above and beyond the call of duty," she reminded him.

"So are most things in life," he said, and she smiled at him.

They left the house together in time for her appointment, and he came into the exam room with her and held her hand. It was painful, as it had been before, but seemed less so with Jack to talk to and provide some distraction. And she thanked him when they left the doctor's office.

"I feel guilty dragging you through that," she said, feeling embarrassed.

"I volunteered. Believe me, I've seen worse." She smiled at him and they took a cab uptown. And for the rest of the afternoon they went through catalogues together. She pointed out why she liked certain paintings for their clients and not others. He found it fascinating, and he was always impressed by how knowledgeable she was. She was a remarkable woman and, in her opinion, he was an exceptional friend.

Chapter Seventeen

Xela felt her visit to Oona in time to see the babies born had been a great success. She was there for a week. Oona stayed at the hospital in Florence for five days, while dozens of visitors, mostly Gregorio's relatives, came to see her every day. And Xela left the day she went home. She had told her what she wanted to say, and they enjoyed some loving close moments while she was there. Xela was still in awe of what she'd seen during the birth of the twins. Gregorio had been pouring champagne and handing out cigars ever since, and he gave Oona a pair of Bulgari diamond bangle bracelets to thank her for their two beautiful new children, Paola and Nicola. It still stunned Xela that her sister was the mother of five children and had only recently turned twenty-seven. She promised to visit them again soon. And Gregorio thanked her for being at the birth. It even created a slightly warmer bond with him, although she recognized now that he would always be what he was. He was part of a culture which fostered both his machismo and his narcissism, and no one could stem the tides of that. Oona loved and accepted him without reserve, so Xela had to do the same, for her sake. It wouldn't be fair to make waves for her. Gregorio embraced Xela warmly when she left, which was a first.

She flew from Florence to New Delhi, and from there drove for six hours with a car and driver to Chandpur in the Bijnor District in the state of Uttar Pradesh, where Theo was establishing the small hospital she had dedicated herself to. Xela was impressed when she saw it and how at ease her sister was in primitive conditions with few comforts and no luxuries. It was a sacrifice she was happy to make for the common good, and the people she served. There was a commissary tent where they served free meals to the locals, who were indigent, and in desperate need of medicine and food. She had warned Theo that she was coming, and Theo was startled that she was coming so soon after her surgery. She was afraid that it meant Xela was sicker than their mother admitted or even knew. She was terrified she had come to say goodbye. They didn't get along, but they were still sisters, and Theo didn't want to lose her.

"What really brought you all the way here?" Theo questioned her with a look of concern the day after she arrived. She said the same to her that she had to Oona, except that she owed Theo more of an apology and told her why.

"I've been cruel and unkind to you all my life, consumed with jealousy of who you are and what you have." Theo was as shocked as Oona had been, but also deeply touched by Xela's humble admission.

"Now I'm even more worried about you," Theo said seriously. "Mom said you had stage one breast cancer. She didn't tell me it had gone to your brain," she teased her with a wry expression. "Who are you, and what did you do with my sister?"

"Oh, shut up," Xela said to her and they jostled each other as they had as children and then laughed. They hadn't enjoyed each other in years, if ever.

Xela stayed with her for a week, and they had a wonderful time together. Theo showed her everything she was doing there, and introduced her to a team of doctors who had come from London to help them, and were staying for several months.

Xela teased her about it later, having noticed that the head of the team had a marked interest in her older sister, and she asked Theo about it before she left. His name was Geoffrey Bates. His father was a member of the House of Lords and Geoffrey was very upper crust, but he liked the rigors of their barren outpost as much as she did, and had just come from a similar setup in Zambia, which Theo was planning to visit with him to see how it worked.

"I see Dr. Bates has a definite weakness for my big sister," Xela said with a quizzical look.

"We're just colleagues," she insisted, "and interested in the same things."

"That's how it starts," Xela warned her. "I always thought you wanted to be a nun when you grew up, like Mother Teresa. If you fall in love with Dr. Bates it's going to spoil everything if you turn out to be human."

"No worries. I'm not going to fall in love at thirty-seven," Theo said firmly. "I'm not the sort."

"Why not?" Xela questioned her further. "You're not ancient, and you'd be gorgeous, if you'd ever comb your hair and get out of hiking boots." The two sisters exchanged a grin, and held each other close for a long moment before Xela left for the airport. She had crossed half the world to apologize to her sister, and she had to go back to New York for radiation treatments now.

"Take care of yourself," Theo said with tears in her eyes. "I love you," she whispered softly. And Xela turned to hug her again. If anything happened to her, she didn't want there to be any doubt in Theo's mind about how she felt about her and how sorry she was for how mean she'd been in the past.

"I love you too. Don't forget that. Even if I've been an asshole for most of your life." But she wasn't anymore. They had grown closer than ever before during Xela's visit and had shared confidences and a new relationship that they both cherished and had vowed to continue in future.

They waved to each other as the car set out for the long trip to New Delhi, and Xela hung out the window, waving until she couldn't see Theo anymore. It had been a good trip, even a great one to see both of her sisters, and now she had to face the music in New York.

She was thinking about it on the plane from London to New York, and what lay ahead for her. She had heard that radiation could be rough. Her mother had promised to go with her, but she was nervous about it anyway, and glad she didn't have to go alone. She felt especially pleased that she had spent the last three weeks visiting Theo and Oona and had made amends for the past. She had a lot to make up for, although they had both insisted that they didn't hold it against her, and appeared to forgive her.

Everything in Xela's life had new meaning now, and she had laid the foundation with each of them for a relationship they'd never had before. Her sisters were both such different women. Oona was the epitome of family, and Theo the soul of solitude, although Xela had a feeling that Dr. Geoffrey Bates was going to try and change that, if Theo let him in behind her walls. He seemed to be making good headway in that direction when Xela left. Theo denied it and said that their interest in each other was strictly professional. It might have been on Theo's part, but from what she'd seen, Xela was sure Dr. Bates had other projects in mind, particularly on the trip to Zambia they were planning, to visit his research facility. Xela was smiling, thinking about it, when the man sitting next to her spoke to her. He'd been looking at her for a while but she hadn't noticed. He was American and had classic good looks, and the appearance of a businessman.

"Business in London?" he asked her, to strike up a conversation. He wondered if she was a model. She could have been.

"No, I've been in India, visiting my sister. She lives there, and is building a hospital in Chandpur, in the state of Uttar Pradesh." It sounded very exotic to him. He looked fascinated by her. He had noticed her when she boarded the plane, and thought she was a striking-looking woman.

"Is she a doctor?"

"No, she's a saint. She's been in India for sixteen years, helping to bring food, water, and medical help to villages, and building medical facilities. It's a vocation more than a job," she said proudly, for the first time. There was no longer an edge when she spoke about her. She'd had to get cancer for that to happen, but she didn't tell him that.

"Do you live in New York?" he asked hopefully, and she nodded. She didn't want to talk to him all the way across the Atlantic, but they were waiting for lunch to be served.

"Yes," Xela answered.

"I work for an international firm on Wall Street. We

have investments in Mumbai and New Delhi in electronics, and partners in London. I go to London a few times a year. And to India about once a year."

"I'm the founder of a struggling startup," she said, with a self-deprecating look. He hadn't expected her to say that, and liked the idea that she was an entrepreneur. They chatted through lunch, and then she put the headphones on and selected a movie, and fell asleep halfway through it. She didn't wake up until they were landing in New York. He decided to take a chance before he lost sight of her at the airport, and handed her his card as the landing gear came down.

"I'd love to meet you for a drink sometime," he said, and she looked amused at how direct he was. He was a good-looking guy and he'd been nice to talk to, but she was in no position to date anyone right now. She had cancer, and she didn't feel she had a right to inflict that on anyone. What if she got really sick? Or worse.

"Thank you," she said politely and slipped the card into her purse without looking at his name, intending to throw it out when she got home.

"Do you have a card with you?" he asked and she shook her head. This had been a strictly personal trip to Italy and India, and she hadn't brought business cards with her, intentionally.

"No, I don't. I'm sorry." She didn't encourage him or offer to write down her number.

"A boyfriend?" he asked and she laughed at the question.

"I don't have one of those in my purse either."

"What's the name of your company?" She told him, and she admired his persistence. "Actually, I've heard of it. Clever idea. Delivery services all over the country."

"Not yet. But we're getting there. Seven cities right now, and we're growing." But she didn't want to talk business with him. She was still basking in the afterglow of a wonderful trip to see her sisters.

They said goodbye, she left the plane, picked up her luggage, went through customs, and didn't see him again. She took a cab into the city, and called her mother as soon as she got home. They hadn't spoken in a week, while she was in India.

"How was it?" Isabelle asked her, anxious to hear how it had gone with Theo.

"Fantastic. Theo is amazing. You should see what she's doing out there," she said with admiration.

"I have." Isabelle smiled. Xela sounded strong and peaceful, and more relaxed than she'd ever heard her.

"There's a cute English doctor following her around too. She says she's not interested, but I don't believe her. And he certainly is."

"It's never too late," they both said in unison and then laughed. "How are you feeling?" her mother inquired gently.

"Fine. I hate the idea of starting radiation in a couple of weeks, but I guess I have to." It wasn't a cheering thought and brought reality into sharp focus again.

"Let me know when you plan to start," Isabelle said seriously. They talked for a few more minutes. Xela was tired and was going to bed, and they hung up.

The phone rang again five minutes later, and Isabelle assumed it was Xela with something else to tell her. She didn't get many calls at night. But the voice on the other end was male and unfamiliar until he said his name. It was Charles Anderson in Boston, her son.

"Hello," he said awkwardly. "I don't know what to call you. Mom seems a little weird by now." She laughed nervously when he said it, and was happy to hear his voice. She had given up hoping for his call, and thought he'd decided not to see her or contact her again.

"You can call me Isabelle if you like."

"That'll work." There was a long silence then for a minute and she waited. "I want to see you," he said in a low voice. "Could I bring my wife and kids?"

"I'd love that. I want to meet them too. Should I come to Boston?"

"Would you mind? I don't get to New York very often, like once every five or ten years." That surprised her. He obviously led a simple, somewhat unsophisticated life.

"That's fine. It's an easy hop for me."

They agreed to meet at the Bristol Bar at the Four

Seasons on Boylston Street, at five o'clock on the following Saturday. She was nervous thinking about it.

"I can't wait to meet you, Charles," she said breathlessly.

"You can call me Charlie. And I can't wait to meet you too." Isabelle was shaking when she hung up, and so was Charlie. It was an important moment for both of them. He had dreamed of it all his life.

Chapter Eighteen

Isabelle asked Jack if he'd mind going to Boston with her on Saturday. She didn't like to ask him to work after hours or on weekends and intrude on his personal life. But she was nervous about going to Boston by herself. It was a short flight but she had to deal with the airport, the plane, and she was nervous about the meeting with Charlie. Jack agreed to go with her and didn't ask until the day before who they were meeting, and assumed it was a client. He asked casually and she gave him an anxious look when she answered.

"My son."

"Wow. That's a big deal." He was quiet for a moment.

"Yes, it is. He took a while to decide if he wanted to see me, and I don't blame him. He's bringing his kids and his wife. We're meeting at the Four Seasons. I'm not sure what to expect. And he probably isn't either. What do you say to a mother or a child you've never met or seen since the day he was born?"

"Hello is always a good start," he said, trying to lighten the moment. He could see how anxious she was.

They took a morning flight on Saturday. They were in Boston before noon. She didn't want to be late or risk a delay, so they had lunch and walked around Boston before going to the Four Seasons. It was March and blustery outside. When it started to drizzle, they walked into the lobby twenty minutes early, and she sat quietly talking to Jack about nothing in particular. He was trying to distract her so she'd calm down. She looked stressed, and went to the ladies room to comb her hair and put on fresh lipstick before the meeting, which felt silly even to her. She had abandoned Charles as an infant, and now she had resurfaced more than forty years later and she was worried about her lipstick and her hair.

"You look great," Jack said to reassure her and wished he could give her a hug to bolster her, but didn't think it was appropriate, particularly in a public place. He wasn't coming to the meeting with her, and he was going to wait in the lobby when she went to the bar. She had made a reservation and asked for a quiet table so they could talk. Jack was just along for the ride.

At two minutes to five, she left Jack and she walked into the Bristol, where they had reserved a seating group with leather couches and chairs around a table. She saw a couple with two children the right ages, sitting on the couches, and she approached them hesitantly. She had worn gray slacks and flat shoes and a short black coat. She looked stylish but not too dressed up. Her blond hair was pulled back in a neat ponytail and she had a pale blue cashmere turtleneck the color of her eyes under the coat. And before she could ask them if they were the Andersons, the man stood up. He was balding but good-looking, slim and athletic, and what shocked her about him was that he was the image of her father, and he looked more like her than any of her girls. She would have known him anywhere. She had been afraid that she wouldn't recognize him in the restaurant, and they wouldn't find each other. There was no risk of that. His son looked like Charlie, and his daughter was cute with dark hair. His wife was a pretty blonde in her late thirties. She was wearing a red coat and high heels and had obviously made an effort, and Isabelle was suddenly afraid she hadn't dressed up enough. She hadn't wanted to show off, but to be real.

Charlie turned toward her and watched intently when she walked toward him, as though he could sense her near him, and she could see in his eyes that he was aware of the resemblance too. She stood looking at him for a moment as her eyes filled with tears, and instinctively held her arms out to him, and he moved right into them and they held each other. Jack had followed her to the entrance of the bar, saw them meet and embrace, and had to choke back tears. It was an incredibly moving moment without a word uttered.

She took a step back then and smiled up at her son.

"Hello, Charlie." Her voice was soft and her eyes brimmed with tears, and Charlie's too.

"Hi, Mom," he said and they both laughed, and their laughter sounded the same too.

"You look so much like my father," she said in a gentle voice, looking him over like a lioness finding her cub in the wild and wanting to make sure that he was all right.

He introduced her to his wife then, Pattie, and his children, Steve and Jaime, and said they were sixteen and eleven. The two children, her grandchildren, were staring at her in fascination. He had explained to them what the meeting was about, that she was an additional grandmother and she was his birth mother. They were old enough to understand what that was, and shocked that she had given their father away. He had explained to them that she had been fifteen at the time, and some of the details she had recently told him.

Isabelle kissed both the children and Pattie, and then they all sat down.

"What do you want the children to call you?" her son asked her politely and she looked confused for a moment.

"Whatever you'd like. Isabelle? Grandma Isabelle?" She wasn't sure.

"Granny Izzie!" Jaime burst out and they all laughed. There was a mischievous light in her eye.

It put it into perspective for her when Charlie pointed

out that Isabelle had been a year younger than Steve, who was sixteen but looked thirteen, when she gave birth to him. It had helped him to better understand too. He wished he had known that all his life. The two women ordered tea, Charlie a beer, and the two kids sodas, as Charlie commented that she looked a lot younger than he'd expected. She was of an age when she could have looked grandmotherly, but she didn't. She told him that her youngest daughter, his half-sister, had just given birth to twins, his niece and nephew.

"How many children do you have?" He had asked her on the phone but was so nervous he didn't remember.

"Three daughters. Theo is thirty-seven, she lives in India, helping indigent starving people there. She's lived there for sixteen years, isn't married, and has no children. Xela is turning thirty-two, struggling as an entrepreneur in New York. She's single too and no kids. And Oona is twenty-seven, has been married for five years, lives in Italy, and has five children, including the twins I just mentioned."

"She makes up for the others," he joked with her, trying to remember the different locations, names, and details. But the essential thing was that he now knew he had three sisters. She had brought photographs to show him, and he passed them around after she handed them to him. He looked at the girls' faces with interest, studying them intently.

"Same father?" he wanted to know. He had noticed how different their appearances were, and none of them looked like him, and they didn't look much like her either, except possibly Theo, who was fair but really looked more like Put.

"Three different fathers," she said, slightly embarrassed to admit it. "Two of them died, one went to jail." She was keeping no secrets from him after her long absence. He nodded.

"Are you married now?"

She shook her head. "No, I'm not. I haven't been since Oona's father died twenty-seven years ago, before she was born."

"That's too bad," he said kindly, "especially if two of them live so far away."

It was her turn then. "Were the Andersons kind to you, Charlie?" She had always worried about it, but convinced herself they were.

"Nice enough. They weren't warm people. They had a daughter after they adopted me, and I became the adopted kid then, and she was the 'real' one. It made a big difference to them." She was sorry to hear it and disappointed for him.

"That must have been painful." And then she felt instantly hypocritical for saying it since what she had done to him was far worse.

"They're both dead now. They never wanted me to find

you, and wouldn't tell me anything. They probably didn't know much themselves. Adoption agencies kept their records sealed in those days." It was an old-fashioned position where an adopted child was prevented from knowing the facts about their birth parents. "Nowadays everyone stays in touch, visits, and sends pictures and Christmas cards. It wasn't like that then. Most of my friends who are adopted know their birth parents now."

"I always wanted to find you. I didn't know if I could, but I was afraid to disrupt your life, and my life was complicated for a number of years with weird relationships, a husband who died, a divorce, and bringing up my children alone. It didn't get easier for a long time."

"Do you work?" He wanted to know everything about her, what she did and who she really was.

"I'm an art consultant. I sell paintings to private individuals." It sounded fancy to him. He hadn't had a fancy life, but he looked like a bright guy, and sounded intelligent. "Do you like your job? What do you do?"

"I'm a sales rep for a publishing house. I don't love it. It's a job. I was in insurance for a while. It's funny, I like art, but I don't know much about it. Pattie teaches sixth grade. She's from New Hampshire. We got married when she was twenty-one and I was twenty-five. It seems to work." He smiled at his wife. He appeared to be a quiet, stable person. He wasn't daring or imaginative or creative, but she had the feeling he was reliable and trustworthy. She wondered how her daughters would react to him, or if they'd be snobbish about him. He wasn't from an elite world and lived in a middle-class suburb, but he seemed to be a solid, kind man, the sort of person who would never put a child up for adoption.

"Do you know anything about my father? I couldn't find him either." He looked pained as he said it.

"Not much. I hardly knew him. I was a sophomore, he invited me to a school dance. He got me drunk, dragged me into a car he'd borrowed, and you can figure out the rest. His name was Stewart Wheeler, he was eighteen the year you were born. My father went to see his, and he denied the whole thing. He went to the University of New Mexico, and I never heard of him again. We were never friends. Our school may know more about him than I do." She gave him the name of their high school in Newport, and he jotted it down with his father's name. Finding his parents had been a lifelong pursuit for Charlie. She was embarrassed at how little she knew to tell him.

"My dad was a really nice man. You look so much like him. He was a museum curator in Boston, and my mother died when I was three, of breast cancer. After that, he took a job as a property manager on a fancy estate so he could be with me more. And I grew up there. He died a long time ago now, twenty-seven years ago. I was an assistant in an art gallery before I started my own business."

"It seems like you did pretty well, in spite of a rough beginning," he said fairly, thinking of her mother. "You have nice kids who sound like they're doing good things. I would have killed any kid who did that to my daughter." He looked protectively at Jaime, as she watched them and her mother stroked her hair. Pattie looked like a warm person, and a good wife and mother. Isabelle could feel her as a positive force among them, without judgment. They all just wanted to know as much as possible about each other. "Are there any health or mental issues that I should know about?" he asked her. "I've always wondered. With that kind of adoption, you don't get to know about those either." It had concerned him all his life whenever he went to a doctor, and they asked about family history. He had none.

"Not that I know of, no mental ones. My father died of a heart attack at sixty-five with no previous heart problems. My mother died of breast cancer at thirty-three, and that just surfaced in my daughter Xela, who's almost thirty-two. She's in treatment now and they caught it early. So for your daughter, that would be her great-grandmother, my mother, which is fairly remote, and now her aunt, your sister, which is closer. I don't know if it's coincidence or heredity but it's upsetting."

"I'm sorry." He looked sympathetic.

They ordered another round of drinks and Isabelle added cookies for the kids, but Pattie and Charlie didn't want anything. He was too excited to eat, and so was Isabelle. The reunion was going well, with kind feelings among them, and some questions Charlie had had for a lifetime were finally getting answered.

They sat and talked until seven o'clock and Isabelle could feel the tension go out of her body. There had always been a place in her that was broken ever since she had given him up, and she felt it was healing. It was the end of the meeting when she remembered what she wanted to show him. She took out her wallet and pulled out a faded photograph the size of a postage stamp of a baby that could have been any infant in a little blue hat and blanket.

"It was the day you left the hospital with the Andersons. One of the nurses gave it to me. The one who told me your adoptive parents' name. She wasn't supposed to take the picture either. I've carried it for forty-three years." His eyes filled with tears as she said it, and so did hers. The meeting had been emotional for them both. And Pattie and the children had been curious and quiet and respectful. They knew how much finding her meant to their dad. They had never seen him cry before.

"It means a lot that you didn't just walk away and forget me. I understand it so much better now. It still hurts but it makes sense. You couldn't take care of a baby at fifteen, you didn't even have a mother to help you." He echoed what she'd told him on the phone.

"My father wouldn't let me keep you," she said again. "I never forgave him for it." Saying the words was like releasing a caged bird she didn't even realize she was holding in her heart, but it was true. She had never forgiven her father for making her give him away, even though she loved her father. It had always stood between them, and she suspected he'd known it. It was why she thought he hadn't fought her any harder than he did about Theo. He couldn't. She was of age then, or very close to it, and twenty-one when Theo was born out of wedlock.

She handed Charlie the photographs of his half-sisters, with their names on the back as to who was where in the photo, for him to keep. She'd brought one of her parents, when they were young, and a few of her at different ages. One of her at fifteen right before she got pregnant. She looked like no more than a child. One when she was studying in France with the Eiffel Tower behind her, and a few taken over the years, and a recent one Jack had taken at her desk for an article about her in *ARTnews*.

She asked for the check then and insisted on paying, and he thanked her, and then they walked through the lobby of the hotel together. She made eye contact with Jack and nodded and he approached them, and she introduced him as her assistant. Charlie shook hands with him, and then stared at him and looked as though the roof had just fallen in on him.

"Oh my God . . . oh my God . . . it's you, isn't it? You were my idol in high school, when you were playing in college. Jack Bailey. I saw your final game. I cried for a week afterward. What are you doing here?" Jack smiled at him.

"I'm Isabelle's assistant. I'm teaching her to shoot hoops," he said and they all laughed.

Jack had brought a camera with him, and offered to take a photograph of all of them, standing in the lobby. And then Charlie asked if Isabelle could take one of him with Jack. He was almost more excited to meet his teenage idol than his mother, and the two women exchanged a look and grinned. Eighteen years of marriage confirmed that Isabelle's assessment of Pattie was correct, she was solid and loved him, and they looked happy together.

They all hugged and kissed goodbye, and she promised to organize a meeting with her daughters soon. And then Isabelle and Jack got into the town car he'd gotten to take them to the airport, as she let out a sigh and leaned back against the seat, drained and relieved.

"How was it?" She thought about it before she answered. It had all gone so much better than she expected. He wasn't angry and he didn't hate her. The meeting had been warm and compassionate on both sides.

"It was like lancing a boil that has poisoned a part of me since I was fifteen. I always knew it was there but I couldn't do anything about it. I think it was like that for him too. So many questions we didn't have the answers to, either of us. His adoptive parents don't sound like great people, just okay. They had their own biological child after they adopted him, and he was treated as second best forever after that. It's a terrible thing to do to a kid. But what I did was worse. I'm glad he has a sweet wife and good kids. They're decent people, and he's the image of my dad. I don't know if he still hates me or not for leaving him, but I think hearing how it happened put it in perspective. Today, his father would be charged with rape. Back then, it was considered normal and a hazard of dating, and tough luck if a girl got pregnant at fifteen. The thought was that if it ruined a girl's life, she deserved it. It didn't ruin mine but it could have, and having him and giving him up have weighed on me for all these years.

"I'd like to see him again, and I want to introduce him to the girls. I told him it would take a while to arrange. They don't come home very often, and not together. I think I might ask them to come home specially and meet him," she said, looking pensive. "I think it's important. They're blood relatives even if they never knew about him, and they don't have much in common." As she looked out the window while they headed to the airport, she wondered how they'd react to him. She thought about her father too and how vehement he had been that she give up the baby. She felt she had no choice. "My father must be rolling in his grave over the meeting," she said softly as she looked at Jack.

"I think he'd understand," Jack said kindly.

"I hope so. I couldn't die one day without having met him, or at least trying to find him." Jack looked shocked at what she said.

"I hope you're not planning to do that anytime soon."

"No, but if I go blind, I wanted to see him before I do. It's funny, he looks a lot like me, more than my daughters."

"Yes, he does," Jack agreed. "He's a good-looking man."

"And he was thrilled to see you. That was so cute." She smiled at Jack.

"I guess a few people still remember," he said quietly.

"Yeah, like every guy under ninety."

"What do you know?" he teased her. "You've probably never been to a basketball game."

"That would be true. But I've read about you now. You were a very big star." He didn't comment.

"I'll take you to a game sometime." She smiled when he said it.

"I'd like that." She remembered how shocked she was by his height the first time she'd met him. Now it made sense, as an ex–basketball player.

The flight to New York was easy and brief, and after

worrying so much about meeting Charlie, with the release of the tension, she fell asleep with her head on Jack's shoulder. He left her there until they landed and he gently woke her up. She smiled and followed him off the plane, and he dropped her off at her house, and then went downtown to Sandy.

Isabelle thought about Charlie and his family all night after she got home. At least he hadn't had a bad home, even if he didn't have warm parents. They hadn't beaten him or starved him. She had worried about it in her worst nightmares all her life and her father refused to let her talk about it, even to reassure her. He felt the subject should be closed and forgotten and never spoken of again.

She got up at three in the morning and wrote an email to her girls. It was hard to find the right way to say it. And she didn't want to worry them unduly, or at all. She changed the wording several times.

"Darling Theo, Xela, and Oona" (she always listed them in order of age). "This is one of those strange motherly requests that you won't understand until later, but it is important to me. *Very* important.

"There is someone I would like you to meet from my past, someone you should know. I think it will be meaningful to you and for him too. I would like all three of you to come home in the next month or two, and indulge me on this. My treat of course. Let's find a date that works for all three of you. With all my love and gratitude, Mom."

*

She didn't want to tell them why, or who he was, and Oona was the first one to call the next morning, since it was six hours later in Italy.

"Are you in love? Did you run into an old boyfriend? Are you getting married? Are you tricking us into coming home for the wedding?" It hadn't dawned on her that they'd think it was romantic.

"No, I'm not in love. I don't have a boyfriend and I'm not getting married. It's a relative of mine you've never met. That's all I'll say. I want you to humor me on this."

"That won't be easy, Mom," she said seriously. "Gregorio doesn't want me to go anywhere without him. And I'll be nursing for the next year or two." She felt like a milk cow nursing two of them, but Gregorio insisted. Anytime one of their children caught a cold, he accused her of having stopped nursing too soon, after a year, which she thought was long enough but he didn't.

"I'm not waiting two years for you to come home. I'll pay for the trip. Bring the twins, and I'll pay for the nanny's ticket too. We'll take turns helping you with them. You don't need to stay for more than a few days, although I'd love to see you. And if he wants, Gregorio can come too."

311

"He hates leaving Italy. He'll complain the whole time. I'd rather come alone, and bring the babies. Thank you for paying for my ticket and the nanny's. I can get them passports at the consulate in Florence. You make it very tempting. I'll see what I can do."

Theo sent an email asking the same questions, and her mother gave her the same answers. They all thought it was a surprise wedding. They could think of no other reason for her to bring them home, to meet a mystery stranger from her past. They couldn't imagine who it was, despite a flurry of emails between them.

And when Isabelle took Xela to radiation she grilled her on it too. She had already been given tiny tattoos to target the radiation with infinite precision.

"I won't say until you're all here," Isabelle said in answer to her questions, and was definite about it.

"I think you're in love," Xela insisted, and then told her mother about the man she'd met on the plane.

"He sounds interesting. You should call him," Isabelle encouraged her.

"I have cancer, Mom. I'm not going to do that to some poor guy and turn him into a nurse if I get sicker. That would be irresponsible and cruel."

"And if you don't get sicker, which you won't," Isabelle said with determination, "you'll have missed an opportunity."

"I'm not going to call him," Xela said stubbornly, and

Isabelle didn't argue with her. The radiation proved to be as draining as they said it would be. It was brutal for her for four weeks, but then at least it was over. She had let her own treatments for her eyes go during the whole month. She couldn't do them and take care of Xela too. She went to radiation with her every day.

"Should you be doing that? Skipping a whole month of your shots?" Jack questioned her.

"I can't do both. I'll go back as soon as Xela is finished." Isabelle made it plain that she didn't want to be nagged about it so he backed off. He was her assistant, not her husband. But the day after Xela finished her radiation treatments Isabelle was in a hurry, ran to catch a cab, didn't see the curb, and fell in the street. She skinned her knees badly and sprained her wrist, and she was mortally embarrassed when pedestrians stopped to help her. She limped home and tried to get through the front door without Jack seeing her, but he heard her come in and came to say hello, and was shocked when he saw blood running down her legs, and her wrist was already the size of a small football by then.

"Oh my God, what happened to you?" He rushed to help her. "Did you get mugged?" He went to get ice packs and clean wet towels for her legs and wrist, as she walked into the kitchen and sat down.

"I'm fine," she insisted. "I just feel stupid. I didn't see

the curb." And the wrist hurt more than she wanted to admit. It felt broken.

"You have to go back to the eye doctor. Is it getting worse?" He looked worried and she shook her head.

"Actually, I think it's a little better. I just wasn't looking and I was rushing."

"We should get an X-ray for your wrist."

"No, we shouldn't," she growled at him. She lay down for a while and a call from Oona cheered her up.

"I can come in a week. My sister-in-law said she'll keep an eye on things for me. My nanny's cousin will come with me, and I told Gregorio that you want to discuss our inheritance so he couldn't argue with me. He gave me three days."

"That's fantastic!" Isabelle was thrilled. "What about Theo? Have you talked to her?" She wanted all of them there at the same time.

"She sent me an email. She has to go to London around the same time. That British doctor helping her has to present a paper at the Academy of Royal Medical Colleges, which will help them get donations. She's meeting him there, and she said she can fly through New York if you really insist."

"I do," Isabelle said firmly. All she had to do was tell Charlie and hope he and his family could make it too. She called him as soon as they hung up and he said he could, and she said she was treating him and his family to the hotel and airfare and he was embarrassed but grateful. They clearly didn't have much money.

She sent out emails then, thanking all of them and confirming the plan. They were all coming to New York in a week. Jack made the arrangements for her.

There was alternating good and bad news. Her wrist continued to be agonizing despite the ice she put on it, and Jack made her go to the ER, where they X-rayed it and told her it was broken, and she had to wear a cast for four weeks. She hated to see her children that way, but there was nothing she could do about it. She went back to the eye doctor after that, and he thought there was some slight improvement.

She could hardly wait for her family to be there for the meeting. The girls were arriving on Friday. Charlie and his family were coming to the house on Saturday morning and had agreed to have lunch with her. She hired a cook since she was useless with her broken wrist, and Theo and Oona, the nanny, and the babies were all staying with her.

It was total chaos once they arrived. Jack had rented every possible kind of baby equipment—two cribs, high chairs, and a swing. The girls arrived on Friday on schedule, and Xela came to dinner the night they arrived. They ate pasta in the kitchen, and Xela and Theo were horrified by how often Oona had to nurse. She constantly had one baby or the other on her breast, and sometimes both.

"Don't they ever stop eating?" Xela was shocked. "They're little vampires."

"I know. I feel like a cow. It never stops with twins. And I have so much milk, I feel like I should walk around with my boobs out all day and offer them to strangers."

"Why don't you just stop," Theo suggested.

"I can't. Gregorio would kill me. They're only two months old. I'd love to stop at six months, though. He'd probably divorce me." With twins, she was either feeding them or changing diapers, and they passed them around between their mother, their aunts, and their grand-mother. And the nanny took them away whenever they got fussy or needed a nap. Someone was always holding one of them to give Oona a break.

"I can't nurse them for you, though, Oona. My boobs are fried at the moment." Xela made a joke of it. But she was in good spirits. She had just had a PET scan and a blood panel and she was cancer free. They celebrated at dinner with champagne when she told them, and Isabelle looked ecstatic. She had all three of her daughters home, got to meet the twins, and Xela was all-clear. It didn't get better than that.

There was lots of guessing about who the mystery guest the next day was going to be, but no one could even remotely imagine who it would be.

"Someone who wants to give us each a million dollars?" Xela teased, but she didn't mean it and they all laughed.

"If they do, I'm getting a breast lift," Oona announced. "By the time I stop nursing, they'll be on my knees."

"Just don't get pregnant again right away," Theo said wisely, and Oona sighed. She knew her husband better than that, and he said he wanted six, and possibly eight, to outdo his parents. She wasn't finished yet, not if she wanted to keep him happy, which was her main goal in life. But at least she had come to New York, despite his grousing. He called her every five minutes to ask what she was doing. She didn't answer his call during their dinner on Friday, and he started texting her. He kept her on a very short leash.

They grilled Theo about Geoffrey Bates then, and teased her about him. She insisted again that they were just colleagues and her sisters hooted and jeered and didn't believe her. And she finally broke down and admitted that they had had dinner a few times, and then confessed they were going away for a weekend in Scotland.

"I knew it!" Xela shrieked, and they all encouraged Theo. It was the first man they'd known about in Theo's life in years.

The girls all stayed up late that night, talking, and Xela spent the night with them. Breakfast on Saturday was as lively as dinner the night before, with the twins being handed around the table, except when Oona had to nurse them, which she did with a shawl over her.

There was an atmosphere of anticipation, waiting to meet the mystery guest that morning. The girls were still dressing when Charlie and his family arrived promptly at noon, and Isabelle led them into the living room, offered them something to drink, and five minutes later all three girls walked into the room, with Theo and Xela each carrying one of the babies. Isabelle introduced them all to each other and invited them to sit down. The girls were looking the Andersons over with curiosity.

"I wanted all of you here," Isabelle said seriously, "because I want to tell you about a piece of my history that I've never shared with you." Theo was staring intently at Charlie as her mother spoke. She'd never met him, but there was something so familiar about him that she couldn't stop looking at him. They were all smiling uncomfortably at each other, and Charlie looked extremely nervous, while Jaime played with one of the babies and Steve looked bored.

As they listened, Isabelle told them about the school dance when she was barely fifteen, and what it had led to. Her father's decision, her own inability to do anything different, or convince her father otherwise, and the baby she had given up that had marked her forever. As the story progressed, her daughters looked at her with amazement at this part of her life that they had never known anything about, no matter how well they thought they knew her. And then Theo understood before the others and realized how much Charlie looked like their mother. Isabelle told them then that she had always wanted to find Charlie, and she had finally had the courage to look for him, and had found him forty-three years later. She said simply that he was their half-brother and she thought they all deserved to meet. There was dead silence in the room as it sank in. Theo was the first to get up and embrace him, Oona started to cry and went to kiss him, and Xela was next and told him that she had always wanted a brother because her sisters were such a pain in the ass when they were growing up, and everyone laughed. There were tears and kissing and hugging, and the girls talked to Pattie and their niece and nephew. There were no recriminations or accusations. There was only compassion and sympathy for what both she and Charlie had been through. They all took turns hugging their mother and so did Charlie, and they realized the courage it had taken for her to tell them.

The noise level in the living room was enormous, and an hour later they all moved into the dining room for the lunch Isabelle had ordered. She sat looking at all of them for a moment. And then Charlie turned to Isabelle with a look of disappointment. "Where's Jack?"

"Jack who?" the girls asked in unison.

"My assistant," Isabelle explained. And with that, Charlie told them his whole story, what a big star he had been and how it had all ended. It gave them a new perspective on him, and Isabelle told Charlie that Jack didn't work on Saturdays.

Xela leaned over to her mother then and whispered that she had called the man from the plane, and they had had lunch, and were having dinner the following week.

"We can just be friends, in case I get sick again," she said cautiously.

"What if he got sick? Would you run away?"

"Of course not." She looked startled and offended.

"Then why assume you will, and he'd run out on you?"

"It's not that. I don't want to ruin his life, Mom."

"You won't," Isabelle said, observing something she thought she would never see in her lifetime—all four of her children at one table.

Oona showed the Andersons photographs of all her children, and the farm in Tuscany. Theo and Pattie had an interesting conversation about the school she wanted to build adjacent to the hospital. Charlie talked to all of them. Jaime got to hold one of the twins.

The Andersons stayed until five o'clock and the girls and their mother sat in Isabelle's office and discussed all of it after they left.

"Why didn't you ever tell us, Mom?" Theo looked hurt that she hadn't.

"I put it away as my darkest secret a long time ago. I never told anyone, not even your fathers. My father wouldn't let me talk about it either. It's not something I was proud of."

"He's a nice person," Oona said about her new brother. "We must be a little overwhelming for him. I thought he handled it very well."

"So did I," Isabelle said, proud of both branches of her family.

"Are you planning to see a lot of him?" Theo asked her.

"Probably not. But I want to stay in touch. Maybe I can be some kind of a mother figure to him now. He's my son. He's a little old to come back into the fold, but I don't want to lose him again." It sounded reasonable to them, and then Isabelle braced herself, to tell them another secret. She knew she had to. In simple terms, without making it sound too alarming, she told them about the problem with her eyes, and that it was improving for the time being.

"That's why I hired an assistant," she explained. "I can't spend hours and hours on the computer, and that's how I broke my wrist, I tripped on the curb. I felt like an idiot." They were sympathetic and handled it rationally but with concern for her.

"This family is certainly full of secrets," Xela commented, and realized that they had been through some major challenges recently. Her breast cancer, her mother's eyes, the baby their mother had had at fifteen.

"Does anyone else have something to confess?" Xela asked and no one volunteered.

"Well, I don't want to go home tomorrow, and that's not a secret," Oona said, looking sad about it.

"Why don't you stay a few more days," they all suggested, but she didn't want Gregorio to get upset.

"He'll survive it," Xela said. "You never come home. Enjoy it. And it's so nice for Mom."

"Maybe another day," she considered. And they talked her into leaving Tuesday, which would mean she had been in New York for four days, which was not overdoing it. She had lots of help at home for her other children. Theo changed her ticket for her, and Oona sent a text to Gregorio, who sent a flurry of them immediately and ordered her to come home. She said she couldn't leave her mother, who was having a problem with her vision and had broken her wrist. He couldn't argue with that.

They had another boisterous dinner on Saturday night and went to the park together on Sunday. Isabelle couldn't remember when she'd enjoyed her family so much, and Xela's turning over a new leaf with her sisters made a big difference. She told them all about the preacher from Texas that Jack had introduced them to.

"What really made a difference, though," she admitted to them, "was when they told me I had breast cancer. And then the preacher said that forgiveness changes things and he was right. I was angry all my life until then, and having cancer woke me up."

"It's what the French call *un mal pour un bien*," Isabelle said gently. "A bad thing happens which leads to a good thing. But the good thing would never have happened without the bad thing first."

"A blessing in disguise," Oona said and they all nodded.

*

Jack called her on Sunday night to ask her how it had gone. She told him it had been perfect and thanked him for everything he'd done to help set it up and make the arrangements.

Theo left for London on Monday with considerable teasing about Geoffrey Bates. And Oona went back to Italy on Tuesday and the house was deadly quiet after that. Isabelle was sitting in the kitchen looking depressed the day after Oona left with the twins, and Jack found her there when he got to work.

"Why don't you go visit them?" She'd been planning to go to Italy anyway and had postponed it to go to Xela's radiation treatments with her, but now they were over. "There's an art fair in Venice in about a month, and another one in Bologna. You could visit Oona, see the fairs, and stop in Paris on the way back. You love it there." He thought she needed some distraction and fun. She liked the suggestion and thought about it as she went upstairs, and by the end of the day, she had decided he was right. She didn't need to sit there feeling sorry for herself. All the dates coincided and the fairs she was interested in were happening in May, which was a lovely month to travel.

"All right," she told him before he left for the day. "Let's go to Italy and Paris. Can you get away?"

"I'll work it out." It had gone smoothly before. "I'll book the tickets on the Internet from home," he said, smiling at her. He was pleased that things were working out well for her, and he liked his job, even more than working for the senator. And it was so varied. There was always some new surprise afoot.

He emailed her later that night. He had booked the plane tickets, with a five-day stay in Paris on the way back. And he would take care of the hotels the next day when she told him where she liked to stay. She thanked him and gave him the names of the hotels she preferred in each city. She realized that so far, he had been a blessing in disguise too. If she hadn't been told that she might go blind, which didn't seem to be happening, at least not for now, she would never have hired him. And he had definitely improved her quality of life. It was an interesting thought, how sometimes good things came from bad.

Chapter Nineteen

The plane took off from Paris to Florence an hour late due to storms in Paris, but the weather was beautiful and sunny when they got there. The car and driver were waiting for them, and this time Jack was staying at the farm with her. They were only staying for four days, and then going on to Bologna and Venice for the art fairs.

The children were happy to see their grandmother, and the twins had doubled in size in two months. Gregorio said it was because she was nursing and had so much milk. Oona told her mother she had decided to stop in the summer, which seemed long enough to her, with twins. It was all she did now. She hadn't discussed it with Gregorio yet, but she seemed just a little bit more independent to her mother. She assumed they'd work it out.

Theo had admitted that she'd had a wonderful time in Scotland with the doctor, and he was coming back to India. Xela was seeing Mark Thompson, the man she had met on the plane, and all her tests were clear, and with luck would stay that way. Isabelle was in touch with

Charlie and Pattie every few weeks, just a friendly email, or a call which made him feel part of a larger family. All of her chicks appeared to be in good order, and when she and Jack left for Bologna after a relaxed visit, she looked rested and happy.

"You certainly came into our lives at a turbulent time," Isabelle commented to him as she watched the Italian countryside slide by, and he smiled at her.

"That's why you hired me," he reminded her. "I know he's the most macho guy on the planet and drives like a lunatic, but I actually like Gregorio, and he loves her."

"He just loves himself more," Isabelle responded and Jack laughed.

"That could be true, but she's happy with him."

"That's because she accepts doing everything his way. I wish she stood up to him a little more." But that wasn't Oona's personality. She wanted to please him and everyone around her.

"Maybe she will when she gets older. She's very young." And she was very grown up in a way too, a good wife, and an extraordinary mother.

"He's a lucky man," Isabelle said, and Jack didn't disagree.

They checked out the art fair in Bologna that afternoon, and stayed at the Grand Hotel Majestic in two beautiful rooms, and drove on to Venice the next day. Jack had never been there before. They both loved it.

"Sometimes I have to remind myself that this is a job. I still pinch myself in the morning when I wake up. I should be paying you," he teased her, as they walked around Venice, comfortably lost part of the time. She tucked her hand into his arm so she didn't trip, but her eyes were definitely getting better. The shots were working, and she had to have more when they went back.

They stayed in Venice for four days, drove south to Rome for two days, and then flew to Paris for the last five days of their trip. They had planned it perfectly.

Isabelle bought four paintings in Paris for old clients and two in Venice for the Caseys' yacht. The job for them was almost complete, and she had an appointment with a new Russian client when they got back to New York. Jack had become very knowledgeable in the last six months. He learned quickly and read everything she gave him.

"You'll be a fine art dealer one day," she teased him. "You'll probably leave me and open a gallery," she said as they walked along the Seine, once they got to Paris. They had dinner at her favorite bistro that night on the rue Saint Dominique. It was an odd arrangement. He worked for her but they were constant companions now. She was uneasy going out without him, and used to him, and their work life spilled over into their private time. She discussed everything with him, and they agreed on most subjects.

"What are we these days?" he asked her over dinner. "Best friends or work pals or . . ." He smiled as he watched her carefully and waited for the answer.

"Does it need a name?" she said.

"It might one day, so I don't get confused and cross boundaries I shouldn't." The boundaries between them had been blurred for months. When he scolded her about something, she told him he sounded like Gregorio, and ignored him. "Where do you see yourself five years from now?" he asked her as they shared dessert. She looked surprised at the question. "Or ten?"

"Hopefully not dead," she said cynically.

"Don't say things like that. You'll probably live to be ninety and I'll be long gone."

"It's interesting how we've both had several lives. As a basketball star in your case, radio, TV, the senator, now art. Me with the kids, and very different men who influenced my life." Putnam probably the most among them, and for the longest. Collin and Declan had been so brief. But all three had left her with wonderful children. "Don't you want children one day, Jack?" She thought it a shame if he didn't. He was so good with her, and so nurturing. No one had ever taken care of her as he did. She had always had to fend for herself, and take care of her kids.

"No," he answered her honestly. "Parenting is so quick. You blink and they're gone, and you're alone again anyway." She couldn't deny that. Her girls had all flown and were doing fine without her. It left one to figure out what to do with the years that were left. She was beginning to think about it. She had her work. But what else? "Would you ever be interested in a partnership, Isabelle?" She was surprised by the question.

"In business?"

"Not really," he said quietly as their eyes met. "I had something else in mind. This seems to work surprisingly well, for both of us. I just wondered if . . ." He wasn't sure how to finish the sentence, and she smiled at him, touched.

"Is this a proposition or a proposal?" she whispered across the table.

"Possibly both," he whispered back.

"Interesting . . . I'll give it some thought," she said mysteriously and they left the restaurant a short time later and went back to their hotel. It had been a lovely evening and she was intrigued by what he had said. She asked him a question in the car on the way back. "The age difference doesn't bother you?"

"No, would it bother you if it were reversed? You were with a man twenty-seven years older than you, with Putnam."

"I was young then." She smiled at the memory. She had been so desperately in love with him. "And if I turn into a blind old woman?"

"We'll figure it out. Then you wouldn't see how old I

was getting. That would be a blessing." She laughed and they walked through the lobby and went to their rooms, which were side by side. There was a connecting door, which they kept locked. They said good night, and he kissed her on the cheek, and they disappeared into their own rooms. Isabelle stood looking at the connecting door for a while and with the same spirit of adventure and willingness to take risk she'd had at twenty, she silently unlocked it and opened it just a crack. He might never even notice. If he did, what happened next was up to the fates. As she stood looking at the door, it opened slowly, and Jack stood looking at her from the other side.

"Is that an invitation, or a mistake?" he asked and she smiled at him.

"Which would you prefer?"

"What do you think?" And with that, he took her up on the challenge, stepped across the threshold and kissed her as he walked into her life.

*

Everything changed for them in Paris. They found their youth again and dared what neither of them had in years. Their hearts were open, and by the time they left Paris, boundaries had been crossed, walls had fallen, and hearts laid bare.

*

They flew back to New York sitting next to each other, eating, talking, watching movies, and he was sad knowing he couldn't stay with her in New York. He couldn't leave his sister alone at night. He wasn't going to desert her no matter how in love he was with Isabelle, and he was very much so. She understood the responsibilities he had to honor, and respected him for it.

He dropped her off at her house, took her inside, and kissed her. They had talked about her children in Paris, and she said she didn't need their permission or even their approval. It was too late for her to let anyone stop her at her age. He lingered and hated to leave her and then he went home to Sandy, who was waiting for him. He thought she looked strange when he walked in, as though something was bothering her, but he was tired and didn't want to ask.

She waited until the next morning to tell him, after asking how the trip was. She thought he looked different too. There was something she couldn't put her finger on, but she could feel it, more than see it. In some subtle way, he had changed while he was away.

"I have bad news," she finally said over breakfast. "Not about my health," she was quick to reassure him. "I feel terrible doing this to you. Your niece finally left the creep she's married to. Nancy wants to come home, Jack, with the kids, and live with me. I didn't have the heart to say no to her." She felt guilty toward him. "You gave up a great job in Washington for me, and now I'm throwing you out. I feel like the worst sister in the world." He looked at her in amazement.

"You're throwing me out?"

She nodded. "She's coming home in three weeks."

"Perfect timing," he said, putting on his jacket, and rushing to the door. "I'm late for work. Sorry. We'll talk later." He smiled at her.

"Are you mad at me?" she called after him.

"Not at all. I love you, more than ever."

He let himself into the house, and Isabelle was still asleep. He took the stairs two at a time, silently opened her bedroom door, dropped his clothes on the floor, slipped into bed beside her, and put his arms around her. She opened one eye sleepily and looked at him, half awake.

"You call this a job?"

"It used to be . . . I just got evicted. By my sister. Her daughter left her husband and she's coming home in three weeks to live with her mother. So I'm out."

Isabelle smiled and pulled him closer to her, until they were pressed against each other and she could feel every inch of him against her skin. "Isn't that what you call a blessing in disguise?" she whispered. He didn't answer her. He kissed her. The fates had smiled on them again.

Danielle Steel

Have you liked Danielle Steel on Facebook?

Be the first to know about Danielle's latest books, access exclusive competitions and stay in touch with news about Danielle.

www.facebook.com/DanielleSteelOfficial

IN HIS FATHER'S FOOTSTEPS

The shadow of war and tragedy defines the relationship between father and son in this deeply moving novel set in post-World War Two New York. Yet to shape his future, Max Stein, son of concentration camp survivors, will have to face the scars of his family's past.

Paperback published June 2019

TURNING POINT

For four top trauma specialists, a Paris work trip is either the perfect or the worst-timed break from the relationships and chaos in each of their personal lives. But when the city is hit with an unspeakable act of violence, the doctors are confronted with their greatest challenge yet.

Paperback published August 2019

BEAUCHAMP HALL

Life is drearily passing Winona Farmington by, until a shocking discovery inspires her to take control. Winona leaves her backwater Michigan town, heading to a picturesque English village she's come to love from her favourite TV show, and a new adventure awaits . . .

Paperback published October 2019

SILENT NIGHT

Emma Watts, heir to Hollywood royalty, is moulded by her ambitious mother into being a child TV star – until an unforeseeable tragedy changes everything. When Emma is taken in by her career-driven aunt, both must embrace hope and the chance for new beginnings.

Paperback published December 2019

THE NUMBERS GAME

A thought-provoking, poignant story of three generations of women by the world's favourite storyteller, Danielle Steel.

Eileen Jackson is forty. Her marriage is on the rocks, and her self-esteem is at an all-time low. Her children are struggling to come to terms with their parents' divorce and she knows she has to get her life back on track – fast. The realization of her talent and the opportunity to pursue a long-held ambition give her the confidence to believe in herself and be the happiest she's ever been.

Olivia Waters is twenty-seven. Beautiful, clever, successful, she is the woman who Eileen's husband has fallen in love with. What she swiftly comes to understand is that while an affair is fun, she's too young to take on the trappings and responsibilities of a father of three children – she has much to do in her life and she's not prepared to sacrifice ambition just yet.

At ninety-two, Olivia's grandmother, Gabrielle, is a talented and internationally successful sculptor. She's enjoying life to the full, she's experienced the highs and lows of youth and middle age and now she knows what she wants out of life and who she wants to be with.

Coming soon in hardback

PURE STEEL. PURE HEART.